MW01281754

Something
SPECIAL
S. MASSERY

Interior Design by AB Formatting
Cover Design by Murphy Rae, www.murphyrae.net
Cover Illustration by Ashley Quick, www.ashleyranaequick.com

For Rebecca,
Thank you for never letting me give up.

Before

WE RAN AND RAN UNTIL THERE WERE NO more houses, no more signs of life. All around us was a blinding array of colors; a forest full of light and promise danced around us. The sun filtered through trees, creating illusions of spiraling fairies. This far exceeded any adventure we had taken before. The sky was too blue, the forest too green, my heart too full.

The backpack started choking me as Jared flickered in and out of sight ahead of me. "Stop," I hollered. It reverberated in the quiet around us, in the stillness of the woods.

I never doubted that he would come back. A second later, he bounded toward me, wearing a grin that slid over his features.

I thought he might be worried. There was something in the shadows and cracks of his smile, but I couldn't think of anything else when his hand grazed my arm. We had known each other forever, but things were shifting. He was becoming someone else. I was, too, but at a slower rate. Our adventures were few and far between now. We were growing up.

"Let go," he said as I stood there frozen. He was taking the pack from me, shouldering it over his own. "Come on, slowpoke."

He spun and followed the trail deeper. He kept up such a brutal pace, I was sure my lungs were going to explode. He'd have to explain it to the police and my parents. I wasn't sure which he would find more terrifying.

I followed him. Of course I did; I always had, I always would.

Finally, we broke through the tree line, and I gaped, mouth hanging open. Jared grinned at me. Any of that worry I had seen earlier was tucked deep inside of him.

"Like it?" he asked. His voice was huskier than usual. At sixteen, his voice had been cracking and deepening for almost a year. Some sort of rush went through me, but I didn't understand what it was. I just wanted to be closer to him. I stepped close enough that our arms brushed. We were nearly the same height, and our arms aligned from our shoulders to our elbows.

What lay before us was magic: it was the rare, hidden beach on the backside of the lake. If our parents knew how we got here, they would murder us. No one would find us, though. We were utterly alone.

I pictured myself turning toward him and leaning forward, pressing my lips against his. It would've been a quick thing. It would've been a peck like Mom gives Dad before she goes out with her friends, or before he leaves for work.

And then...

Jared groaned, softly, and I thought it was directed at me.

But no. A jet ski flew toward us, skipping across the water. "Don't do anything stupid," he muttered. I wasn't sure if it was directed at me or the boy coming to the beach.

"Colby?" I guessed. He had stuck to Jared like glue since they met just a few months ago. Colby was the new kid, the rising basketball star, and a jerk. He leered at me in a way that made my skin crawl. He said crude things to me, but then he would smile and say, *It's okay, Charlie, I was just messing with you.*

"Yeah," Jared muttered. The muscle in his jaw tensed for a moment. "How did he find us?"

Colby, always showing off, killed the jet ski engine at the last minute and skidded onto the sand. He leapt off before it was fully stopped. "You made it!" he yelled at Jared. "About time. The others should be here soon." He pointed at a kayak in the distance, in the middle of the lake, flanked by at least three more.

Jared grabbed my hand and finally met my eyes. I had always admired the brilliant sapphire of his eyes and how they said so much and nothing at the same time. "Don't..." He stopped and shook his head. "Please don't let him touch you, okay?"

Of course not, I wanted to say. The metallic taste of fear was spreading through my mouth, and it sealed my lips closed. This was not how I pictured our last adventure before starting back at school. I had pictured something quiet, somewhere secluded and alone and *ours*. We were on the precipice of a big, unknown change.

The three girls and one boy in the kayaks arrived within minutes, and Jared and Colby lifted two mini coolers from the kayaks. I sat and watched the action unfold: how one of the girls, Leah, kept touching Jared's arm and laughing at every word that passed his lips.

I knew Jared: he wasn't *that* funny. Colby encouraged their interactions, and it made me hate him even more for shining a light on Jared's attraction to Leah. Already, Jared was standing straighter and smiling easier. He was bolstered by the laughter of people we wouldn't remember in ten years. It didn't make sense.

Part of me wished Jared would realize I wasn't quite there; I was mostly camouflaged by the tree line, half there and half not.

The sun flickered over the water, and the trees swayed in the breeze. I was getting tenser by the minute. I wished for a book or a phone, neither of which I had thought to bring. I had Jared. I was safe. And yet—my Jared was quickly vanishing, replaced with a colder, social version.

Older kids arrived on a pontoon boat. They got as close as they could and splashed their way to shore with beer bottles in their hands. I recognized one of the new five.

I glanced over, toward Jared, and caught Colby's eye. *He* saw me. He smirked, silently lifting a beer bottle in my direction. It was either an invitation to come closer or a *cheers*— I couldn't decipher it. I could never read him. Uneasy, I shouldered my pack. It was time for me to go.

In the water, Jared was making out with Leah. My heart seized, and I turned and fled.

Part I

JUNE

He seemed like an angel
Gracing me with his presence.

Chapter 1

H E FLIES THROUGH THE DOOR LIKE A BLIZZARD, bringing in a fresh crispness that I had yet to experience in a New York summer. It makes me straighten in my seat. He says something to the cashier, and she beams at him. All I see are his lips, his smile, his golden hair that curls at his collar. I need to knock off this type of thinking immediately, but something about him captivates me.

Stop staring, I order myself. I look back at my book and force myself to swallow a paragraph of words, but then I look back up toward the cashier. He's gone. I'm surprised when it hollows me out for a second.

I feel a presence over my shoulder, and I slam the book against my chest—both in an effort to preserve my cleavage from prying eyes and in surprise. I look up at him. Of course it's him. He's even more beautiful up close. It has been too long since I kissed a boy, and here I am, thinking about kissing this stranger.

"Do you mind if I sit with you?"

His words are faint over the music in my ears. I nod, and then shake my head. What did he ask? I don't think I have ever seen eyes quite like his: a unique blend of brown and gold. We watch each other for a beat, and I realize I gave him two opposing answers. A hot blush seeps up my neck, staining my cheeks red, and I use my foot to slowly push the chair across from me away from the table. He looks from me to it, then takes a seat. I drop my eyes back to my book and contemplate turning off my music.

"My name is Avery," he says, extending his hand at me. I shake it and think, *Wow*. It's so proper of him to do it like that. When's the last time a guy introduced himself any other way besides grunting his name in my ear over the loud music at a bar? I couldn't say.

I pull out my earbuds and wrap the cord around my iPod. The café noises swarm in my ears like bees.

This time, I focus on his nose instead of his eyes. It's safer territory.

"Charlotte," I say. Everyone knows me as Charlie—even my professors call me Charlie. A part of me must want to come across cooler—or more mature—than I feel. I wear a loose pair of shorts and an old *Relient K* t-shirt that has some holes in the sleeve. It has a single flower on the front from one of their older albums.

I find myself picturing his face on the latest Calvin Klein advertisements that have been plastered over all the subway platforms for weeks. It's always the eyes that draw you in, but the body sells the product. *Two seconds with him and you're already undressing him? Nice, Charlie.*

"Well, Charlotte, thank you for letting me join you. I didn't expect it to be so crowded." Like we're in sync, we glance around the tight cafe. He pulls a thick book from the briefcase resting against his chair and smiles at me.

"No problem."

We sit in silence for at least twenty minutes. It's long enough for me to notice the way he sucks his lower lip into his mouth right before he turns the page of his book; I start fantasizing about tasting his lips for myself. I'm doing that *thing* where I try to pretend I'm not staring at him, but I am. If I'm being honest, I'm not great at it. A table across the room opens up, and I see that he notices it, too. But he still doesn't move. I don't know whether to be happy or worried with this new information. I suppress a shiver. What if he's a creepy serial killer? Ted Bundy was charismatic, too...

"What are you reading?"

I flash the cover of the latest spy novel, and he nods. He looks impressed... or maybe surprised. "It's because I would do anything to escape my reality of my summer job," I say. *Why would you say that?* I ask myself. I imagine my mother hooking her arm around my waist and pinching me, telling me to control myself.

Inhale, exhale.

He's just a boy. My imagination is running wild picturing him as Ted Bundy's cousin.

He smiles at me, and I want to look at the dimple in his cheek forever. "That's quite interesting. I'm reading a book my sister recommended, since you asked. It's about a girl and a boy, and they're in love but they don't know it."

I raise my eyebrows. "You don't strike me as the romantic type."

He sighs, leaning forward. I wonder what type of man he

will turn out to be—he could hardly be older than I am.

"Charlotte, if you learn anything about me today, know this: I am *definitely* the romantic type." He flashes me a smirk that makes me run hot and cold inside.

I can't stop the shy smile that creeps across my face. My heart is swooning. My brain is having a meltdown.

"And you? Are you romantic?"

"No," I say. My heart may be swooning, but my brain is still in charge of my voice. "I have historically not gone out on Valentine's Day. I'm terrible at remembering birthdays and anniversaries. And declarations of love aren't *really* my thing."

"That's quite sad. Dinners lit only by candles and the moon? Spontaneous trips to Paris? A surprise picnic in a field of flowers?" His grin is lopsided. In that moment, I have no doubt he would try—or maybe already had tried—to do all of those.

"Truth?" I cock my head to the side. What did this boy see when he looks at me? Dumb, murky blue eyes and dirty blonde hair and a figure that has a few extra pounds strapped across the middle? Did he see that I was drowning in boredom? I was itching for something to happen to me—something straight out of my spy novel.

He nodded.

"Dinners by candlelight and the moon seem like a headache in the making. Squinting to see what the menu says or what you're eating? No, thank you. And who can afford a spontaneous trip to Paris? What kind of job must you have? A picnic... does sound nice. Except for the whole field-of-wildflowers thing. They tend to have a surplus of bees." My eye twitches, because clearly I want to show the insane side of me today.

He throws his head back and laughs. "Oh, wow. You really

are anti-romance, aren't you?"

I lean forward, resting my elbows on the table. He seems rapt, suddenly, with something over my left shoulder. I glance back, see a few people standing in line, and turn back to him. His eyes shoot up to meet mine. "Were you looking at my boobs?" I ask.

The question is ridiculous, but I couldn't stop it from coming out of my mouth.

His ears turn red.

"Oh, wow," I laugh. "It's okay if you were," I offer, because now he can't look at me at all.

He rubs at the back of his neck. "I just—"

"They're there." I glance down. "It's a revealing shirt. It's hot out."

He chuckles. "You sure do know how to make a guy feel better."

"Stare away," I say. I start to blush. "But, actually, maybe..."

"I'll only do it when you aren't looking." He winks at me.

I nod, because I can accept that. Plus, his wink made something flutter in my stomach.

"So," Avery says. "The anti-romantic. Tell me more."

I shake my head. "No, that's a boring story. You know what I do like?"

His raises an eyebrow. I'm immediately jealous, because I can only raise both or neither.

I tell him, "Adventures."

"You like adventures," he repeats. There are wheels turning in his head. What will he do with the information?

He holds out his hand as he rises from the table.

I look at it, dubious.

"Well, come on, Charlotte. Let's have an adventure."

I smile.

Inhale, exhale.

Take his hand for the second time.

This time, I don't let go.

Avery leads me down street after street, and I can't fathom where we're going. He won't tell me, either.

"You could be kidnapping me," I protest.

"I'm not," he says. He grins at me and lets go of my hand. "You're free to go, miss."

We laugh, and I keep following him like a lost puppy. When we round the corner, I have a clear view of the harbor and the ferry docked at the end of a pier.

"No," I say. I don't think I can stomach a boat—even a huge ferry.

He looks at me, absorbs my fear, and takes my hand again. "Yes. Have you done this?"

I shake my head.

"No, of course not. Yes, we're doing this. Ellis Island, here we come!"

He pays for the ferry, which I try to stop. He pushes me back, gently, his arm going against my collarbone. A flash of heat moves through me. The attendant, a high school student from the looks of him, looks at us with big glassy eyes and waves us in the right direction.

"Charlotte," he says.

"Avery," I reply.

"Tell me something."

I think and come up with: "I go to college in Chicago."

He glances at me. "Why are you in New York? Reading in a cafe?" He clears his throat and motions me up the ramp ahead of him as an elderly gentleman checks our tickets. "Reading a *spy* novel in a cafe?"

I smile. "Because I had the day off of work, and I like

reading."

"Oh, right." He nudges me with his elbow. "You like spy novels on your day off. And coffee."

"Coffee keeps me nice," I say with a straight face. "But you're one to talk. You were there with a romance novel."

"I can't believe you don't like romance."

We find seats on the top deck. There are almost too many people around—kids yelling, teens leaning over the railings. For a minute, the noise is overwhelming. I shift toward Avery, focusing on the brown and gold eyes that remain steady on mine.

"I can't believe you abducted a stranger and took her to Ellis Island," I joke.

He puts a hand to his chest. "Oh, how you wound me."

I laugh and gaze out toward the Statue of Liberty. "Are you from here?" I ask.

"No." He looks out across the water, too. "No, I'm from California."

"Oceans away."

He turns to me and smiles. It's so blinding, I might die. "I'm glad I'm here. Otherwise, I wouldn't have met you." Our knees touch, but neither of us move. It feels like we are growing something fragile between the two of us.

Once we're off the ferry, he tugs me to the side. We follow a path around the edge of the island. "You don't want to go in there," he says.

I have had a lot of people telling me what to do in my life. My mother, my father, professors, bosses, ex-boyfriends... "Why?" I ask. I stop and glance back toward the doors that tourists still file through.

"Because it's boring in there. It's dead. Literally, everything in there is dead. Out here? This has been here the whole time. It changes as the years go on, it grows, it dies, it breathes. Come with me," he says. I hear Jared in my head over him, whispering, *come with me*.

Taking it as an omen, I go.

Chapter 2

PAST

MOM URGED ME OUTSIDE, BUT I COULDN'T GO. I couldn't do anything except stare at the bus idling at the curb. How on earth was I going to start my sophomore year of high school like *this*? I was a mess. I had spent most of the morning—and last night—crying. My eyes were still puffy even after I held frozen spoons on them for ten minutes.

"Get going, Charlotte," my mother snapped.

"Yes, ma'am," I whispered. I hoisted my new backpack further up my shoulder and stepped out the door. I almost tripped going up the stairs, and I froze at the top. This was so much worse than last year: I'd had Jared, then.

Now? He was gone. Poof. Three weeks ago, just shy of his junior year of high school, he got into a fight, and his parents retaliated by throwing him into a boarding school in the middle of nowhere. There was a rumor that they had taken his laptop and cell phone, too. Mr. and Mrs. Brown were friends with my parents. Even between the four of them, I couldn't figure anything out. I just missed my friend.

When the bus pulled up in front of the school, I leapt to my feet and practically pushed people to get off of it. I stood on the sidewalk and inhaled the damp September air. It was foggy, heavy, wet air. I pictured Jared next to me, looking off toward the parking lot. I looked, too. Rows of teachers' cars on one side, and around the corner, the older students' cars.

Come with me, he said. I shook my head at my imagination and entered the building.

Go away, Jared, I thought, but I didn't mean it. What I meant was, *Come back.*

The first person I saw was Colby.

I tried my hardest not to flinch, I really did, but the wicked smile he gave me told me he saw it. He saw *me*. Instead of coming toward me, though, and leaving the embrace of the girl draped over him, he turned into her and nuzzled her neck.

It took me a minute to realize it was Leah—the one that Jared had made out with only a few weeks ago. Now that Jared was gone? It was just Colby sitting atop the social pyramid. I wasn't sure how to feel about that.

My first class was entirely made up of sophomores, which was a comfort. We were all pretending not to be scared little chickens in the hallways, like the freshmen outwardly were; they tucked together and tried not to ruffle feathers. In this classroom, though, we were bolder. We spoke louder.

The second class was mixed. I stared at the whiteboard, letting people fill in around me, until someone kicked the back of my chair. I glanced behind me and felt the blood rush away from my face.

Colby.

"Hey, hot stuff," he whispered. "I was hoping we'd have a class together. Maybe two or three..."

I ignored him. I always ignored him. But when I felt him so close to me, his breath on my neck, an uncontrollable shiver rushed up my back.

"I knew you were affected by me," he said before he leaned back.

I couldn't concentrate the rest of class. My eyes darted all over the place. Third period, I waited by the lockers down the hall—they weren't even close to mine—and waited to see who would go inside. A minute before the bell, Colby sauntered in, and my body froze.

Jared whispered, *Come with me.*

I glanced toward the doors at the far end of the hall. It was in the opposite direction of the classroom, and I couldn't make myself go anywhere near that class. I didn't want to feel Colby staring at me for another minute.

I walked quickly toward the doors, pausing only to fiddle at a locker that wasn't mine when a teacher hurried past. And then, I pushed through the doors, and I was free.

Where are we going? I asked the Jared in my imagination as we scanned the deserted lot.

On an adventure, he said. I jogged toward the parking lot, ducking around cars, until I got to the edge of the baseball field. The right edge was lined with a low fence; the ground dropped down beyond it, into woods. A shiver ran through me.

I wandered through the woods until I found a large boulder that seemed a good spot to sit. I pulled out my notebook and pen, hovered for a second, and started writing.

Dear Jared, I wrote.

It has been three weeks, and I miss you. It's the first day of school. Colby looks at me like I'm a piece of meat. It doesn't matter, whatever you said to him, because he's gotten worse. How could you get in trouble when he didn't?

I miss you. I said that already. I'll say it again: I miss you.

Why don't you return my calls?

A tear dropped onto the page, startling me.

I'm on an adventure, I continued. *Although, I'm sitting alone in the woods behind school writing to you, so, I guess I need to step it up a bit. It's the first day of school and I'm skipping a class—can you believe that? I hope they don't tell my parents. I remember you used to skip your last period to come get me from the middle school.*

I groaned and threw down my pen. I couldn't do this.

I closed the notebook and went back to school.

Chapter 3

"HI, MOM!" IT IS BEST TO START OUR conversation on a cheerful note, even if it's slightly forced. She can never tell the difference.

"Charlie, honey, we miss you!"

I roll my eyes. She starts every conversation this way: by buttering me up before dropping me in the frying pan, depending on how the conversation goes.

"I miss you, too. How's your week?"

I hear her start to settle into her chair. That thing has developed a nasty squeak. She converted the side parlor into her office, and she always looks tiny behind the massive oak desk. It is where she takes care of all her event planning, as well as the phone calls to her daughter. That action alone says, *Charlie, you're work.* "Well, the Browns were sad to hear that you weren't coming home this summer. Jared was asking about you! He's gotten quite a bit cuter, I think—"

"No, that wouldn't happen." I haven't seen him since we were kids... since he was whisked away before his junior year of high school. "Isn't he in D.C.?" I cringe on the inside when I realize I know—and admitted to—his whereabouts. It'll just spur my mother on further.

"Yes, dear, but he came home for the summer. I'll text you his number in case you want to catch up with him. Your father has already booked your train ticket home for the weekend before school starts, so make sure to clear your schedule for then. You can reconnect with the Browns, as well, although Jared may be back in school...." I sense her frown through the phone.

I close my eyes as she continues to prattle on about the neighborhood gossip. Every time I blink, I see Avery's face. His smile. His hand in mine. I can't believe he took me to Ellis Island. I can't believe we didn't go *in*. We were there for under an hour. We made a short circuit around, bought some food, and got on the ferry back to land. We parted ways shortly after that, which left me feeling suspiciously empty. I hadn't even gotten his last name.

My mother stops talking with a feeling of expectation; I had probably missed a question hanging in the air. I lie, "Sorry, Mom, you broke up for a minute there. Do you have bad service?"

"Well, there is one corner of my office that seems to fade in and out quite a bit. It must be all the wires and such. I wanted to see if you needed anything from me. You good?"

I swallow. Crying or complaining would just make her angry. She likes a happy, perfect daughter. She doesn't ever ask how my week is going; she expects I can handle it. Before tears can form in my eyes, I say, "Yeah, I'm great."

"Remember, *yes*, not yeah."

"Sorry, Mom. *Yes*, I'm great. Can you have Dad send over the train ticket information if he hasn't already?"

"I can do that. And look up Jared—they were quite insistent on your renewed contact!" The fact that she has brought him up more than twice makes me uneasy. I come up with an excuse to get out of the conversation that is quickly unravelling. Something about dinner on the stove. She accepts that without objection, and ends the call with, "Love you, honey! Don't forget to eat your veggies!"

Chapter 4

A WEEK PASSES BEFORE I MAKE IT BACK TO THE cafe where I met Avery. I have a knot in my belly, directly related to the possibility of seeing him again.

I order an iced coffee, barely glancing around at the few patrons. He isn't here.

Biting back a wave of disappointment, I leave the cafe and head toward one of the small residential parks in the neighborhood. My favorite book is in my purse, and I am not going to waste the last hours of sunlight. There are some benches around the edge of the park and along the pathways. But the true draw is the maze in the center. Of the many parks scattered around the neighborhood, each one has a maze with a different configuration. In the center are the more comfortable benches, a sacred thing in New York City. Of the many decisions I've made in my relatively short life, this is a good one. Finding a haven.

New York City is almost three hours from my hometown in Northampton. That seems *almost* far enough away to escape my parents. My mom called twice since I spoke to her about their Labor Day party, which is legendary among my parents' friends. It's an extravagant display of excess wealth. Men are required to wear ties, although coats are optional depending on the weather. Women either wear dresses or are refused entry. *That* had happened one summer. My cousin, Nathan, had brought a date and forgot—or "forgot," depending on who you ask—to tell her the dress code. My mother and her sister, my cousin's mom, threw fits. He and his date walked out and didn't come back. I guess the shame was too much to bear. Or it was an elaborate excuse to get out of a stuffy party.

Speaking of shame, I am loath to admit that I dislike my job with the blog that has employed me this summer. I hate the research, and the political lean of the site is in an undesirable direction. My coworkers don't trust me, and I have found that my fact-checking is often double checked. It irritates me more than I care to admit, but since my boss refuses to tell them to stop or tell me that I'm not doing a good job, I force myself to ignore it. Whining would do no good. My dad would turn red in the ears and say, *Are you trying to embarrass this family?* Maybe, Dad. I haven't quite decided yet.

The iced coffee is gone by the time I circle the outer edge of the park—a ritual to ensure I won't be followed into the maze by someone dangerous. I follow the curve of the shrubs until I find the entrance. The hedges extend a foot above my head, making it impossible to see out. After two turns that lead to a dead end, I find the center and let the victorious thrill roll through me. When I get there, I can't help the grin that spreads across my face.

Avery sits on one of the benches, reading the same book as

27

before.

"Well, this is a surprise," I say.

He jerks upright, caught off guard. And then he, too, smiles.

"Charlotte." My name sounds so rich coming out of his mouth. I step closer until I stand directly in front of him. He watches me. Takes my hand in his. Tugs until I am seated next to him. "What brings you here?"

I blurt exactly what I think: "I'm not stalking you, Avery."

He laughs, the sound exploding out of him. I almost flinch. The birds behind us do the same, twittering and flying away. I watch them with a vague envy of their wings.

"I like you, Charlotte. Why have I never seen you before at my favorite coffee shop and my favorite garden?"

"Your favorite coffee shop?" I raise my eyebrows. "I've been going there for almost a month now and have never seen you." Quieter, "I would've remembered you."

My hand is still in his. He easily threads our fingers again, palm pressed to palm. I hope my hand isn't too sweaty.

"I feel..." He stops. "I would have remembered you, too. I don't know you yet, but I want to."

My heart skips.

Is that it? Is that the warning your heart gives you before falling in love? Another ten minutes of sitting with Avery, and I will be doomed.

His free hand comes up and cups my cheek. He brushes his thumb across my lower lip. His hand slides down, as light as a feather on my neck, his thumb capturing the rapid beat of my heart.

Slow down, heart. I'm not ready for this.

Avery smiles again. It's softer, the creases at the corners of his eyes not as prominent. My heart squeezes again.

I haven't kissed anyone in over a year. What if I don't

remember how?

And then I don't have time to think anymore, because he leans in and I close my eyes like I've done this with him a million times. His hand is still at my neck, his thumb hovering over my pulse. It moves a bit, a gentle caress, right before his lips touch mine.

It's everything a first kiss should be. Sweet. Innocent. A close-mouthed affair. We pull away and stare at each other some more; all we do lately is stare into each other's eyes, and then we are kissing with fervor. Our teeth clash once, but the awkwardness is lost as his tongue runs along my lower lip right before he nips it. He tastes like peanut butter.

My hands slide up his arms, trailing my nails along the back of his neck as my fingers push into his hair and scrape his scalp. He groans into my mouth; his hand leaves my throat and twists around my braid. He tugs on my hair, tilting my head for better access. His other hand works its way up my rib cage, splayed fingers dangerously close to my breasts.

And all at once, it hits me that I am making out with a stranger. Kissing a stranger with more passion than I ever had for any ex-boyfriends. Sharing germs with a guy who I haven't talked to for more than two hours total, whose last name is a mystery, whose *life* is a mystery.

Avery must sense my sudden hesitation. He pulls away, eyes cracked half open.

I lean away. Just because it was a good kiss doesn't mean I want to invite it to happen again.

"Are you okay?"

"What's your last name?" It comes out as a mumble. My cheeks burn.

"Rousseau." He winks. "And my middle name is Carter."

"Avery Carter Rousseau," I say. It's a pretty string of names.

"And you, Charlotte? What is your last name?"

His phone starts ringing before he can finish speaking. He raises an eyebrow at me, prompting me to answer him as he digs out his phone.

"Galston."

I don't see the caller ID, but his face darkens. He leans forward, pressing a quick kiss to my lips. "I'm sorry, Charlotte Galston, I have to take this."

And then he is gone.

Chapter 5

I CAN'T WAIT TO GET AWAY FROM THIS PARTY.

My dress is suffocating. The high neckline presses against my collarbone in a way that feels like fingers strangling me. I wind through the house, avoiding hallways and rooms where people are gathered. It's a yearly thing: my parents hosting an end of the summer party filled with coworkers, friends, and family. It is always a weird combination of people they don't quite like, people they do like, and people they love. My parents are masters at encasing everyone in the same phrase: *So good to see you!*

I make it to the kitchen without being called upon, into the pantry, and up the antiquated servants' staircase to the second floor. I pause outside my bedroom door, pressing my forehead to the cool paint for a second. Further down the hall, in one of the other bedrooms, it sounds like people are arguing. After a minute, a girl bolts out of the room. She freezes when she sees me, one hand on her hair and the other tugging the hem of her dress down. I get the distinct impression of watching a deer frozen before an oncoming car, or a predator—*Am I the predator?* She is delicate and beautiful, but in a chaotic kind of way. Her eyes are bloodshot, dark brown orbs, open wide as if she's seen too much, and can't stop seeing too much. Her full lips hang open, mouth gaping. Her whole body is still until she sniffs, swiping a hand under her nose.

I let that action settle into me. *Please,* I pray, *don't let one of my cousins be doing something stupid like cocaine or making girls cry.* Ignoring the knot forming in my stomach, I stride towards the girl and the open door. She flattens against the wall until I pass her, and then she flees toward the main stairs. I don't have to guess that she is someone's daughter, brought here to impress someone and wrangle her either a husband or a job. Her short black dress and dark makeup—a bit much for a *summer* party— spell out her intent: husband.

I pause in the open doorway. It isn't a cousin in the bedroom, but someone I don't immediately recognize: short dark hair, muscular, a crisp lavender shirt with a white bow tie. He sits on the bed, elbows on his knees and his hands holding up his head. A defeated position. The urge to back away slowly dances through me. But then, he looks up and pins me with a gaze. His head tilts to the side, like he doesn't quite recognize me, either.

My eyes travel over his nose and his lips and his square jaw. My gaze settles on his eyes—dark blue like a pair of sapphires. Recognition jolts through me, an electric zap, quickly chased by confusion. Jared isn't supposed to be here. He isn't supposed to be anywhere *near* here, because he is supposed to be back at school, and I am mourning Avery and New York City.

I blink, and Avery's face swims in front of mine. *Don't forget about me*, he tells me in my dreams. I wish he had really said that.

The suffocating feeling creeps back. Jared still stares at me, looking a little more lost than he did before. And just as miserable. Maybe he doesn't recognize me. The last I saw of him was three weeks before I started tenth grade, when he showed up on my doorstep to say goodbye. *Off to boarding school*, his parents had proclaimed. The Browns were strict, and Jared was decidedly unruly. He was kept away, even during the summers. My fearless leader was banished because of one incident, with a four-word declaration. That was six years ago.

He opens his mouth, but I hold up my hand to stop him. "Making girls cry at parties is in bad taste. Especially when a few words can get twisted around and ruin reputations. Go back downstairs. Or better, just leave."

My legs decide to cooperate, then, and I walk as quickly as I can back to my room. I shut the door behind me with a soft click, leaning against it. It hurts to inhale. I wish, with all my might, that everything was different.

Everything.

That thought nearly unhinges me. I slide down the door until I am on the floor. Wrapping my arms around my legs, I let that thought wash over me. I wish I had more understanding parents. I wish I had less pressure. I wish I had kissed Avery more. I wish I had, at the very least, followed Avery. Gave him my phone number. Waited for him to come back.

The last one is a lie. I did wait, for almost an hour, but he didn't return. I reread the same paragraph of my book over and over again, distracted by every twig snapping, every bird fluttering around in that damn maze. And then it was like I was possessed by a ghost. I couldn't stop haunting those areas. Almost daily, I passed through the Culture Espresso, sat, and then fidgeted until I forced myself to leave. I took the long route past the ferry for Ellis Island. I trampled through the maze, memorizing the turns, only to feel lost at the center when he wasn't there. Finally, around the end of August—a full two months since meeting him—I realized: Avery had left the city. And with it, me.

This damn dress still strangles me.

I claw at the back until I get the zipper down, pulling the top down until it pools around my waist. I kick off my heels while I'm at it, frenzied motions made more difficult by still sitting on the floor. Once free, I shakily exhale.

Life would be different if he and I had stayed in the same city. If he had come back after that phone call, picked up my hand, kissed it, and let us read our books in silence. Took me out to dinner, then a string of dinners, and then we would be dating. Easy.

But then I would have left New York, Chicago bound by the end of August, leaving him... where? To follow me to Chicago? To go wherever the wind blew? He struck me as the kind of man that followed his feet wherever they led. Whimsical, romantic, dire. Maybe not my perfect match for a relationship, or even within my comfort zone, and definitely hardwired to fail.

"It doesn't matter," I say aloud. It wouldn't have worked, anyway.

That's what I tell myself on repeat as I pick myself up off the floor.

"Charlie," a voice says on the other side of my door. I step away as it inches open. "I'm coming in." Jared slides through, closing it behind him. He leans against the door, blocking my escape. I'm not in any position to escape, though, so I take a few steps backward.

"Hi," I mutter. I realize that I'm standing in my nude shift, but there's nothing to do except pretend it isn't happening.

"Are you okay?" He looks at me with concern. "Why is your dress off?"

I shake my head. "It was strangling me."

He rolls his eyes. "You did love to deflect."

"My mother taught me that." I contemplate him when he doesn't say anything. "Why—" But I can't get any more words out. *Why are you in my room?* I want to ask, but I can't. *Why was that girl crying?* I also want to ask. *Why are you back home?* And maybe, *Why did you forget about me?*

It's been too long. There's too much empty space between us.

He exhales. "I don't know what to tell you, Charlie," he says.

"Okay," I say. I throw my hand toward the door. "Get out, then."

He does.

My mother knocks on my door as I finish freshening my makeup in my bathroom. She peeks her head in, a small frown on her face. She is barely an inch shorter than me, and at least twenty-five pounds lighter. Plus, she somehow manages to never have a hair out of place. I missed those genes.

"Your dress, Charlotte?" The disappointment is evident in

her voice.

Still, I meet her gaze in the mirror as I swipe on fresh lipstick. My new dress is the same base color as the first one—dark blue—with a wide scoop neck, and cut in an A-line style that flares out gracefully from my hips. It's what I would have picked from the beginning, if I had a choice in the matter.

"Someone spilled a drink on the other one," I tell her.

Her expression relaxes, shoulders lowering slightly. "You should be more careful," she says. With that, my body seems to let go of the last bit of tension in it. But then, she ruins it. "Honey, you don't have to lie. You found out about Jared, didn't you?"

I shake my head, confused. Does she mean him and the girl in the bedroom?

She steps forward and, in a moment of rare affection, puts her hand on my shoulder. We look at each other through the mirror. Something stops us from directly facing the other. Sometimes love is easier when you don't have to look at someone.

"He came with his family, as invited. I told you he might be back from the capital. But then this girl showed up..." She sniffs. It isn't a sad sniff, either. It's a *someone screwed up* sniff. "He got her pregnant."

Oh.

I didn't expect that.

The way the girl had swiped under her nose—clearly crying and not on drugs. Her other hand pressed against her stomach; it was indicative of something much more than just being upset. She looked young, too. Younger than me, and I haven't even graduated college, yet. I had guessed her look correctly, though: she was husband hunting. But apparently it was Jared that made her show up, not a clever parent. Is she blackmailing Jared into marriage? Or was this the first time he had heard of her pregnancy, and he didn't react the way she'd hoped? Why else would you ambush a guy at a party filled with influential people?

I want my mother to take her hand off me as much as I want her to hug me. She is doing this because she believes I will be upset. Her perfect match for me is suddenly unworthy, and it's a slap in her face as much as she perceives it will be a slap in mine. I'm sure she is already taking Jared's name off of the invitation for next year. From *Mr. & Mrs. Brown and Jared* to, simply, *Mr. & Mrs. Brown.* Couldn't have a scandalous man running around impregnating women.

The thought of having kids petrifies me. My hand floats over my stomach, but I can't picture growing a baby inside of me. Mom always said she only needed two angel grandbabies. Dad never said anything about it, but his eyes glowed at Mom in an unfamiliar way when she talked of it. *Plenty of time for that later,* was how my mom would end the conversation, smiling. After all, I was barely twenty-one. There had to be an actual boyfriend, who then had to become a husband, before there could be any talk of babies. Or so I thought.

Apparently, Jared skipped a few steps.

"Ready to go back downstairs, Charlotte?"

I jerk. Mom's hand has disappeared from my shoulder, and she is already out in my bedroom. She is probably looking for my dress, for evidence of a drink soiling it. I had thought ahead in that regard and poured water down the front, leaving it air-drying on the hook behind my door. She makes a noise in her throat, which I take to mean that she found it.

"Five minutes," Mom says before the door clicks shut

behind her.

I sag against the sink counter. Five minutes to get my shit together.

Chapter 6

PAST

I SLAMMED THE NOTEBOOK CLOSED MID-THOUGHT and squeezed my eyes shut. I tried to remember the day Jared told me he was moving back into his own house. Our true friendship began after his house burned down and my parents offered the two guest rooms to his family. I was nine.

I stared at ten-year-old Jared, who had just told me he was moving out.

"The house is done," he declared. "Daddy toured it yesterday and said that it was ready." He told me this *after* he had packed his little suitcase of clothes. There was a box of baubles and knickknacks he had collected while he lived with us sitting on the bed. This was *his* room. It was blue. There was a toy airplane on the dresser, and a helicopter—the blades actually spun—next to it. His stuff was always thrown around. Jeans on the floor, shirts on the chair in the corner, boxers *everywhere.* At nine, it was gross, but I wasn't sure why. Cooties, probably.

His parents had the room down the hall, which had been my room before their house burned down. I was temporarily evicted, because his parents deserved the room with the private bathroom. Jared and I shared the one in the hallway.

He had been a pain in the butt in the beginning. He took my favorite chair at the dining table, drank all the orange juice, and burped out loud. I marveled at that, and the way his dad only gently reprimanded him with a quiet, "Manners, Jared." His dad was always quiet, but in a nice way. If my dad got quiet, there was something dangerous brewing inside of him.

Also, if I were to belch like that, I would not be allowed to speak at the dinner table for a week.

"You're leaving?" I asked. Somehow, I couldn't quite fathom it. I'd thought he was going to stay forever. My eyes welled up with tears.

He dropped the suitcase and came over, awkwardly patting my shoulder. As I cried harder, he wrapped me in a bony hug. "It's okay, Charlie, we're still going to go on adventures together." Charlie, because he was embarrassed hanging out with *Charlotte*, and referring to me as such would only dampen his rising social status.

I brightened, the tears momentarily abated. "When?" I breathed.

"Tonight. We can meet tonight, in your backyard."

"Why not your backyard?" I asked.

He shook his head like I was a silly girl. "Because you're nine. You're not allowed to cross the street alone, remember?"

When we went back to school and everyone found out about the house fire, Jared's popularity soared. At first, I watched from the sidelines. I didn't have friends—I was the quiet nerd girl, after all—but I pretended to play with some of the girls at recess. I pretended I didn't know that they were running away from me on purpose; I always ended up *it*.

One day, Jared jogged over. I was standing there, panting, as all the other girls giggled and bolted around in circles around me. I knew they were giggling *at* me, but I couldn't catch them. They were all too fast. He stood there with me as I caught my breath, and, slowly, the girls stopped running.

Some of them kept touching their hair, and giggling at nothing. They seemed surprised, too, that the older, popular boy was paying attention to me.

He ignored them all, tugged on my hand, and said, "Come play with me." He waited for me at the bus when school got out, as well, and sat next to me for the ride home.

That was the same routine almost every day, and I feared that, now that he was leaving, it would all be ending. Everyone would return to their regularly scheduled broadcast. I would return to being the invisible girl I used to be.

"Are things going to change?" I asked him as he went back to his suitcase.

"Us?" he asked. He was always on the same page as me.

I nodded.

"No, of course not, dummy. We're best friends."

I grinned at him. It turned out he was right. Nothing changed.

That night, I snuck out of my house and waited, huddled, on my back porch. It was October, and the nighttime air had a bite to it. There was one spot that was hidden from view of both the automatic porch light and my parents' bedroom window. Waiting for him, I felt more alone than I ever had. It wasn't a feeling that I was accustomed to; for all of my life, I had been surrounded by people.

"Charlie," Jared whispered.

I jumped. He materialized out of the darkness. I stood and met him on the grass, grinning at him. He messed up my hair and started jogging toward the old tree in the far corner of my yard.

A simple platform had been built almost two years ago by some guys doing work for my parents. One of them spotted me playing by the tree, glanced around, and then walked over. He had spit out a quick question, *Little girl, do you want a treehouse?* I smiled at him, and he smiled back. My mother came out of the house, then, and yelled for me to get inside. I edged around the construction worker and went to my mother. She had palmed the back of my head, hugging me to her. *Don't go outside without me,* she told me. I didn't—I wasn't allowed— but as soon as our roof was finished and the men left, I raced outside to find that platform built twenty feet in the air and some planks nailed into the trunk to help my ascent.

We climbed up and sat facing each other. Jared pulled a backpack off of his shoulders. From it, he pulled out a small flashlight, a blanket, and a jar of peanut butter with two spoons. "Storytime," he said.

"I hope that's smooth," I said, pointing at the peanut butter.

He puffed his chest. "Only the best for you, my dear." We burst out laughing, and I opened the jar while Jared spread the blanket over our shoulders. "Okay." His voice dropped a bit. "Storytime," he repeated. "A long time ago, a boy had a lot of things."

I nodded. Yes, he *did* used to have a lot of things.

"The boy didn't really care about much except his basketball and the cool shoes his mom had gotten him a few weeks ago. He liked to shoot hoops and play with his friends. He barely noticed the people around him, especially the girl with the boy's name. Sure, she could hit like a boy, and she could run like a boy, but she was a girl with girly—Hey!"

He rubbed his arm where I had punched him.

"*Anyway*, she was really cool, but for a while the boy ignored her because she was a girl and he had friends that would've made fun of him for hanging with her." He shrugged. "And then the boy's house was stolen away by a fire breathing dragon. All he had left were the clothes on his back. But it wasn't his other friends who rushed him on the leftover grass that didn't burn. It was the girl who crushed him with a hug and told him it would be okay." He sighed. I imagined, for a second, that he was picturing himself as an ice dragon, freezing the fire.

"That's a good story," I said. He stuck his finger in the peanut butter and scooped a glop of it into his mouth. "The boy would probably go on to be a dragon hunter, don't you think?"

His shoulder bumped into mine and he smiled. "Maybe. But until the boy was older he wouldn't be able to do crap." My eyes widened. "Don't tell my mom I said crap."

I licked the last of the peanut butter off of my spoon.

"I don't want to close my eyes in the new house."

He looked so lonely, even sitting next to me, that I threw my arms around his shoulders. I buried my face in his neck. "You're not alone, Jared," I whispered.

I heard him groan, but he didn't try to dislodge me. "I see it burning, over and over again."

I rubbed at his back the way my mom would when I cried. He exhaled, but it was shaky. "It'll be okay. Your house isn't going to burn down again."

"I forgot to add, 'and the boy realized what a true friend was.'"

I leaned away from him. "You're nice."

"I wasn't talking about *you*."

I punched him again, and he laughed.

We stayed there until it was too cold, and too late, to stay any longer. "You can sleep over," I offered. He shrugged and glanced toward his new house.

"I'll sleep over next time," he said.

"Night, Jared."

Part II

THIRTEEN MONTHS
LATER | AUGUST

The third time I see Avery,
He is broken

Chapter 7

M Y BEST FRIEND, GEORGIA, HAS A BIG GLASS OF
wine in front of her when I get home. There is an
empty glass waiting for me, which makes me love
her more. I had texted her this morning that I had the potential
to be fired from my brand-new job.

"I have ice cream in the freezer," she says as I drop my purse
on the counter.

"I didn't get fired," I say.

"Get out."

I grin and shrug. I'm not sure how I pulled it off, either. "He
made me go with him to a meeting with the CFO. I somehow
didn't screw it up."

Georgia grins. "Celebratory wine, then." She points to my
glass, and I pour myself some. "Cheers!" After we both take a
sip, she giggles. "I definitely thought you were going to be out
on your ass."

I pretend to be insulted for a second.

"Just imagine your mother's face."

We burst into laughter.

"I think she would disown me!"

My mother had been generous enough to cover my rent for last month. I wouldn't have been able to stay in Chicago without her help. "Asking for help builds character, Charlotte," she had told me when I called her in July. I was shocked that she didn't condescend. And then she had continued, "I'm glad you're trying to make a name for yourself out there. We want you to be successful, and that doesn't happen overnight."

I had shed a few tears when she said that.

But, still, she had made it clear that failure wasn't an option.

"Seriously," Georgia says, "you're good?"

"Seriously," I confirm.

"Well, there's still ice cream..."

We laugh again, and I join her on the couch. Before I accepted the job, I had consulted with some people I had worked for at my internship. I asked if they thought it would be a good job opportunity or if I should look for something else. I was warned that my new boss was a hard ass and went through assistants like cigarettes. Based on today, they weren't exaggerating.

"He was nice in the interview. Remember? Kind of gruff, but he said I had an interesting resume for someone who was just graduating college." I snort. "*Interesting* should've been my first clue. Why not something like *impressive*? And then today..." I tip my head back and let out a sigh. "I don't know, it was like he was Dr. Jekyll in the interview and Mr. Hyde for most of today."

She pats my knee. "We all have horrible bosses at some point."

"I think my mother gave Jared my phone number," I tell her.

Georgia and I met in college, and we've lived together since our junior year. She has ventured home to Massachusetts with me on occasion and knows the history surrounding my neighborhood—most of it, anyway. Just this past September, she came with me to my parents' Labor Day party. Jared was absent, which made me guess that he was too busy with his baby and its mother. I was too ashamed of my thoughts to ask my mother or his parents.

Georgia glares at me. "Why would you think that? Why would she do that?"

I fiddle with the wine glass in my hands. "Because I have a message on my phone from him." My heart had stopped when I realized it was his voice in my ear.

"What did he say?"

"Uh." I stop and roll my eyes. Why did I bring this up to her? "I don't know. Nonsense, really. Something about wanting to catch up."

"And you *believe* him?"

I think I laid on my grief about never hearing from him once he left a *little* too thick, when I told Georgia about my childhood. She would go to battle over anyone that hurt me, past or present.

I shrug again. My heart has picked up speed, thundering out of my control. Maybe I should call him back. Maybe not.

Hey, Charlie, it's... uh, it's Jared. Jared Brown. Ha. Anyway, I figured... I don't really know. I guess I just wanted to hear your voice. Call me back when you get this.

I leave Georgia to her television show and walk into my room. I stare at my phone and listen to the message twice more before I press *call back.*

"Charlie?"

I have a lump in my throat that I can't seem to swallow around.

"I'm sorry for calling..."

There are so many feelings racking up inside of me.

"Are you there?"

"I'm here," I say.

He chuckles. "Wow. You've never been quiet."

I shake my head. *Yes, I have.* I lost my voice, and it took a while to get it back.

He laughs in my ear, because I haven't responded. His voice is low and smoky, and so different from how it was before.

"I'm sorry—"

He cuts me off with one word: "Charlie."

I close my mouth. I can't read his voice like I could when we were children.

"I wanted to apologize for last year."

"What happened last year," I repeat. I feel like *I* should be the one apologizing—I yelled at him, after all. "That wasn't..."

He sighs. "No, really. I didn't—Macie shouldn't have been there. I didn't know she was going to show up."

Pregnant. My mind supplies the word that Jared hasn't acknowledged. He didn't know she was going to show up pregnant.

"Jared," I start, and pause at his quick intake of breath. When he doesn't interrupt me, I continue, "It isn't your fault. And you shouldn't be apologizing to *me.*" Jared may have fractured my soul in one moment, but it wasn't his fault. I should've prepared for the eventuality of him moving on because we hadn't talked in years. It just surprised me how much it hurt.

"Okay," he says. There are notes of uncertainty in his voice that I don't understand. "I just—I was a shitty friend, at the end,

50

and then..."

I shake my head again, and I want to say, *No, no, don't go there.* I don't want to talk about the past. A shiver runs through my body. I've done so well at blocking out what happened after he left. "I have to go," I say instead.

There is silence for a moment. I wonder if the call dropped, or maybe he hung up first. And then, "Okay."

"Bye, Jared," I whisper. Tears prick my eyes, because this feels final.

"Goodbye, Charlie."

Chapter 8

PAST

D EAR JARED,
       Are you coming home for Thanksgiving? I am
       hopeful because I miss you, and I keep crying
       randomly. It's been forever and a day, and
sometimes it feels like infinity is just stretching on in front of
me. It's this stupid road that just goes on and on and I hate it.
I want to veer off the road and crash into the trees.

Halloween was awful. It was just Halloween last week,
and I went to a party. Colby invited me. My mom was so
excited that I got invited. I think she's always wanted me to be
popular, but friends (besides you, obviously) just haven't
worked out for me. So she pretty much forced me to go...

Colby was leaning against my locker when I walked up to it.
My arms were full of books, and I stared at him, willing him to
move. He eventually did, sliding to the side and tugging the

books from my arms. Half of me expected him to drop them on the ground and stomp on them.

Instead, he held them and watched me with steady eyes. After I opened my locker, he shoved them inside and closed it. "Lunch," he said. He had been offering in the past, but this time seemed different. I felt a thrill of danger under my skin; it was the look in his eyes. It was too intense. "Charlotte, come to lunch."

I shook my head. I didn't like that feeling. One step closer, and I would get shocked. "I have plans," I said.

He quirked his lips. "Plenty of girls would kill to have lunch with me, and I want to eat with you."

"No," I said again. I move around him, headed toward the library. I had a date with a book. He watched me go, and my skin crawled until I rounded the corner. I let out a sigh I hadn't realized I was holding.

But in the library, Colby found me again. He had a lunch tray with him, and he plopped down across from me with a clang that made me cringe. "Halloween," he said. I looked at him blankly. "Come with me to a party."

He never asked me, and maybe that was what irked me the most. When Jared did it, it was okay. We were friends. Colby had come sauntering into our lives with his hard eyes and brash language and demanded things that I didn't want to give.

I shook my head and ignored him.

I thought, later, that maybe it was *that* point that fueled him on more. He went to my house. He talked to my mother, made up some story about how I was worried she wouldn't say yes to an older boy—a *junior*—and told her how he really wanted to take me to a Halloween party at his friend's house. So then it was my mother, standing in the doorway of my bedroom, glaring holes through my head until I agreed to go.

It was a disaster.

Mom picked out the costume; at that point, I had given up hope of controlling the situation. That night, she walked into my room with a bag in her hand. "I had this made," she said to me. "Look what I found! We can do your makeup to match." She pulled out a green leotard, and I realized that I had unwittingly become Tinkerbell.

Well, she didn't have a voice, either.

When Colby showed up an hour later, I saw it had been planned: he was the spitting image of Peter Pan. "Ah, Tink," he whispered to me. And then, to my mother, "Should we get some pictures?"

It felt like the ultimate betrayal to smile and stand close to him.

I got into his car, and it was the beginning of the end.

I'm sorry, Jared, I can't... I don't want to talk about this anymore. I hope you come home for Thanksgiving. I realize that you're never going to read these unless I mail them, and I'm not going to do that. We were always on the same telepathic wavelength. Why can't you know that I need you?

Please come home.

Charlie

Chapter 9

MY HAIR TANGLES IN MY FACE AS I RUSH down the sidewalk, late. Literally, I am running toward the hotel. They didn't nickname Chicago *The Windy City* for nothing. Tom and I have a meeting with some executives from a firm in Boston—some sort of merger deal. My heart sinks when I see him waiting for me, because he looks perfect, as usual. What kind of hair gel does he use? It never moves. I take a deep breath, slowing my pace to a brisk walk and approaching him with fake confidence. When he turns toward me, I am shocked to see him holding two cups of coffee.

Nice generally hasn't been in his playbook.

"You're late," he snaps. And then he looks me over and blinks a few times. Maybe *he's* going into shock. I can't stop staring at the coffee. My zombie brain can practically imagine its taste. "Go fix your hair in the bathroom. You're a damn disaster, Galston."

"Sorry, Tom." I glance from him to the coffee. "Is one of those for me?" The hopeful tone in my voice kills me. I struggle against the blush creeping up my neck. *Every damn time.* Tom is attractive. And married. Besides, I learned in college that my first love would always be coffee—and that's clearly the case, the way I'm giving it moony eyes.

He passes it over, then uses that hand to push me toward the restroom.

True to form, my hair is a nest. I am surprised there are no leaves or twigs to pull out. I keep a hairbrush in my purse and a hair tie on my wrist for these exact reasons. It takes a few minutes to get it sorted. When I return to the lobby, Tom is leaning against the receptionist's desk. There are three receptionists behind the long desk, but only one focuses on him.

I approach as the receptionist tells Tom, "Mr. Henley will be down in a minute for you."

Tom nods. "Charlie, we need you to sign in, as well."

The receptionist's eyes widen a fraction before she laughs. "Oh, Mr. Kasper, I was expecting a man!"

Do not roll your eyes.

I say, "It's short for.... Avery?"

There he is.

"How is Charlie short for Avery?" The receptionist wrinkles her nose.

I don't answer. I barely give her another glance before I start walking toward him.

"Where are you going?" Tom's voice echoes behind me.

There he is.

He has a suitcase next to him and a folded newspaper on his lap. His hair is longer, pulled back into a low ponytail. He has a slight scruff. When I get closer, his eyes flicker up to mine.

For a second, I think he won't recognize me. It has been just over a year, after all. A year since we kissed, and then he disappeared from New York altogether.

And now? He's in my city. In the same building as me. On the same day, at the exact same time. Fate. But only if he remembers me.

"Avery?" My voice quivers. This should not affect me so much, and yet there it is. All the emotion I had blocked out is shoved to the forefront of my mind. He looks gaunt, from either lack of sleep or unhealthy eating. Maybe both. I need to know how he ended up in Chicago.

I see the minute it clicks. He stands, the newspaper forgotten. It falls, scattering on the floor and drawing attention, but he doesn't react to that. He comes closer and closer, and he wraps his arms around me, pulling me flush against him. I inhale into his chest, letting a small smile flicker across my lips. He's taller than I remember. My head tucks under his chin. Hesitantly, I hug him back.

He sighs a long, slow breath that tickles my ear. Our bodies easily melt into each other. It's like we've done it a million times before and couldn't forget how. Like riding a bike. It's strangely intimate.

"Charlotte," he whispers. "I was hoping—"

"Galston," Tom calls. He hasn't moved from the desk across the lobby, and his voice rings across the open space. I cringe at his tone. "We're late." I could hear him thinking, *again*.

I pull away from Avery and look into his golden-brown eyes. Thirteen months later, and they are just as I remember them. There are so many things I want to say, or do, but can't. I smooth his tie, and even that feels too familiar.

"Dinner? Tonight? Please, Charlotte?" One of his old smiles slips over his face like a mask. "We can catch up."

"Are you staying here?" I ask. I take a few steps backwards, toward Tom. Maybe it would be enough to appease him a few more seconds.

"Yes."

"Okay, I'll meet you here."

"Seven o'clock," he answers.

I keep backing up, grinning, until I hear Tom say my name again.

Once in the elevator, with Tom tapping his foot next to me, I let my grin fade. If he's just visiting Chicago, I can't get my hopes up about us working out.

"Do you have my paperwork?"

I swing my purse in front of my body. It's large enough to double as a briefcase most days. He takes the file, flipping through it. Maybe he won't ask any questions about Avery. I don't know how to answer them, anyway.

"Okay." Tom takes a deep breath. Is he nervous? "You'll take notes?"

I nod. Life as an executive-slash-personal assistant... not always exciting. But today? I'm happy for it, because it's brought Avery and me together again.

"And, Charlie. Don't be late again."

Chapter 10

I WALK INTO THE APARTMENT AND FREEZE WHEN I see Georgia in only a bra and shorts. "Why are you not wearing clothes?" I try not to snort, but it slips out anyway.

Georgia laughs. "I stayed over at Henry's last night," she whispers. They had been steadily getting more and more serious. While I am positive they've had sex before—I got all the details when *that* happened—they had never slept over at each other's places. The fact that they are at this point now is promising. It isn't just another fling.

I raise my eyebrows. Sometimes I cover one of my eyebrows with my hair so it looks like I'm just raising one. It doesn't fool anyone. "And?"

"And... it was good." She presses her lips together, looking down. "I'm scared, Charlie. Maybe it was *too* good."

Georgia is a romantic. She lives for the roses and fireworks and whatever else. I go over and hug her, because she looks like she needs it. "He didn't disappear in the middle of the night?" That had happened before.

Her hair swings around her with the force of her head shake. "No, no. We made breakfast together," her gaze becomes dreamier, "and had morning sex—"

"You know I love you, but I don't need to hear about that."

Georgia bites her lip to hide a smile. "Sorry, babe. It scared me, letting him in like that, but he made it seem okay. He made me not worry."

I chew over her words.

At the beginning of our senior year of college, Georgia and I moved in together. One year later, we were still in the same apartment. Over our years of friendship through college and beyond, I've witnessed Georgia's taste in men. Which is to say, she really didn't have a particular taste, except for the fact that she always chose the one that was going to leave her ass for the next best thing.

There was Chad of freshman year, who proclaimed he loved her on the third date, and by the fifth date was cheating on her. There was Mark, a "nice guy" who freaked out when Georgia talked to any male besides him, including coworkers and friends. Then Anthony and Chad #2; Lorenzo was a foreign exchange student, so that was bound to end badly—and it did. They all did. Epically, loudly, and with a resounding echo.

After that string, Georgia gave up dating. She claimed to be working on turning into a lesbian, but we weren't sure attraction worked like that. To test that theory, she made out with a girl in a club and "didn't feel anything." After *that*, she vowed temporary celibacy—a six-month cleanse. I was on board with that because, by that time, it was three months post-Avery, and I hadn't been on a single date since high school. It felt too raw. With one kiss, Avery had mixed up my insides. It took too long to put the pieces back in order.

We survived the six months boy-free and plunged back into the dating world. Georgia found Henry almost immediately, and they've been dating ever since. I had no luck—not that I was willing to push it. Any guy who showed interest was met with a scowl.

Tom was right: I am a damn disaster.

"If this thing with Henry scares you, maybe you just need to jump in with both feet." I don't ask her if he's *the one*, although if I did, she might have answered yes. I'm not ready for her to not need me anymore. Soon, I'd be replaced by him—that's what long-term boyfriends did. They became the best friend, too.

She nods, accepting my advice.

"I saw Avery," I say, unable to keep the sudden delight off of my face.

Her mouth pops open. "What the hell is he doing in Chicago?"

"I have no idea." I tell her everything.

When I'm done, she squeals. "Charlie! This could be it! You've been waiting for this for a fucking *year*. You better get his number and have sex with him. Whether it's in that order is debatable."

My heart picks up speed. Could I do that?

"It just... feels different with him, Georgie. It makes me want to pass out. Or throw up."

Her expression turns thoughtful. She knows my tendency to avoid romance... or rather stomp all over romance. I like order, and keeping everything neat, and keeping my feelings compartmentalized. Romance does not have a place beside practicality. Plus, I've never had such a visceral reaction to a man before.

"He could really hurt me," I whisper.

Georgia counters, "It's true, you could never see him again. Like last time. But *this* time, you can end it on a good note."

I glance at my watch. I have about two hours to get ready to see Avery. Butterflies wiggle in my stomach. *Since when does that happen?* I shouldn't allow him to make me feel so irrational.

"Does a good note mean sex?"

She smirks.

I throw my head back, laugh, and say, "I guess that means I should shave my legs."

Chapter 11

PAST

COLBY WAS MY BOYFRIEND, AND I DIDN'T KNOW how it happened. One minute, I was shrugging off his arm and dodging invites. The next, we were 'official' and girls much prettier than me were trying to befriend me.

It wasn't until after Thanksgiving, though, that he insisted on taking me to the movies. He asked in front of my mother, who lingered whenever he was around, and he smirked when she said she was *so* happy for me. To her, he was everything I wasn't: popular, charming, social. He was light to my dark, and I needed him to balance myself out. In reality, I wasn't sure he had a speck of light in him.

In the theater, he held my hand so tightly that I felt my bones grind together. Ten minutes in, I slid past him and bolted to the restroom. Fifteen-year-old me didn't know why I was throwing up or why the sight of my red hand made my head spin. When I got back, he picked up my hand again and put it on his thigh. He grinned at me, but there was something hard about it.

And then later, in his car, he waited until I was buckled in before he leaned over and kissed me. He palmed the back of my head, pulling me into his mouth. Blood rushed in my ears. This was my first kiss, and I was petrified.

"Open your mouth," he whispered against my lips. When I hesitated, he nipped my lower lip. I gasped, and then his tongue was invading my mouth. I thought I would die, then, from the way my stomach flipped, and my thighs hurt from how hard I squeezed them together.

All I thought about was how my mother would be nodding, pushing me forward.

He kissed me for minutes, but it felt like every second was a year. When he let go of my head, when I was able to lean away, he frowned at me. He started his car without looking at me again. Even in my driveway, nothing.

I didn't say anything, either, as I got out of the car and went inside.

That night, I snuck out of the house and climbed up to the platform in the tree. The toes of my boots peeked over the ledge, and I dared myself to let go of the branch I was holding onto. It wasn't high enough to kill me if I fell; for a moment, that fact disheartened me. There was a layer of snow that had made climbing it difficult, and it seeped into my sweatpants as I sat.

I shivered in my coat, but my thoughts cleared for the first time in a month.

I pulled the small notebook from my pocket, clicking my pen open.

Jared, I'm sorry it's been so long. I guess I was waiting to see if you'd grant me the wish from my last letter—you know, where I begged you to come home for Thanksgiving? Spoiler alert: you didn't.

I think I would hate Colby if he didn't remind me of you. I always saw the confidence you carried around inside of you, but he broadcasts something more extreme. Something more dangerous. He struts around like a freaking peacock, and the world bends at the waist to accommodate him. I shouldn't tell you, but he kissed me. I don't think I liked it, but I haven't ever been kissed before. What if that's the best I'm going to get? Honestly, sometimes I look at him and expect your words to come out of his mouth.

He's the worst parts of you, Jared, but those are the only pieces left.

I sighed and looked up at the sky. The clouds seemed so far away. But then, I exhaled, and suddenly the clouds were around me. I could barely make out the stars through the boney tree branches. I was utterly alone, and I hated it.

I laid back, kicking my feet, and thought about what I had just admitted.

No. It wasn't right. Colby wasn't the worst parts of Jared, or any parts of him; Colby was his own person. He was intimidating and crass, but he hadn't done much to hurt me. Didn't boys pick on girls they liked?

That was it.

I closed my eyes and chewed on that thought.

Chapter 12

I SEE AVERY BEFORE HE SEES ME. HE IS DRESSED like he was this morning, except his shirt is now a different color. Suit, tie, beautiful long blond hair tied at the nape of his neck. He shaved, as well. He stands by the windows, peering up towards the sky. I am tempted to leave him be, to watch him for a minute. He radiates sadness. When he isn't putting up a charade in front of people, I can tell that he is miserable.

I try not to fidget with the hem of my shirt when Avery and I lock eyes. The sadness that I glimpsed earlier is erased—or perhaps overlaid—by his smile. He meets me in the middle of the lobby, lifting my hand. His fingers are calloused, but his palm is smooth and warm. He brings my hand up toward his face and kisses it. I am a ball of nerves, and his lips on my skin send lightning bolts through me.

"Hi," he murmurs. I want to hear him say that forever.

"Hey," I answer at a whisper. My heart better stop galloping out of control. My brain can't keep up.

He threads his hand with mine, fingers laced, and tugs me outside. We wind through the streets of downtown Chicago, all familiar to me from my years in the city. I keep my mouth shut, though, because I feel a bit rebellious. College Charlotte had developed her voice and wasn't afraid to use it; this new version of me was practicing moderation.

"Here we are," Avery says. "Is takeout okay? We can bring it back to my room."

I had been excited for a night out, but I nod.

After we get the food, we backtrack toward the hotel and talk. I ask him why he's here.

He sighs and squeezes my hand. "You mentioned you lived in Chicago," he says. "I'm on my way to Boston, and I scheduled myself an overnight layover here."

"Not to see me," I say. I mean it as a question, but it comes across as an accusation. "How would you have found me?"

He shrugs. "I was hoping to get lucky waiting outside of your work later today... I may have searched for your name on Google. It surprised the hell out of me when you appeared here this morning. My flight had only just got in an hour before."

Wow. "We had a business meeting," I tell him. I don't say that they were from Boston, too, or that the meeting—and possible future merger—went very well.

Once in his hotel room, I put my purse on the table by the door and slide out of my jacket. He moves through the room, turning on lights, and turns and pins me with a look. I feel a blush rise up through my whole body, a flash of heat. "Charlotte," he says. "Or do you prefer Charlie?"

I raise my eyebrows. I don't recall telling him about my nickname.

"I heard the man you were with call you Charlie this

morning."

"Well, you can call me whatever you want. Except Charlotte Harper—that's my mother's favorite go-to when she's angry with me." I laugh.

His eyes soften. "I like Charlotte. It's how I thought of you... before."

"I know what you mean. I only thought of your full name in my head. Avery Carter Rousseau. Every time." I wink and add, "Not that I'll admit how often that was."

"Probably not a lot. It has been a year, after all."

"Well, a little more than that." I slowly close my eyes, trying to control the blush. I open them again and meet his gaze. He looks tanner than the last time we saw each other. "What have you been up to? I'll admit, I was pleasantly surprised to find you here. Although definitely shocked." I study my fingernails. "I didn't really think I'd ever see you again."

"Hey," Avery mutters. He crosses to stand in front of me. "I'm sorry about that."

A well of emotions surges in me. Anger that he is sorry. Relief that he is sorry. Disappointment that he didn't come back to me. All the feelings from before: the worry, the confusing heartache after having met him *twice*. The fear that I'd never meet anyone that made my stomach twist.

"I looked for you."

Oh, god. There is a lump in my throat, but it's nothing compared to the avalanche of misery flowing across Avery's face. I just pulled up some pretty painful memories.

He bows his head for a minute, then meets my eyes again. "That phone call, in the garden?" He waits until I nod. "My dad was calling to tell me that my grandmother had passed away. That's one of the reasons I decided to pack up and move back home."

Impulsively, I grab his hands. They are familiar already, and I can count on one hand the number of times I have been able to touch him. It would be so easy to lean forward and kiss him. And why shouldn't I? I pull him toward me, tilting my face up. He raises an eyebrow for a split second before meeting me halfway. Butterflies swirl in my stomach, but this kiss feels different. It lacks the intensity from our last kiss. I press away the doubt and redouble my efforts, opening my mouth and sliding my tongue into his.

Suddenly, he responds. He presses me against the wall, caging me in and taking over. I don't object when his hands go to the button of my pants. It feels hurried and unreal—all before we've eaten dinner—but I push away the thought that he's anything similar to my past. Finally, I have him alone. His fingers slide into my underwear, eliciting a gasp from me.

He pulls away and unzips his fly, freeing his erection. He has the nerve to push down on my shoulders.

And *that* pulls me out of the mood.

"Stop it."

I don't have enough air in my lungs, and I'm trapped between the wall and him. I push at his chest until he takes a few steps backwards.

Avery blinks at me.

"I don't really like how that just went," I tell him. "You went from nice to demanding a blow job in about two seconds."

He sniffs, and his eyes get distant. "Charlotte, I'm sorry, but—"

I'm not interested anymore, I fill in. Message received. It stings a bit, especially after the warm welcome this morning. I nod at him. I smooth my hair down and stride toward the door.

I can't believe this.

Before I make it very far, he latches onto my wrist. "Wait,

please," he says.

I stop but don't turn to face him. I feel like I am going to burst into tears. I had put a lot of weight on this date. Why? Why had I done that? We don't even live in the same city!

He sighs. It moves my hair a bit, and he wraps his arms around my waist, still behind me. His hands lace together over my navel. There is a pressure at the top of my head, and I know he is resting his chin there. I am encased, anchored to him. "Please, I'm sorry, I lost myself for a moment. Let me explain and we can finish dinner." He slowly turns me to face him. We're close enough to touch, but we aren't; there's a hair's breadth of space between us. "We have more than a year to catch up on. And... all the time before that, too."

I wait, watching him. He lets go of me and wrings his hands together. He steps back, dropping his head. Perhaps he assumes I will say no, run away, and never look back. The defeated look, more than anything, spurs on my answer.

"Okay." We both sit on the edge of his bed, angled toward each other. I'm not sure what to do next, because he just stares at me.

I wish the urge to kiss him would go away, but it doesn't. It thrums under my skin like an extra pulse. It feels like I am on fire when he brushes my hair back from my cheek.

No fair, I want to say. He can touch me, but I can't do the same?

"I met someone back home," he says. "But it just—"

I tilt my head to the side when he abruptly closes his mouth. "Ended?" I supply.

"Do you ever look at someone and only see their good pieces?" he asks.

I do when I look at you, I think. Instead, I ask, "What do you mean?"

"It means I was foolish. She turned my world upside down and I didn't even realize until...." Avery rubs at his neck. It's hard to watch him fumble his way through this.

I look away, my eyes burning. I feel a desperate need to save him from his past working its way up my throat.

"It was the kind of break up that made me leave the state," he finishes.

I wonder who did the breaking: him or her. It's clear that he hasn't moved past it. He can barely look at me. "I'm sorry," I tell him. And I am: I'm sorry that he had to go through that, I'm sorry that I wasn't there to save him, I'm sorry that he's not staying in Chicago so I can heal him. I'm sorry for a lot of things that aren't my fault.

"I meant what I said earlier. I wanted to find you. I had some idea that you'd give me the closure she couldn't."

Closure.

How does one word echo and bounce around in my skull as if it's the only thing left in an empty room?

He lifts my hand and holds it like I'm the delicate one. "Charlotte, I'm glad I found you. I felt like we were unfinished, and I needed to see you."

"I'm glad you found me," I murmur.

"I missed you, even when I barely knew you."

I wish the urge to kiss him had gone away, because those words are undoing me.

The first time I met him, he had been a flurry of movement, a bit chaotic, and utterly devastating. Now, he is quiet. There is a storm locked beneath his skin.

I want to bring it back out. He's a shadow of who he used to be, and I need to remember that he's only in my city for a night. I manage, "You're going to Boston."

Avery looks down at his fingertips, which are pressed

together. "That's probably just as well."

What?

My face pales, and then I feel it turn an ugly shade of red, so hot it burns. "Why do you say that?"

"I think I'd push myself to get into something with you and I'm still effected by my past relationship. It would end badly; can't you see that?"

Suddenly I, too, see the future he talked about: fighting that disintegrates our relationship before it's begun. Misunderstandings. We would be unable to talk about our feelings, or learn about each other, or grow.

Well, on that note... "You're right." I smile at him. Perhaps I show too many teeth, because it doesn't make him relax. "I'm going to go. Avery, it was really nice to see you. To... close this chapter in my book."

He shakes his head. "That's not..."

"No," I say. The word snaps out faster than I intend, sharp like the crack of a whip. "No," again, softer, "that is what you meant. I'm going home. I am not foolish enough to think that after meeting me three times, you'd want to pursue me. So. I'm going to walk out of here with my dignity intact. We won't see each other again."

Silence.

He can't even look at me anymore, but his lips press into a thin line. He knows I am right.

We've ended before we even had a chance to begin.

Part III

ELEVEN MONTHS
LATER | JULY

Life is about to change…
Forever.

Chapter 13

GEORGIA SMIRKS AT ME. I CAN'T SEE HER LIPS behind the giant box she is carrying through my door, but her eyes are twinkling. I almost tell her to shut up— but I realize that I'm acting like a giddy fool. She goes to set the box labeled *Pillows* in my bedroom.

I've been on turbo-speed all morning. The movers finally arrived from Chicago with all of my stuff. The apartment that I've been drooling over for a month, ever since I put down the deposit, is finally mine. The windows are large, the space is perfect for one person, and who cares if my view is of a muddy little river?

Mom breezes into the apartment, carrying another box. *Kitchen* is written on every side. "Charlotte, I think there are utensils in here. Should I start putting things away?"

I take a sticky note and write *Utensils*, slapping it to a large drawer. It was her idea to label where everything should go, so everyone can help put things away. And then I'll be able to find everything. I keep labelling the kitchen while the movers shuffle my bigger items into the apartment. Bed frame and mattress, dresser, an embarrassingly large bookcase, couch, coffee table. In and out they go, and in between them slip Georgia, me, and my mother with other boxes.

When it's all unloaded, I pay the movers and close the door. Dad had to work, otherwise he would have come, too. It's been awhile since I've seen my parents, but not long enough. I'm just waiting for her to start nitpicking. Now that I'm only two hours away, I don't have nearly as good of an excuse to avoid them. I slide the area rug to about where I want it, giving it a shove to unroll it. Georgia helps me lift the couch, and we continue setting up the living room in silence while Mom handles things in the kitchen.

"Honey, you've done a lovely job," Mom says. She stands in the center of my living room. It feels borderline claustrophobic in here; her judgement rolls off of her in waves. "If I could suggest moving the couch, though, the feng shui in this room is off a bit." I glance at Georgia, puff my cheeks for a second, and then nod as I blow out the air. It isn't worth arguing with her. Mom claps her hands together. "Excellent! Georgia, please help me." Together they shift the living room until it is to her satisfaction.

Mom comes over and hugs me. We're nearly the same height and have a lot of the same features. Sometimes I look at her and see how I will look in twenty-five years. I mentally have to add in some wrinkles, of course, because I don't think I would be able to stomach the Botox.

"Shall we set up your bedroom?"

And so we go. Mom arranges it, crowing about feng shui and energy. It isn't how I would've done it, but it works just fine.

I can always rearrange once they're gone.

It feels like hours later when Mom finally heads out. "I'm sure you want to have the place to yourself for a little while. Unpack your clothes and toiletries," Mom says as she heads for the door. Georgia is staying on my couch, and I'm grateful that she took an extra day to help me get settled.

Once we're alone, she says, "Well, should we put everything back to where you wanted it?"

I laugh and shake my head. It's been a long enough day as it is.

Georgia flops onto the couch, and I join her. "Six month leases aren't typical, are they?"

I shrug. "They offered a year or six months. I figured it was best to start small. Who knows where we'll be in January? Maybe Tom will finagle another company takeover and we'll wind up in Hawaii."

"Yeah," she says. "Or you could stumble upon your dream job and leave your boss to get a worker that isn't overqualified within six months." I ignore this. "You're such a pushover."

"What's that supposed to mean?"

She has the grace to look sheepish. "I mean it with love, Charlie. But... you do whatever your mom wants, and whatever Tom wants. You'd probably have two-point-five kids if you could, just because she ordered it. And as for your boss, he snaps his fingers and up and moves you to a whole new city."

I pat her leg. "I love Boston," I whisper. "It was hard to choose to leave you, but you have Henry..."

She groans. "Does this job even make you happy?"

I consider her question.

"Charlotte. Everyone needs to have something that makes them happy. It can't just be a boy, work, or a nice apartment. Yes, those things are great. But what do you do when you don't have those things anymore?"

What makes me happy?

I laugh, suddenly stricken. I swallow my next words: I'm afraid that I don't have anything. Take away the apartment—which isn't even decorated how I want—and take away my job, I have nothing. There's a boy who broke my heart, a city filled with strangers, and parents who wish I was just a little different.

"Painting," I eventually say.

Georgia grins. "Excellent. And you know I'm going to send you the supplies as soon as I get back."

Soon after, we settle in for bed. Who cares if it's only eight o'clock?

I close myself in my room, and I am wrapped in silence. It seeps down my throat and crawls in my ears, and I wonder if I'll ever hear again. The sound of traffic doesn't penetrate the apartment. There is no ticking clock on the wall. No loud neighbors.

I turn on every single light in my room. The lights make me feel better, but my heart still beats a chaotic rhythm. I can feel it in my throat, in my fingertips, struggling against my ribcage. It realizes: in a day and a half, I will be alone. Madly, truly alone.

Chapter 14

PAST

COLBY TRANSITIONED FROM SOMEONE I couldn't get away from to someone I couldn't get enough of—and I didn't notice that I was losing myself in the process. The notebook I wrote to Jared was lost in my closet. Instead of sneaking out to hang out in our tree, I snuck out to meet Colby and his friends.

"Hey, baby," he said when I climbed into the car around the corner. "Swallow."

I blinked at him, and he stared until I opened my mouth. He put something on my tongue and handed me a water bottle. I gulped, closing my eyes. A large part of me didn't care what it was, although I knew I wanted to hold onto my virginity a little bit longer. Whenever he got close to my jeans, fingers toying with the button, I froze up and asked him to stop. He was always vocal about how that wasn't how he had imagined things playing out; he would pout and growl, and then ratchet up the charm as if that could convince me.

He nuzzled my neck, and I turned my lips toward him.

"You're a good girl," he said before he kissed me. I leaned into him, wondering when I'd start to feel the effects of the pill. His tongue swept into my mouth, eliciting a shiver down my spine. Abruptly, he pulled away. "We're going to Marco's house."

I shivered again. Marco's parents were out of town for a week, celebrating New Year's Eve somewhere fancy. There was a party at his house the other night, but I was forced to leave early due to a curfew about which my father wouldn't budge. Colby's hand settled on my thigh as he drove. I let my head fall back against the seat and closed my eyes.

Seconds later, Colby said, "We're here."

I cracked my eyes open and smiled at him.

He smirked at me, looking me up and down. "Damn, you're hot," he said. He got out and circled the car, squatting in my open doorway. I fell toward him, and a tiny ripple of surprise ran through me at the looseness of my body. He caught my arms, shifting them around his shoulders, and bit my neck.

I groaned, letting my head tip back again. His hand on my skin felt like fire as it traced its way up my side, palming and squeezing my breast. "Inside," he grunted. He helped me stand, half supporting my weight until I located my feet. We stumbled up the walkway together, and he opened the door without knocking. In the living room, pairs of people were sprawled on the furniture in various states of undress.

"Colby," I heard. "My man! You made it!"

"Hey, dude," he answered. He used his free hand to do a weird fist bump handshake. My own fist tightened in his shirt at his waist, and he grinned down at me. I couldn't hold his gaze; my eyes kept skating around the room.

"You have her on something?"

"You know how she likes to cut loose," he said. "I'm gonna take her up."

"Go right ahead," his friend answered. I didn't see his face. "Just don't do it on my bed, yeah? Virgins bleed a lot."

I shivered again.

"Don't psych her out with that shit."

Colby turned me toward him and backed me against the wall. His mouth landed on mine, nipping at my lips, and that fire came roaring back. I moaned into his mouth. His hands slid down my thighs, and he lifted me up and off the ground. I wrapped my legs around him.

"You need to lose weight," he muttered, walking quickly toward the stairs. I rested my chin on his shoulder and watched the people in the living room. My eyes felt so heavy. They drifted closed.

I jarred awake when Colby dropped me on a bed. He crawled over me, pushing my shirt up as he went. When he pulled down the cup of my bra and sucked on my nipple, I saw stars. For the first time, I didn't flinch when he unbuttoned my jeans and pulled them down my hips. There was a trickle of inhibition, but it blew away when he pushed his fingers under my underwear. He eventually yanked those off of me, too.

His weight disappeared for a second, and my eyes fluttered closed again.

"Open your eyes," he said from above me. As soon as I did, blinking them open slowly, I felt a pinch and burn in the most vulnerable part of me. My mouth parted, and then slacked. It felt awful and good at the same time.

Colby's weight was mostly off of me, and he moved quickly inside of me. After a few minutes, he buried his face in my neck. "You feel so good," he whispered. "So fucking tight."

I whimpered.

"Relax," he ordered. My muscles responded before I could process, and I sank back into the mattress.

He continued to make noises above me, but I was checked out.

Inexplicably, I thought of Leah and that day she made out with Jared in the water. I wondered what it would've been like to kiss him, to press myself against his chest like she had done. She was now dating a senior—she was moving up in the world, I supposed. It didn't matter than she had made out with my best friend. She apparently owed me nothing.

Colby groaned and trembled over me, his full weight pressing into my body. He was heavy enough to suffocate me. His hands stilled by my head, forcing me to meet his eyes. The world was blurry, but his green eyes stood out. He kissed me, his tongue immediately taking possession of my mouth. I clenched my muscles, and he bit my lip. I could still feel him in me, but it was mixed with a feeling of being untethered.

After a minute, he pulled out and away.

"Fuck," Colby said. "You're fucking bleeding."

A tear slipped loose and rolled down my temple, into my hair. And then another. Another.

"Stop it."

I held my breath, wondering if that would smother the black hole within me.

He pulled me upright, roughly dabbing my thighs with a cloth. He touched my cheek. "You need to stop. They're going to think I forced you."

I shook my head, disjointed. I was wholly unattached.

He stood and left the room while I sat there and stared at the bloody cloth.

When he returned, I was flat on my back with my eyes

closed. "Hey," he whispered. He pulled me upright again. "Drink."

I opened my lips when he put the rim of a cup to my lips. Cool liquid burned as I drank. Vodka, maybe. One, two, three swallows.

He pulled it away and kissed me again. I watched him pull my clothes back on me; he clasped my bra on the wrong hooks, and my underwear bunched under my jeans.

"Good job, baby, now let's go party."

He lifted me from the bed, carrying me down the stairs and dropping me on a couch. His friends greeted us, but I couldn't make my mouth function. The room kept swaying—or was that me?

Minutes later, or maybe hours, Colby jarred me awake. "Fuck, baby, you slept like a rock," he laughed. I rubbed at my eyes, looking around. We were parked in front of my house. "Go on," he said.

"What?"

He got out of the car and circled it, opening my door and unbuckling me. "You should pretend to have the flu or something." The way my stomach suddenly rolled, that wouldn't be a problem. "Go inside."

He helped me stand, then stood back as I walked unsteadily up the front lawn. I tripped and caught myself on the side of the house, but kept going. Almost to the back, I glanced back toward Colby.

He was gone.

I felt the ache so keenly, it doubled me over.

Chapter 15

THE BUZZING IS LOUD, NON-UNIFORM, AND wholly annoying. Lifting my head from the pillow, I am temporarily frightened of the unfamiliar room I am in. The move comes back to me, as well as last night's panic. I had fallen asleep without turning any of my lights off and slept through the night.

Getting up, I stalk toward the noise. I haven't the faintest idea what time it is.

The buzzer to let people into the building is flashing. I press the *talk* button.

"Hello?" My voice is scratchy.

"Charlotte Harper, you let me up right now," Georgia shouts.

I wonder how she got outside. The buzzing starts again. I wince, pressing the button to open the downstairs door.

"I forgot a key, and you pick today to sleep in?" Georgia

looks very put together this morning. She raises an eyebrow, which makes me want to punch her. In her hands, though, is a drink tray with two cups.

I scramble toward her. Bad mood forgotten, she laughs and hands me my cup, which—*yes*—is a cafe mocha.

"I love you," I sighed.

"Are you talking to me or your coffee?"

"Both."

She stomps into my bedroom, looking for evidence of... something. Bottles of booze? Pills? I wince. "Did you sleep on top of your duvet?" she yells. When she reappears, she looks at me with pity.

I hold up my hand, warding off any more questions. "It's fine. I'm fine."

"Babe, you went to sleep with all the lights on? That's not normal. I was right outside your door... why didn't you say something?"

No, it's not normal. There's an adjustment period. Before I realize what's happening, I'm tearing up. "I'm the *definition* of not normal right now," I say. The tears slide down my cheeks. The sadness comes out of nowhere like a summer thunderstorm.

Georgia looks as shocked as I am. Probably because she can count on her hands the number of times I've cried in front of her.

"Okay." She claps her hands. "We're going to get you in the shower. I'll find your clothes and towels, and we'll get ready and go to a museum or some touristy shit today. Okay? Your mom gave me money." She forces a cheerful smile. Touristy things are not in her nature, and she has always fought the idea of my mom giving her money. Her family believes in earning their money. But it makes me feel a little relieved, if not guilty, that she's doing this for me.

I nod, letting her lead me to the bathroom. Despite a spider mishap, and the fact that I was done with my shower long before Georgia found a towel, things were looking better.

"I was thinking the Museum of Fine Arts," Georgia says once we're on the street. "Or the Museum of Science."

We end up at the Museum of Fine Arts. It's closer, and the building is intriguing enough to entice us in. We stare at different types of art in different sections of the building for what must be an hour before finding our way to a section dedicated to odd paintings and drawings.

There are a few that remind me of my father: they are dark, with pockets of light. John Singer Sargent's *Rehearsal of the Pasdeloup Orchestra at the Cirque d'Hiver*, for one, is a whirling mass of dark and light. My father has always wanted the best for me, but his route to get me there has been difficult. There was always a test, and I never had the correct answer.

Worse, yet, were the times when I unintentionally made him angry—the C in Introduction to Economics in college, the lack of boyfriends after Colby, the drawing class. Once I was out of the house for college, he would wait until Christmas break when I was trapped at home for a month before creeping into his anger. It would be brought up at dinner, when my mother was onto her third glass of wine—I guess, after over twenty years of marriage, she could read his moods and medicate accordingly. One minute we would be discussing the latest neighborhood gossip, or what the local politicians were doing wrong, and the next I would be slinking further and further into my seat under Dad's seething face as, like a judge, he wrought my sentence for the crimes of which I was guilty.

His anger was thunder. It rolled on and on. It blustered. Intimidated. It contained a certain spark of manic glee. But he was not lightning, and no one ever got hurt because of a little noise. The painting, though, was like someone saw straight through me. I couldn't move, staring at it. Lost.

"Charlotte?"

I break away from the painting, confused. Georgia is just a few feet away, looking at a different painting. Besides her, no one here knows my name.

"Charlotte?"

A handsome man strides across the room in my direction. Short, short blonde hair. Brown and gold eyes that have always held the power to melt my heart.

He nods when he sees the recognition on my face. I start walking toward him.

Behind me, Georgia whispers, "No shit."

Avery's hug is better than the last time we saw each other. He crushes me into him, inhaling sharply while his lips are pressed against the top of my head. Peace washes over me, easing the anxiety that has been holding my lungs captive all day. I breathe him in, as well, locking my arms at his back. He feels thinner than I remember. My eyes are squeezed shut, and I would prefer not to open them. Public displays of affection are *not* my thing. And here I am, having shown him affection in public three times. *Three!*

"What are you doing here?" he whispers into my hair. "Are you real?"

I nod. My heart threatens to gallop out of my chest.

"That's a fucking terrible painting that you're looking at," he continues, moving back a step to look at my face.

I force a laugh, because I had been drawn to it. Even now, I can see it behind my eyelids. "I know," I lie. "I don't understand it at all."

He grins and then glances at Georgia. "Hi, I'm Avery—"

"I know who you are," she says. Her voice is cold. "You've got some nerve, showing up here after that *fiasco* of a date." She looks ready to bite him, which isn't normal for her. I have the urge to check her for a fever. This type of protectiveness only comes out in her once in a while, and it's usually reserved for her siblings.

Avery's smile falters.

"This is Georgia, my best friend," I say. I don't try to explain away her behavior. I can't.

He looks at me with a question in his eyes. I have never been the greatest at reading strangers—it made a life of sales out of the question for me—but I can see him crystal clear.

"Uh." I thread my fingers together. "You know, I wasn't in the best shape when I got home after seeing you. So."

"We're not going to be so easy this time around," Georgia says. She grabs my arm, hauling me toward the door. "Catch you around, Avery!"

I let her pull me as far as the entrance before I dig in my heels. "Seriously?"

"Yes, seriously. That boy has issues. I was more relieved than anything when you finally started dating again." She winces and purses her lips, staring outside. It had started to rain while we were inside. "Let's get lunch, and then we can go see a movie since this weather sucks."

We exit from a different door than we entered. Two large brass baby heads frame the stairs leading to the doors. "Creepy," I mutter. Georgia makes a noise of agreement.

Avery bolts out of the depths of the museum, catching up to us by the time we get to the sidewalk. "Please, Charlotte," he pants. Who knew the guy was so out of shape? "I can't let you go again. Are you just visiting? Only here for the weekend?"

Georgia shakes her head, blowing air sharply out of her

nose. "I can't listen to this." She points back to the museum. "I'll be inside... staying dry while you sort out this nonsense."

He takes my hand, turning me so I face him. When he doesn't say any more, I realize he is waiting for me to answer his questions. I look up at the sky, blinking at the rain. It's going to make my hair get weird waves in it.

"My boss was transferred to Boston," I say. "I'm his assistant, so he brought me with him."

Avery narrows his eyes. "Are you together?"

I let go of his hand, stepping back. "Seriously? He's married. I'm good at my job."

He nods quickly, his face relaxing. "Sorry," he says. "I just…. Now that you're finally in my city, I needed to make sure you were available."

I laugh at the same time that my stomach twists. Something rankles about the California boy calling this city *his*. "You didn't ask me if I have a boyfriend. You only asked about Tom."

"Do you?"

I consider telling him I do. I consider telling him I don't, but that feels like admitting defeat. Right now, it feels like we're playing a game. It's a spark of excitement that has been lacking in my life.

"I suppose you'll have to wait and find out."

He grabs my hand as I turn toward the street. "Please, Charlotte," he whispers. "Can I have your phone number? I can't rely on these chance meetings anymore."

I pretend to contemplate it with my head cocked. "Three chance meetings is probably all fate would allow," I say. He grins, handing me his phone. I put my number under *CHG*—can't make it too easy for him—and close out of the app.

His fingers graze my hand as he takes his phone back. It sends goosebumps up my arms, but I try to lock down the

S. MASSERY

shiver. He smiles anyway, leaning forward and pressing a kiss to my forehead. When his lips linger against my skin, I frown and pull away. It feels much too intimate, too familiar, too comfortable. We aren't there yet, even if I want to fall into his touch.

Avery nods, almost like he can hear my thoughts.

"I'll see you soon," he promises.

It feels too much like the last time we parted for me to turn my back on him. Instead, I nod and wait. He walks backwards for a few feet, keeping his golden-brown eyes on mine. Then he turns, navigating around a family coming down the street. I watch the back of his head, the new cut of his hair making it more difficult to track, until I can't see him anymore.

Shaking out of the trance-like stare, I realize Georgia has returned. Her eyes are narrowed at me.

"What?" My voice is a squeak.

"You know what," Georgia grumbles. "He's just going to break your heart again."

I shake my head.

"You don't know he *isn't* going to break your heart." Her voice softens as she adds, "I'm not going to be here to help put you back together again. I'm going to be a three-hour plane ride away. So you have to be safe and guard your heart."

I link my arm through hers, tugging her down the street. "Retail therapy," I say, "and then lunch. And we're not going to talk about this anymore."

Chapter 16

PAST

HE SHOWED UP AT MY HOUSE WITH A DOZEN red roses. My mother looked *thrilled* because, of course, Valentine's Day was on a Saturday this year and she answered the door. I blushed so red that my cheeks matched the flowers.

Colby winked at me when I tried to subtly pass the armful of flowers to my mother. She whisked them away, murmuring about trimming the stems and getting them into water. He leaned forward and kissed me.

"Happy Valentine's Day, baby," he whispered.

"Mrs. Galston," he called. If it were *me* calling her like that, she would've ignored me until I found her. But for Colby, she came running. He sent her a charming smile. "You don't mind if I steal your daughter for the day, do you?"

She looked at me and narrowed her eyes. "She didn't mention having plans."

Colby hooked his arm around my shoulders, cinching me to him. "Ah, she didn't know. It was a surprise..."

My mother beamed at him, nodding. "Okay, as long as she's home at a reasonable hour."

"Midnight?" he asked.

She looked from me to him, back and forth, until her eyes landed on him. "Fine. But just this once."

I begged Colby off for a minute to change my clothes and put on makeup. He nodded and followed me up the stairs into my room and sat on my bed watching me. "You ready to have fun tonight?" he said.

My body heated. "What did you have in mind?" I met his gaze in the mirror.

He winked. "Didn't you hear me? It's a surprise."

At that, I turned and rested my hip against the counter. "Please?"

His eyes flashed. He stood and came closer, pinning me against the counter. "You didn't hear me." He leaned in and claimed my mouth. I whimpered when he bit my lower lip, sucking it into his mouth. He moved down to my neck, biting and sucking, until I felt like I would combust. His fingers easily undid the button of my jeans, slipping down and teasing me. I moaned because I knew I was supposed to, shifting my legs wider and clutching his arms. One finger slid inside of me, in and out, and then two. He suddenly stopped, withdrawing and stepping away. "It's a fucking surprise."

I leaned back, panting. His eyes glowed in a way that said, *I own you*, and I felt another blush crawl over me when he put his fingers—*that had been inside of me*—in his mouth.

"Button your jeans. I hear your mom."

I turned back to the mirror, fingers trembling on the button.

"You kids okay up here?" My mom flew in; I hadn't realized my door was wide open. "Thank you for respecting my open-door policy, Colby," she said. He was back on my bed, his phone in his hand.

I tried not to make a mess of my eyeliner, but my hands wouldn't stop shaking.

"No problem, Mrs. Galston. I'm happy to follow the rules." I saw her nod, glance in at me, and then leave.

"I'm finished," I said.

He stood and kissed me again. "You haven't finished," he said. "You need a scarf or something." He pressed his thumb into one of the spots he had bitten earlier.

I wondered how much my mother saw and if I would need to explain them later. But I wound a scarf around my neck, and we left the house. She didn't so much as bat an eye at me. It was barely noon.

We drove to his house. He took my hand and pulled me into the family room, pushing me down on the couch. He followed, hovering over me. "I've always wanted to fuck a girl on this couch."

I grabbed his shirt and pulled him down on top of me, kissing his neck. He growled, pushing my hands down his body. I felt his erection through his pants and palmed it. He rolled off of me and unbuttoned his jeans, his dick springing out.

"Suck it," he told me.

I licked my lips. A shiver ran up my back.

"I got you roses. What did you get me? It's a two-way street here, Charlie." He smirked at me. I felt the guilt well up. In the months of dating, I had managed to avoid this. "Do you need to be fucking drunk to do anything?"

I eyed it. Him. He grabbed my face and pulled me to him, until we were so close our noses touched.

"Charlie, for fuck's sake."

I barely nodded. He let go of me and leaned back. I felt his eyes as I tentatively put a hand on him, rubbing up and down before I put my mouth over him. I was terrible, though, clueless, because when his hand slid through my hair at the back of my neck, I froze. He thrust into my mouth, and I tried not to gag.

"Relax," he ordered on a sigh. He grunted as we moved, over and over. Tears streamed from my eyes for eternity, drops falling on his pants, before he decided that was enough. He pushed me away roughly, stripping out of his pants and taking mine off, too.

He plunged into me so fast I cried out.

No condom, I wanted to scream. I opened my mouth to speak, but he covered it with his palm. He buried his face in my shoulder, groaning, before attacking my mouth.

We swallowed each other's noises, and I forgot that he wasn't wearing a condom. I forgot that I wasn't on birth control yet. "Fuck," he growled. He pulled out and yanked my shirt up over my breasts as he squirted hot liquid on my stomach.

Colby fell backward on the couch with a sigh, closing his eyes. I laid there, tears still in my eyes, in shock at what had just happened. I had a pulsing beat in my core, unsatisfied. And I was relatively happy that I wouldn't have to worry about getting Plan B at almost-sixteen. I silently laughed that I would be turning sixteen in exactly a month.

Eventually, he picked himself up and touched me like he liked me. Like he cared about whether I felt good. He moved methodically, mechanically, and stared at me as I gasped and arched my back. He smirked as I came on his fingers.

He stood up and left me there, panting.

I stood up and went into the bathroom, bringing my underwear and jeans with me. I wiped at the come dripping

94

down my stomach, grimacing. It was gross.

My stomach turned, and I immediately knew I was going to throw up. I dove for the toilet, trying to vomit as quietly as possible. When I could finally stop heaving, I stood and rinsed my mouth out. I stared at myself for a while until someone pounded on the door.

"Get out here, Charlie," Colby hollered.

I inhaled, smiled at myself, and opened the door.

"You look so sexy, baby," he said. He smirked at me. "My parents are gone for the weekend. I'm so fucking happy that you let me fuck you without a condom."

My cheeks turned scarlet. I felt the burn of it.

"I'm going to take you out for a romantic dinner because you deserve that shit. And you're going to call your mom and ask to sleep at Leah's house."

I looked into his eyes. "I'm guessing I'm not staying at Leah's house."

He laughed and kissed me. *I own you*, his kiss said again. I opened my mouth, welcoming his tongue. I moaned when his hand palmed my breast and tweaked my nipple. "I need more of you," he whispered. He had said that before he took my virginity, too. He dug into his pocket and pulled out a small bag of pills. "Pick one."

I chose randomly as a small flutter of fear raced through me. He picked one, too, and gave me a look that should've had me running away. I should've never stopped running away from him.

He didn't break eye contact as he put the pill in his mouth and swallowed.

"I haven't—" *I haven't been high since we first had sex,* I thought, but I couldn't voice it. He already knew, since he was the one who pushed the pills on me. I had felt so vulnerable, but

I still found myself sneaking out a few nights later to see him.

Colby nodded. "I know. I've got you."

I put the pill in my mouth and swallowed it without water.

"Call your mom, baby." These past few months, Leah had been my steadfast excuse for all things wrong in my life. She commanded the popular girls. If I had been hanging out with Colby too much—according to my mother—Leah was the one I was going out with that night. If I was late getting home from school, it was because Leah needed help. Colby had seamlessly manufactured my friendship with Leah, so when I finally asked about sleeping over her house, my mother sounded relieved instead of irritated.

I stared into Colby's eyes, my breath short, as he traced his finger across my collarbone. "Yeah, Mom," I answered. "Her parents will be there." I leaned into his touch. "No, his surprise was actually a picnic in his living room." He smirked.

My mother agreed, and I said a quick goodbye.

I could feel the pill at work; my mind was coming apart, and my tongue was loosening. "You're great," I told Colby. "The flowers turned me on, but then you took care of that, which was really considerate of you."

His smirk bloomed into a hard grin. I gulped. "I'm considerate? Is that all?"

"You're the greatest boyfriend," I said. I took a step away from him, sensing danger but not sure how.

He cocked his head. "Do you love me?"

I blinked at him. Time warped and slowed, and all I could hear was my heartbeat. Every pulse said, *Do you love me?* He came over and claimed my mouth, pinning me against the wall. He held my arms above my head and grinded himself against me. He was hard again.

"I asked you a question," he said in my ear.

I wondered if his parents loved him.

"I don't know," I answered. I didn't know; I could only compare him to Jared.

My heart fractured at the thought of my long-lost friend. Where was he, now? Now that I had become wrapped in his friend. Now that I was high on pills that made me feel lighter than air.

Suddenly, I giggled. I moved my hips against Colby. I tipped back and smiled.

"Baby."

I met Colby's eyes. They were such an unusual mix of green and brown. Right now, in the sunlight, they were absolutely green. I loved his eyes.

"You love me," he said.

Slow, slow, I felt my head bob up and down. I was untethered again, floating away.

"Say it, Charlie."

My mouth was gone. My body was coming apart. I heard myself. I said, "I love you, Colby." By my voice bounced around my head. *Do you love me, too?*

He didn't answer.

Chapter 17

I ALMOST RUN HEADLONG INTO AVERY. IT'S FIVE o'clock on a Friday, almost a week after I first saw him. Almost a week since I gave him my number, and got *nothing*. To say I was pissed is an understatement. I almost threw a fit. Georgia had her fair share of ranting phone calls. And now, here he is. He looks rather smug, too. It makes me want to punch him in the face.

"How did you know I work here?" I demand.

"I asked around." *Smug.* I can't seem to be flattered beyond the annoyance.

I keep walking. My day is *finally* over, and I just need a cold shower and a glass of wine. Maybe some pizza.

In the hectic week of moving in, I was surprised to learn that there was a whole private space just for me. When we were in Chicago, Tom had a small office and I was in a cubicle around the corner with the other assistants. Now, the door from the hallway opens into my office, and the door to his office is next to my desk. The wall that separates our offices is made of glass, with giant blinds that can be closed from his side for privacy. Security detail has been added to my job description, as I now monitor who has access to his office. It's been just another exhausting duty to add to my plate.

Avery keeps pace with me as I fly down the sidewalk. I've gotten quite familiar with the fastest routes from my apartment to work, as well as which is the safest at different hours of the day. I have an hour before I need to be back with a car for Tom, dressed for a high-profile dinner.

The smugness is slowly draining from his face. "Aren't you going to say anything?" He looks put out by my silence.

I contemplate holding my tongue. The annoyance is like an itch that I can't scratch. Finally, I ask, "What exactly were you expecting?"

He pulls on my arm, slowing us down. I huff. "I don't have *time* for this, Avery. You would've known that if you had, oh, called or texted me?"

"I..."

"Yeah," I cut him off. "I'm in a hurry. Did you lose my number?"

It had occurred to me that he may have forgotten my last name, and not been able to find my number under my initials. *But* after four days of silence went by, even that excuse fell flat. When I resume walking, he follows. He stays behind me for a minute, and then suddenly he is next to me again.

"I didn't lose your number, Charlotte. I just..." He groans and runs his fingers through his hair. "I couldn't text you and be casual about it. I couldn't say *hey, what's up?* I couldn't make myself pretend that the last time I asked you out, it didn't end miserably. I couldn't delude myself into thinking that maybe you'd give me another chance. So I stared at your phone number for five days and couldn't say anything... until I remembered that the H stood for Harper, and I was quite sure you never told me what your middle name was. But you did, I remember it now. I'm sorry I forgot. I finally found your social media about six hours ago. I needed to see you in person, to apologize for the last time we saw each other."

I glance sideways at him. I feel lifted, floating out of control, by his admission, and it's an uncomfortable feeling. "You've been waiting outside the office for six hours?"

He snorts, but his cheeks are flushed. "No. I've been waiting out here for more like three. The receptionists wouldn't let me up."

"Why didn't you have them call me?" We're almost to my apartment building, now, but I don't tell him that. It would be dangerous to invite him inside. I've had enough danger to last a lifetime.

"You would've let me up?"

My lips twitch as I try not to smile. Damn it, I'm supposed to be mad at him. "No, I wouldn't have."

He follows me all the way to the front stoop of my apartment building. I turn, intending to tell him he can't come in, but he has already stopped a few feet behind me. "I guess I don't have to ask where you live," he murmurs.

"Are you going to call me?"

"You haven't accepted my apology." He watches his feet, as if he doesn't know I've already started to forgive him.

Now is my time to be courageous. I walk closer to him, until I'm close enough that, with a large enough breath, our chests would brush. He is still enough to be made of stone, and still looking at his feet. Being forward is new to me. Showing affection in public is new to me. And yet, there is nothing awkward about the way I tilt his head up a little, how I stretch up on my toes, and brush a kiss to his lips. I pull away, looking into his eyes. There is a fire smoldering there, hot enough to match the flames in my belly.

He wraps an arm around my waist, pulling me flush against him, and kisses me again. It feels like my first breath after almost drowning. His lips are oxygen, and I can't get enough. It feeds the fire inside of me, enough that I am desperately close to inviting him upstairs.

I yank away from him, panting. My lips feel tender.

"Lunch. Saturday. Call me, or something."

His laugh is a beautiful sound. I am almost to the door when I hear him mutter, "You're going to bury me." Morbid, but it makes me grin from ear to ear.

Chapter 18

ONLY A DAY LATER, AVERY CALLS AS I AM stepping out of the shower.

"Hi, stranger," I say.

He laughs and then says, "Wow, we actually are strangers."

A small smile flickers across my face. I had the same thought earlier today; there is so much I don't know about him, and so much that I want to know.

"How are you?" His voice sounds like honey pooling in my belly.

I shift the towel around me. "Tired," I answer.

"I figured that might be the case."

"You figured I would be tired?"

"Yeah," he says. "So I also figured you might not want to cook."

I pull on leggings and a sports bra. It's true: I've been so busy, I wasn't able to make it to the store at all. My fridge is mostly empty, and I was going to have oatmeal for dinner.

"You'd figure correctly," I answer.

"Great!" The intercom at my door buzzes twice. "I hope you like Chinese."

"Oh my god," I say. I cover my mouth and hold in a giggle. We hang up as I buzz him into the building.

A few minutes later, he stands in my doorway and asks, "Is this too romantic for you?"

I pull down the hem of the shirt I threw on, shrugging.

"A shrug. That's a good start."

We sit on my couch and dig into the cartons he brought. I am immediately impressed with his choices: he even hit two out of my three favorites. After most of the food is gone, I set down the fried rice and ask, "Have you been stalking me?"

"What? No!"

I lean away, widening my eyes and trying not to laugh. "That was *not* convincing. At all."

Avery shakes his head. His hair is so short, I miss how it used to be. Not long, like our disastrous first date, but somewhere in the middle. I used to dream about running my hands through it and tugging. "Charlotte, I would never stalk you."

I blow air through my lips and smirk at him. "Yeah, right, only a stalker would say that."

"You have beautiful eyes," he blurts out.

I cock my head. My eyes are nothing special; blue but not *really* blue, they're a murky lake on a cloudy day.

"You're a brewing storm," he says. And then, he leans toward me and puts his hand on my cheek. His thumb brushes my lower lip. I lean toward him, too, instantly desperate to get closer.

"Can you handle this?" I whisper. Our breath mingles.

"I can handle anything you give me."

We both jump forward, into each other's arm, and our lips collide. I swing my leg over, straddling his lap, and we both make noises in the backs of our throats at the new contact.

All of a sudden, I can't stop thinking about the future. Are we dating, now? Do we have sex? Is he clean? Do we use protection even though I have an IUD? Are we *serious* dating? I'm still kissing him, but my gusto is gone. I want to go crawl into my shower and cry, because I'm not ready to be an adult in an adult relationship. My last relationship was *Colby*, and he broke me. After him, there was so much damage, so many walls that I built.

Now...

Avery breaks the kiss; I've frozen, he had to have felt it. Instead of shoving me off of him, telling me, *Go fuck yourself, Charlie*, he smiles and rests his forehead against mine. I watch his mouth, because I can't bear to look at his beautiful eyes.

"It's okay, Charlotte," he says. My heart's guard splinters; I feel so vulnerable.

"I'm scared." I hate how quiet my voice is, how small I have shrunk myself.

He presses his lips to my temple. "Me, too."

My arms are still around his shoulders, but I hug him tighter to me. We haven't even known each other a full week, and I already don't want to let go.

I climb off of him and excuse myself to the bathroom. I stare into my own eyes in the mirror and dare myself not to cry. It also makes me flinch because, for the first time tonight, I realize I don't have a shred of makeup on my face. It's just another layer he's stripped away from me.

When I come back out, Avery has poured a refill of my wine and whiskey for himself. I point to it, because I certainly do not stock whiskey in my apartment, and he laughs. He shows me the flask he has in his jacket, engraved with ACR. His initials.

"Carter Rousseau."

"I didn't forget."

"Ah," he mutters. "Is that your way of making me feel bad? Guilt tripping me for forgetting your middle name?"

"No," I laugh. "I just have a good memory." *Especially around you.*

He nods to the television. "Should we find a movie?"

It feels too heavy to sit in darkness and silence.

"How about a game?"

He quirks his lips to the side. "I'm not sure we're ready for strip poker."

"Funny," I say. "A game of questions."

His eyes light up. "I presume the premise is to tell the truth?"

"That would be it." I push my hair behind my ears. "Let's start easy, okay?"

"Of course," he says. "Should you start?"

I pretend to consider, although I already have a few questions lined up. "Favorite color?"

"Blue." I open my mouth to answer, and he holds up his hand to stop me. "Blue like... a storm is coming on the horizon, and you see it coming from miles away. It's a bit dirty and dark and wholly terrifying." His gaze drops to my mouth. "You're wholly terrifying."

I blink at him. That may be the nicest thing anyone has ever said to me. My mouth opens and closes, but no words come out.

"I'm sorry that I wasn't ready for you before," he whispers. And then he leans back and clears his throat. "My turn. Who's your favorite actor?"

I smile at his diversion.

"Kit Harington," I say.

"Oh, no," he says with a laugh. "You're a Game of Thrones fan?"

I grin. "Absolutely! Who wouldn't love Jon Snow?"

"Doesn't he die?" Avery starts chuckling at my expression.

I press my palm to my forehead. "Don't say that so loud. George R. R. Martin is evil, and if you ask about it—he's *definitely* going to die. So just, shush."

He eyes me. "I haven't seen this geek side of you—oh, except the spy novel. Does that count?"

I can't believe he remembers that. "Are you judging me?"

"Never," he says. He takes my hand away from my face and rubs his thumb in circles on my palm. My heart picks up speed, and I squeeze his hand.

"So, um…"

He winks. "I think you were going to ask me a question."

"Right," I say. "Ice cream."

"What about ice cream?"

"Are you for or against?" I narrow my eyes. "Ice cream and popcorn have gotten me through some pretty dark times."

"So, this could make or break the relationship," he says.

"Maybe!"

He pretends to wince. "You're not going to like my answer."

My cheeks hurt from smiling so wide. "Just tell me, Avery."

"Vanilla," he says, like it's a dirty secret.

"Oh, no."

"With rainbow sprinkles. And whipped cream."

"That's so…." I shake my head.

"It's so vanilla of me," he laughs. "I know."

"I'm going to pity you and tell you that my favorite is Phish Food from Ben and Jerry's."

His eyes, I swear, they twinkle at me. "Noted."

We sit and watch each other for a second, before he says, "I need to kiss you again."

We do.

It's just as good as the first time, and the second, and my heart beats fast enough to fly out of my chest. My mind stays calm, though, because his hands don't wander. He doesn't cop a feel under my shirt or stray down toward the button of my jeans. I am so used to rushing that I am surprised when he doesn't. He holds onto my face and neck, and I love how gentle his hands are.

After a few minutes, he tilts away and grins when I groan. I immediately miss the taste and feel of his mouth on mine. "Tell me about your family," he says.

I grimace, wondering how on earth to capture the personalities of my parents. At one point, I try to describe my mother and make her out to be some sort of a witch.

"She can't be that bad," Avery interjects.

"She's not!" I sputter. "Well," I think for a second. "Everything I said was true. She's controlling, insists that she knows what's best for me, and is *very* pushy. But she does it out of love." I laugh again. This night has been filled with laughter. "I think!"

He tells me about his family, too. His sister, June, is two years his senior. She knows everything about love, he says, and has always been available for support and advice. "Even if I don't want it." His lips quirk to the side, which makes me wonder if June advised him on past girlfriends. I wonder if she advised him about me.

"She sounds nice," I say. I imagine they have the same eyes and nose.

"What's your favorite song?" he asks.

I roll my eyes. "I have a different song for every mood."

"Right now."

I make a humming noise in my throat, trying to pinpoint my feelings. "Slowly, by Son Lux," I tell him.

"I don't know it," he says. He glances at his watch. "Oh, shit, I have to go."

I nod, because it's late and he's stayed longer than I thought he would.

"Be free on Saturday," he tells me.

"Why?"

"Just be ready to go at noon. And bring a bathing suit."

I shake my head.

He stands with his hand on the doorknob, waiting for me to agree. "Charlotte?"

"No," I say. It comes out firm, and not at all shaking.

"What?"

I flinch. "You're supposed to ask, Avery, you can't just demand me to be free."

"That isn't what I meant—"

"I would hope not—"

"Stop." He wraps his arms around me. I love that I fit so snugly against him, tucked under his chin. "Let me try again."

I nod against his chest.

"Charlotte, are you busy on Saturday afternoon? I want to take you on a date."

I shake my head. He takes a step back, dislodging me, before leaning forward and kissing my cheek. "What time?" I manage.

"One? With a bathing suit."

I let myself smile. "Yes."

He touches my cheek and leaves.

I cross to my phone, trying to will my hands to stop trembling. I turn on "Slowly" by Son Lux and close my eyes.

Please be careful what you say,
I may die this way.
Be careful how your mouth pulled apart,
I can see your lips, I don't wanna feel your heart.

Chapter 19

SATURDAY MORNING, I STAND ON THE BOW OF A small yacht while Avery hustles around, doing something with ropes and engines. A man named Mark, who introduced himself as the captain, orders him to various tasks.

I duck into the cabin, finding a cozy sitting area with a bed all the way in the back. I stash my bag and peek up onto the deck. Avery catches me looking as he passes. Stopping for a second, he plants a quick kiss on my lips. "Sorry for the third wheel," he whispers. "It would've been doable to take it out on my own, but I'm in unfamiliar waters." Figuratively *and* literally.

We both look at Mark, who squabbles with someone on the radio by the controls. "Unable to be helped, I think," I say. He kisses me again before finishing his tasks.

The day on the boat is glorious. His boat was docked at a marina north of the city. We sail out south, along the coastline.

It is a calm day on the ocean, which puzzles me. "It's because we're protected by Cape Cod," Avery tells me.

There's a cove that looks more private than not; it seems like a hidden gem in the Massachusetts coastline. They toss an anchor over, and Mark disappears below deck. Avery has been by my side the whole time while we nursed lime-a-ritas and held hands. For the most part, I kept my eyes peeled open behind my sunglasses. I didn't want to miss a second of this. Now, I look around the boat and wonder what else he has up his sleeves.

"Swim with me?"

I had wondered where the swim suits would come into play. "Is it cold?" When he shrugs, I surprise myself by agreeing. I watch him pull off his shirt, and his torso nearly makes me drool. His skin has a golden glow, and baby abs are carved across his stomach. I want to touch them and whisper, *Are you real?*

Slowly, I pull off my shirt. I blush when I catch Avery staring, lingering on the topline of my tankini, and keep blushing when he steps forward and lifts my hand. "You're gorgeous," he tells me. I follow him to the back of the boat, where he slides a ladder into the water. He leaps over it, arcing into a graceful dive. His head breaks above the gentle waves, and he motions for me. I jump without fear.

When I surface, he is sputtering. I had landed as close to him as possible, knees tucked into the infamous—at least, to my uncles—Galston Cannonball. I giggle, and he laughs with me. He pulls me by my arms until we're chest to chest. I wrap my legs around his waist to anchor me to him, and tread water with my arms.

"You're pretty cute," he says. He kisses my nose, and I feel his erection poke into my thigh. His eyes darken when I reach down and palm his length through his swim trunks. "Naughty," he breathes.

It's is the first time I've touched him this way. A tiny part of me wants to swim away, to climb back into the boat and put on all my layers of clothes. But another part is excited, wild, and completely new. I unwind my legs, and we somehow kick to stay afloat without knocking our legs together. His hands hold my waist, while one of mine strokes him and the other balances on his shoulder.

"Kiss me," I say. I feel a rush of adrenaline at my own words and the power they hold.

He does. I slide my hand down into his shorts, gripping him fully, and he hums into my mouth. "Faster," he grunts. After another few breathless minutes, he jerks and lets out a moan, pressing his forehead to mine. He comes in my hand, a hot contrast to the cool water. I pull my hand out of his trunks, letting the salt water wash me clean.

"I think I owe you one," he says with a smile. I shiver, because I don't want to think in terms of being owed. He kisses me and releases me, angling back toward the boat. "Hungry?"

"Sure," I murmur. The ache between my legs is an annoying pulse that demands attention. I touch myself briefly, lessening the pressure, until Avery is almost all the way back to the boat. A small tendril of fear creeps through me about being alone in the deep ocean. Anything could reach up and snag my leg. Only then do I follow him.

We finish the rest of the afternoon on the boat with laughs and smiles. Even Mark loosens up, drinking a lime-a-rita with us after we promise to keep it a secret. I sit in the back with Mark, watching as he checks weather dials and whatever else. Clouds have appeared, blocking out the sun for a few moments, but otherwise it has been a deliciously warm day. It's hard to believe that it's almost August.

I watch Avery, who moved to the front of the boat once we pulled up the anchor. He sits at the bow, staring out at the water. He looks a bit sad, or lonely. When I go to him, he doesn't look at me. I curl my fingers into his, giving a short squeeze. He squeezes back, but his gaze stays trained on the sea. We sit in silence as Mark steers us home.

Chapter 20

PAST

HIS DINING ROOM WAS COVERED IN CANDLES. There were two place settings at the corner and a bottle of wine between them in an ice bucket. A vase of flowers in the center of the table. "Happy birthday," Colby whispered in my ear. He drew his tongue up the shell of my ear, and I shivered.

My eyes got damp, because no one had ever cherished me like this. "I love you," I told him. He spun me around, kissing me hard. He already tasted like vodka, but I ignored it. The best way to keep him happy was to suck him off or tell him I loved him.

"Baby," he said against my lips, "I need you."

He didn't wait, pushing me against the wall and hoisting me up by my butt. I had worn a dress when he demanded it; I had hesitated, but complied, when he told me to put my panties in my purse as he drove to his house. I knew why, now. Colby never did anything without a plan.

I barely registered that he already had undone his jeans and freed himself; he pushed inside me without warning, and we groaned in unison. We moved together, panting, for a few minutes, until he stilled inside of me. "When are you getting on birth control?" he asked.

In order to do that, I would need to admit to my mother that we were having sex. I wasn't ready for that—I didn't think I'd ever be ready for that conversation. I shook my head at him.

He pulled out of me, dropping my legs back to the floor. "Is it in your fucking five-year plan to entrap me with a baby?"

"No—"

"God," he growled. "Did that even occur to you?"

"I'm fif-sixteen—"

"*Sixteen* is old enough to buy fucking Plan B at the pharmacy," he yelled. "And you can't tell your doctor you want the fucking pill?"

"I don't..." I choked out, but I didn't have a plan for where this conversation was going.

He grabbed my hand and dragged me out of the dining room, up the stairs, and into his room. He shoved me on the bed, face down, and said, "Shut up, Charlie," when I made a noise. "This," he tore open a condom wrapper, "is *fucking*." He pulled my hips up, butt in the air, and pushed into me. We both groaned again, because even though part of me was scared, I couldn't deny that it felt good. "So just shut up and enjoy it."

I felt depleted when he finally finished. He fell on top of me, pressing us into the mattress. A tear slid from my eye, down my nose, and onto the blanket. I watched it go and concentrated on Colby's heartbeat. I could feel it just over mine, pressed into my back. When it finally slowed, he got off of me.

He pulled his pants back on and went downstairs. I went

into his bathroom. My tears had streaked my mascara a little. I dabbed at it, but it seemed futile. Everything seemed futile. *His mom probably has mascara*, I told myself. I crossed the hall into his parents' room, and I was shocked at how... different their styles were. While Colby's room was tones of grey, his parents' room was a soft mint green, with fluffy throw pillows on an impeccable bed. I was lucky if Colby made his bed at all, even when he knew I was coming over. His room screamed cold; his parents' room looked lived in, cherished, happy. It made me shudder; I let my eyes unfocus as I ducked into her bathroom.

I found her makeup stash and fixed my eyes. How long did I have until Colby came looking for me?

The answer: he didn't. I stayed upstairs for another few minutes, waiting for the redness in my eyes to fade. When I went back to the dining room, half of the candles had gone out. He sat at one of the seats, already eating.

"About time," he muttered. When I sat, he lifted my hand and kissed my knuckles. "Did you like that position?"

I shrugged.

"It's called doggy." He smirked. "We'll use it when you're being a bitch."

My face flamed red.

He went back to eating.

Happy birthday, Charlie.

Colby dropped me off at home after we ate. Neither of us were in any mood to be nice to each other, and I wasn't feeling like being a punching bag on my birthday. For once, when I told him

I wanted to go home, he agreed.

My mother was surprised to see me walk in the door—she probably assumed I was staying at *Leah's* again—but I made up some excuse about studying for a test. Somehow, my grades had remained steady. I had friends, now, who I sat with at lunch and nodded to in the hallways. I had Colby to make out with against my locker before the bell. But I knew that these friends of mine were really Colby's friends, and Jared's old friends.

Sitting in my room, I had never felt so alone. I had no one to call, no one to talk to... just, no one. Period.

My eyes drifted toward my closet, where I had thrown the notebook with my letters to Jared. He would hate this version of me. He would hate that I listened to Colby so willingly, that we had unprotected sex, that Colby touched me, that I swallowed whatever pills Colby gave me, that they made me feel like a new person.

Don't let him touch you, Jared had told me. Sorry, Jared.

I crawled over and dug for it; it was under a pile of summer shoes. It was hard to look at the words I had written.

"Colby looks at me like I'm a piece of meat. It doesn't matter, whatever you said to him, because he's gotten worse."

I cringed. I flipped to a new page and grabbed a pen.

Jared,

I haven't written in a while. December. I told you that Colby kissed me, and I didn't love it. Well, I'm fucked now, because I do love him. I think. He makes me cry, and feel all these emotions that I never really considered before. Sometimes I think if I just close my eyes and he can take over, life will be so much easier that way. Giving up control. But then I panic, because I don't actually want that. I want to steer my own boat.

Why haven't you called me? It's been seven months, Jared.

It's my birthday. My 'sweet' sixteen. And Colby yelled at me after I botched his romantic gesture. And I have no friends, because apparently I could only land one friend when I was nine, and now he's gone.

I couldn't remember the last time I tried to call Jared. I was more afraid of his rejection than anything else. I couldn't call and say, *Look how far I've fallen.* He'd hate me.

I brushed a tear from my eye, sick with myself that I couldn't stop crying.

I glanced back down at the paper and wrote one more thing.

Don't hate me, Jared.

Chapter 21

"POP QUIZ," AVERY SAYS. IT'S BEEN ABOUT A week and a half since we went out on the boat. A week and a half of crazy, intense courting. But we haven't done anything else sexual, except for giving each other orgasms with our hands. A shadow crosses his face after he speaks, as if two words can dredge up bad memories. I know how he feels; I keep remembering ghosts of my past more and more.

I wave my hand, telling him to continue. My mouth is full of food.

"We've been dating for how long?"

I swallow. "A few weeks."

"And have we discussed exclusivity?"

"No." *Is he about to break up with me? Is he about to tell me he's been sleeping with other women?*

Avery leans forward. He captivates me: the way his nose

flares slightly before he says something important, the way his eyes jump from my eyes to my lips and all the way around my face as if he is trying to ingrain me in his memory. He takes a sip of wine, but doesn't look away from me.

"Have you been seeing anyone else?"

I shake my head. "You're the only one."

Avery exhales tension that I didn't even know was there. His smile blinds me before he asks, "Charlotte, will you be my girlfriend?"

I squeal and break out into a huge smile. He circles around the table and leans down, kissing me long and slow. "I love that you didn't do something romantic," I mumble against his lips. I picture dying candles around a cold meal and dead flowers in cracked vases.

We get to his apartment in a tangle of limbs and clothes that we can't shed fast enough. I pull his shirt off as soon as we are in his apartment, running my hands down his chest. He kisses me as if his soul depends on it, nipping my bottom lip. He turns us, pushing me against the door. He leans over me, demanding with his tongue that my lips part. He claims every inch of my mouth, while his hands roam down my body. I jolt when he squeezes my butt, simultaneously grinding his hips into mine.

I am not super skinny, and Avery, while fit, is not too muscular. He doesn't try to sweep me off my feet and carry me to his bedroom. He nibbles on my neck until I am weak in the knees, and then he leads me through his apartment.

He points to the bed, and I climb onto it. He already took

my shirt off, forgotten by the front door, and he unbuttons my jeans while I kick off my shoes. He leaves his shorts on, crawling over me. He starts kissing my throat and works his way down my body. The anticipation makes me shiver. His fingers work their way under the hem of my panties. My body is reacting like I've never been touched before. I fall apart in his hand, gasping and gripping the bed sheets. Only then does he shed his shorts and roll on a condom. He hovers above me and bites my breast at the same instant he pushes into me. I have never been loud, in bed or out of it. But he makes me gasp and whisper things that make me blush. He finishes with a shout that makes me cringe, burying himself inside of me. His face is tucked against my neck, and has been the whole time. I feel his hot breath on my throat.

After a minute of stillness, of silence, he pulls out and moves to the edge of the bed.

"That was good," I say.

Avery chuckles darkly. "Thanks."

Thanks?

"Are you okay?"

"I'm fine." He doesn't turn around, though, he just stands up and disappears into the bathroom.

Somehow, I doubt that he is fine.

I sit up, scooping my hair up into a bun. By the time Avery reemerges, I'm almost fully dressed. I squeeze past him into the bathroom, fixing the smudges in my makeup and cleaning myself up. *Pee so you don't get a UTI*, Georgia tells me in my head. I listen to her, as I always do. Meeting my own eyes in the mirror, I evaluate myself. Still flushed from the sex, eyes slightly dilated, lips pinker than normal. In my wide eyes, I see vulnerability that hasn't been there in years. I can see every flaw anyone has ever said about me. The mirror holds nothing back:

just brutal honesty.

I don't really like what I see.

"Enough," I tell myself. I straighten my shoulders, schooling my face into something close to indifferent happiness, and march into the bedroom.

Avery stands when I enter. "I'll see you tomorrow?"

I immediately frown. I can't seem to control my face around him, and it disappoints me how easily my guard has lowered. It *is* late, but my expectations were higher than this. My heart plummets, falling down, down, down. "Excuse me?"

He meets my eyes, but he is expressionless. He's better at this *stupid* game than I am. Anger takes over my body. This is a wildfire of rage, all consuming, and in this exact moment, I hate him. If I were a different person, I would let loose this fire. Throw things, scream, cry. But at the end of the day, I am who I am. Controlled. Quiet.

I inhale through my nose, locking all the emotions away, deep inside of me. My voice barely wavers. "We can't do this. We can't be all happy, new boyfriend and girlfriend, and then you turn into an ice box after sex? The *first time* we have sex? No." I shake my head and stare at the ceiling for a second. My hands clench into fists. I need to move before I hit him. "You don't get to *treat* me like this."

He follows me into the living room, where I pull on my shirt and snag my purse.

"I'm sorry," he says. "I just—"

I look into his eyes, waiting to see something like regret or remorse. Willing him to *show* me something. To my surprise, I do see those things; they're just shuttered behind a wall of misery that I don't understand. Right now, I don't want to understand.

"I'll see you later."

Is he someone I would take home to my parents? Is he someone I could *trust*? Love? Marry? My feelings for Avery spiral out of control.

As quickly as my anger came, it vanishes as I walk out. Leaving this way reminds me too much of the last time. My lungs are frozen in the absence of my anger, and no amount of air can fix it. *Don't look back,* I tell myself. *Never look back.* I made that mistake once in my life already.

Chapter 22

I VOWED TO MYSELF THAT I WOULDN'T SPEAK TO Avery until he apologizes.

For three days, I am a mess.

On night two, I start to go stir crazy. I contemplate calling Georgia, but I know she wouldn't want to listen to me complain again. She would repeat information that I already know: just get out of the relationship. *You don't deserve that hot/cold treatment again*, she would tell me.

With those thoughts in my head, I go to bed early.

On the third night, I pace my apartment with a glass of wine in my hand. Does Avery know I keep crying myself to sleep? Probably not. *Some boyfriend*, I keep repeating.

My opinion of him wavers, and I wonder if it was worth it. I didn't move to Boston *for* him, but the thought that he might be here was certainly a factor, no matter how small of a factor it was at the time. Now, it seems like the only thing I based my decision on was Avery, and I regret every inch of that decision. My hands shake, sloshing wine almost over the rim.

At eight o'clock, I turn off my phone. Anyone calling beyond then would have to talk to a tipsy Charlie. That would be mortifying. Plus, I need to save myself from calling Avery and giving him a piece of my mind. I don't want to break my promise to myself.

I fall into a restless sleep, dreaming of Jared and my childhood. While he wasn't perfect, he was safe. I dream of him lying beside me, our fingers entwined. He looks at me and says, *Char, it's okay to be upset. But don't let a dumb jock ruin your life.* He kisses my fingers, each one, before setting our hands back down between us. My heart hurts, but it slows down. The pain ebbs away. And then, I sleep.

My phone rings while I am walking to work.

"Hello?"

"I'm sorry."

"How long did it take you to figure that out?" A curt impersonator has taken over for me. Walls that were seamlessly dropped around him have been resurrected and fortified. But after three days of wallowing, last night I decided that was enough: I was my mother's daughter, and I needed to take her life lessons to heart. With that in mind, I channeled my hurt into annoyance and anger until I couldn't feel sad anymore.

Avery sighs through the phone. I have a thought of hanging up on him, but part of me is curious of what he needs to say.

"I should've called you sooner," he says.

I wait a minute, letting the silence build up. Sometimes, silences get so heavy that they're hard to break. They suffocate you. I swing my hammer and crack the ice. "Is that all, Avery?"

"No—"

I round a corner, and there he is, standing outside of my office building. I end the call, stashing my phone in my purse. He walks toward me, meeting me halfway. His shoulders are hunched, and his eyes have lost their shine.

"I'm *so* sorry, Charlotte."

I love the way he says my name. No one calls me Charlotte anymore, except my mother when she's angry, and even then it's *Charlotte Harper*. I've been Charlie for so long, sometimes it's hard to imagine myself as the original Charlotte. How might I have ended up if Jared hadn't come along and nicknamed me Charles? How might I have been if my mother hadn't been so eager to prove she had the perfect family? How would we have grown had she not forced us into different shapes?

I breathe, and realize it is completely within my power to not forgive him. I can say, *Fuck off, Avery*. I also realize that it's okay if I forgive him. He isn't anyone from my past. Why should their sins be held against him?

"Okay," I say.

"Okay?"

"Yeah, Avery, *okay*. It's an acknowledgement. It doesn't mean I forgive you, or that I've forgotten, or that *it's* okay. What you did isn't okay. It hurt and it sucked."

He rubs at his face, eyeing me like I'm about to explode.

I clench my abdomen, putting all my tense feelings into those muscles, and let myself wear a smile that says, *Everything's fine*. He flinches. I say, "I need to get to work."

I move past him, trying not to run to the doors.

"Are you going to hold your anger against me?" he yells.

I wheel around. "Shouldn't I?" I stalk back toward him, stopping close enough to smell him. "Shouldn't I be angry that you treated me like garbage? Shouldn't I want better for myself?"

His face falls. I'm a ball of emotions, and I almost can't control what's coming out of my mouth.

"Do you have an answer, or are you going to stand there gaping at me?" I snap. I have a sense of déjà vu for a split second, flashing back to conversations with Colby. He once accused me of *gaping like a fish* when I floundered for a response to his anger. This close alignment of speech and personality to *him* makes me uncomfortable.

I picture my anger as fire, when in reality it is mud—thick toxic sludge—that clings and builds. As hard as I try to scrape it away, there's still the stink of it.

"I understand you're angry," Avery tells me.

I shake my head, trying to reign in what I'm feeling. I need to sort through these feelings. I need to get a grip. I need to remember to breathe. "I just need *time*, Avery," I say. I'm much quieter now. "Thank you for apologizing, but I need time to accept it."

He inclines his head a bit, which I take as acceptance. I stare at him for a beat. Isn't he going to push the issue? But, no, he doesn't. He stays silent and unmoving.

I turn and walk into work, feeling more conflicted than ever before.

"Charlie, good morning!"

I manage to smile at Rose, the office manager, as I move through the lobby. She abandons the receptionist and follows me to my office. I flick on the lights, hanging my purse over the back of my chair. Rose sits in the chair opposite my desk.

"Dude," she says.

She is only a year or two older than me, and within a few weeks she has gotten very comfortable around me. She was the receptionist in the office before the merger. During, she was instrumental in assisting Tom. He recommended that she be promoted, and the higher-ups agreed with him. In front of clients, she is nothing but professional. But privately, her vernacular is... interesting.

"*Dude*," she repeats. "You've been a zombie all week, and now you look like..."

I raise my eyebrows, waiting for her to continue.

"I guess you resemble a volcano right now. Smoking. Ready to unleash your lava everywhere. What happened?"

"What *happened* is my boyfriend is a dick." Mentally, I roll my eyes at myself. Her easy way of speaking crudely is easy to fall into. My mother would have a stroke if she heard me.

Rose chuckles. "I can't believe you just said dick, Miss Proper. What did he do?" She leans forward, a mischievous look on her face. "Can you call him an asshat next?"

I lean back in my chair, trying not to glare too hard at her. I doubt she would care, though, since she's a true Boston native. Nothing breaks through her thick skin. *She's just being friendly*, I tell myself. "He just froze me out..." I sigh. "After sex. And then asked me to leave."

She shoots out of her chair.

"That *asshat*! Are you kidding?"

I keep my eyes trained on the ceiling, a trick of my mother's. I feel the starting prick of tears. "That's not even the worst part."

I swallow the lump forming in my throat. "It was our first time together. He literally asked me to be his girlfriend at dinner, and then I'm getting the boot by nine."

Rose growls. She pushes her dark hair away from her face, tying it back in quick motions. "I'm going to kill him myself. I don't even know him, and I want to kill him." Her face softens into something resembling pity, and I hold up my hand.

"Don't get on the pity train, Rose. Please. I don't think I could handle it."

She cocks her head. "But murder suggestions are okay? Is that what you're saying? Blink once for yes, twice for no. Or wink with your left eye for yes, right eye for no." She winks with each eye, exaggerated.

After a minute of staring at her, straight faced, I give in and laugh. Together, we laugh and cackle and howl until tears stream down our faces. "Oh, god. I needed that."

I'm wiping my eyes when Tom walks into the office. Rose scrambles up, straightening the chair she was using.

"Hard at work, ladies?"

Rose mumbles something and dashes from the office, shooting one last look at me. The door swings closed behind her, and we're alone. I swallow, until I see his smirk.

"Looks like you're feeling better."

I nod. "Yes, thanks."

"Well, you've been in quite a mood. I almost resorted to desperate measures."

I purse my lips. "You were going to fire me over a mood?"

"No!" His laugh astonishes me. "I was going to drag my wife in here and have her girl-talk you to death."

I smile.

"Thanks, Tom," I murmur before he disappears into his office.

At six, Rose pokes her head into my office. My phone has been going nonstop, and I have a stack of messages for Tom to handle tomorrow.

"Hey," she says. "Up for drinks?"

I am tempted to shake my head, to tell her no. But I picture how I would spend my evening: pick up takeout, sit in front of my television watching Jeopardy and a Lifetime movie, drink half a bottle of wine and pass out by ten.

"I'd love to," I say. New city, new friends. It's about time.

"Great! Eve is coming with us. Have you met her yet?"

I shake my head, closing down the computer and picking up my purse. I follow her down the hallway and into the lobby, where she pauses. "Eve is really cool. She works for Mr. Carpenter—seriously, that's his name—who works in accounting. He *is* accounting."

"Oh, okay."

"I think she got off at five, so she should be there already." Rose has a quick walk, and by the time we get to the bar—which turns out to be three blocks away—I'm puffing. She glances at me. "You could've told me to slow down, girl! I run everywhere. Fit is my middle name." She laughs and eyes me. "If you ever want to work out with me...."

I shake my head again. "I walk places. That's my exercise."

The bar is filled to the brim with business people. Rose takes my hand, and we wind through the crowd to a table in the back. "Hi, Eve!" Rose plunks down at a chair, gesturing me to the other chair. "Eve, Charlotte."

I look at the woman across from me. She is older, maybe in her early thirties, with white blond hair pulled back in a tight French braid. Her green eyes examine me, and I get the sense that she doesn't miss much. After a moment, she extends her hand. "Nice to meet you, Charlotte," Eve says.

"Please, call me Charlie," I say as I shake her hand.

Rose hops up, saying, "We need drinks. What can I get you, Charlie?"

"Vodka soda?" I try to hide my immediate wince; I don't know why that's the first thing out of my mouth. I haven't had vodka in a *while*.

She gets up and moves to the bar, leaving Eve and I alone for the moment.

"Are you enjoying Boston, Charlotte?"

I let my gaze wander around the bar. Some are already drunk or finishing dinner in the dark booths around us. Others are on the hunt: women with plunging necklines and bright lipstick, who sip drinks they haven't bought, and men who leer at them or try to charm them.

How different are they from Avery and me? The way he used me for sex makes me burn with shame, because he's proven to be just like every other guy. I thought he was different, that he cared about me, but maybe he just doesn't understand that I'm not like that. I have had experiences that shape my views of sex and romance.

Rose reappears at that moment, sliding my drink in front of me.

"I'm so sorry, Rose," I say, "I have to go."

I finish the drink in three long swallows, wiping my mouth when I'm done. It burns slightly on the way down. I'm not usually such a drinker, but I have a feeling I'll be needing some liquid courage. The smell of vodka brings back unpleasant memories of Colby, and I wish I had chosen something else.

Rose frowns. "Off to see the asshat?"

"Yeah. I need to talk to him."

It takes me fifteen minutes to fast-walk to his apartment. In that time, the drink kicks in and heats me from the inside out. I press the buzzer a few times, until his voice comes through the speaker. "Yes?" It's irritated.

"It's me," I say. "Charlie—Charlotte, I mean. Can I come up?"

The door buzzes, and I haul it open.

He opens the door to his apartment before I get there and leans on the door jam. It effectively blocks me from entering, but that's okay. I can talk in the hallway.

I stop in front of him. "I need to say something."

"Okay," he says.

"What you did hurt me." I run my hand through my hair, stepping back and leaning against the wall across from his door. "It hurt because I expected more from you." I watch closely, to see if he will flinch. He does not. But he does look like he regrets it.

I sigh. "When I was in high school, I had a boyfriend. I was a virgin. I wanted to make sure that he liked me before we had sex. He was the epitome of outward perfect. He said the right things, he did the right things. He was affectionate in public, charmed my mother, and happily talked about the Patriots with my dad. Eventually, we had sex, but it wasn't—" I try to remember to breathe, choking on my own words. "It was a fucked-up situation, okay?"

"Charlotte, I—"

"I'm not done," I hiss. I take a deep breath and continue, "We broke up, and I was crushed. After that, I didn't date anyone. I slept with a few guys, but none of them fixed me. Maybe you meant to be better or different, or you want to keep dating me. I don't hold any of my past mistakes against you. I don't compare you to them. But when you *did* that—damn it," I pause, wiping a tear as it rolled down my cheek. "When you did that, it brought up all the past feelings of being hurt and angry and confused and transposed it with magnification onto my current feelings."

I stared at him, willing him to understand while I wipe more tears from my cheeks. They just keep coming.

Avery has an expression of horror on his face.

"Charlotte, I'm so sorry. It wasn't my intention to hurt you. I just... had my own freak out, I guess, and I didn't know how to deal with it." Softer, he says, "You're the first one I've slept with since... my ex." He clears his throat. "I didn't handle it the right way, and I sincerely apologize."

My lips tremble, and I don't know how to feel now that my anger is gone. "Thank you, Avery." But do I forgive him?

Chapter 23

PAST

WHEN I GOT OUT OF THE BATHROOM STALL, Leah was standing there, leaning against one of the sinks. She was just so pretty, my lungs burned with jealousy. Every now and then, I would look at her and think, *Why did Jared pick you?*

She stared at me for a minute, and then stepped to the side. I walked up to the sink, eyeing her in the mirror. Although we ran in the same circles, and I frequently used her as an excuse to stay over Colby's when his parents were out of town—which was, frankly, a lot—we never spoke. She pursed her lips and shrugged. I thought she might be having an internal debate. And, where she stood, she blocked the door.

Finally, she locked us into the bathroom and then turned back toward me, crossing her arms.

I wanted to tell her that I had to get back to class, but I think we both knew that I didn't care that much. My skipping record had proven that already.

"You've always been at the peripheral," she said.

I narrowed my eyes.

"I don't mean in a bad way, Charlie, it's just a fact. You kind of floated around and never talked to anyone except for Jared. He was your voice, or something." That was true—but none of them spoke to me, either, and it was a two-way street. Leah sighed. "I've noticed you more in the last few months. Ever since..."

She didn't want to say, *Ever since Colby sunk his claws into you.* I didn't blame her. That was a scary sentence.

"You seem worse," she admitted. "You seem like you almost flinch every time he touches you. You've must've lost, what, fifteen pounds? You look—"

I was a walking skeleton. I knew it. But Colby liked it this way. He liked that he could touch my ribs, and touch the skin that dipped and sucked around my collarbone and hips. He liked that my breasts were smaller, now, and that he could pick me up easier.

"Is he—" she shook her head, and then started again. "I'm worried. I've seen how he can get. He's fine one minute, and then in a fit the next."

It was the freedom, the money, that his absentee parents afforded him. He didn't suffer repercussions like the rest of the world. I knew that. He knew that. He enjoyed it, gloated and reveled in it, while the rest of us shrunk away.

She was waiting for me to respond. She looked at me with such expectancy. My mother had started looking at me like that when I only picked at dinner, and when I stopped talking so much, and when I stopped hugging her.

Leah, like my mother, should get used to that disappointment.

I didn't answer. I hadn't spoken the whole time, so I didn't know why Leah thought I would answer now. My voice was buried so deep inside of me, I didn't know how to pull it out.

Eventually, her shoulders fell, and she stepped aside.

I unlocked the door and slid into the hallway.

Two days later, Leah came for me again. She hovered by Colby's car after school, fiddling with her phone, when we walked up.

"Leah!" Colby greeted. "What brings you to my neck of the woods?"

Leah's eyes flitted from me to him and back again. "I was hoping to steal Charlie sometime this week for help with my math project. We're in the same class."

His hand squeezed mine in a painful warning, and then he shrugged. "Yeah, we don't have plans." He let me go and stepped away. "Take her."

My heart beat faster; where was my consent? Why didn't I get a chance to say, *Yeah, Leah, let's hang out* or *No, sorry, Colby and I had plans to get high by the lake.* He had just been whispering that to me, not five minutes ago.

Leah nodded, and I followed to her car. Once we were in, the silence felt stifling. We watched as Colby talked to one of his friends by his car. We watched him get in and drive away, never once glancing at me.

Finally, we left. I kept my mouth shut when she got on the highway. We didn't need to go this way, but I was checked out. I didn't care where she was taking me.

"I saw you," she said.

I glanced over at her.

"Before I made out with Jared this summer, I saw you. I saw your face, and how you looked at him. I did it anyway because..."

My chest suddenly hurt.

"I just... I'm sorry, Charlie." She sighed and blinked a few times. "I kind of saw that he was looking at you, too. If I didn't make a move, I figured I would never get a chance again."

I looked up, willing my eyes to stay dry. Her words passed in one ear and out the other.

"Do you want to talk about Jared?"

No, I didn't want to talk about anything. I wanted to sob because my best friend was gone, and I couldn't remember how I used to be *before*.

"Do you want to talk about Colby?"

I glanced out the window again. *Nope.*

Leah took an exit, drove for a few minutes, then pulled over onto a shoulder. We were on an empty road in the middle of the woods; I had no idea where we were. She unbuckled her seatbelt and turned toward me. "Do you realize he's taken your voice away?"

I opened my mouth and closed it again.

"You haven't said a word. I can't remember the last time you spoke to someone other than Colby. Do you know how alarming that is? How *not normal* that is?"

I rolled my eyes, because, *I spoke.* I spoke too much, sometimes.

Leah grabbed my hand. "Say something, Charlotte."

There was cotton in my throat and, under that, fear.

For the first time, I acknowledged my fear. I let it soak through me, giant waves that would drown me if I didn't start swimming. Why was I so afraid?

"I have a notebook," I whispered. When I flinched against

the sound of my rasping voice, Leah squeezed my hand and didn't let go. "I used to write to Jared, wishing he would come back." I shook my head. "He told me that day—the day you made out with him at that beach—not to let Colby touch me." A tear slid loose from my eye; I thought it might break me into fragments. "But..."

Leah didn't react. She just waited.

And then, suddenly, we're back at the beach, months ago.

I caught Colby's eye. He smirked, silently lifting a beer bottle in my direction. It was either an invitation or a *cheers*—I couldn't decipher. I could never read him. Uneasy, I shouldered my pack. It was time for me to go.

In the water, Jared was making out with Leah.

My heart seized, and I turned and fled.

It was easy to find my way back; I ran like my hair was on fire, following the barely-there path. In reality, it was my heart that was burning. *Why did* she *have to kiss him?* I held onto that anger, the adrenaline, and forced myself to run faster.

But eventually, the pack started hurting when it bounced against my back. I slowed to a stop. I didn't just stop, I collapsed to my knees and let myself *feel*. Ugly sobs burst out of my mouth, spit flew everywhere, I choked and tipped my head back and howled my agony.

And that was how he found me.

"Charlie," Colby said. I looked over my shoulder, and he stood on the path with his arms crossed. "Jesus, you're making a fucking racket."

I swallowed my groan.

He stepped toward me and smiled. It looked so wrong on his face.

"You saw Jared and Leah, yeah? I thought you might be in

love with him." He shrugged. "Oh, well."

I stood up when he walked closer. My fingers tightened on the strap of my backpack, every muscle tensing. He was close enough to breathe in; I didn't want to do that. I wanted to step back and back. In fact, that's what I did—right until I bumped into a tree.

He touched my face. I knew this moment would haunt me, but fear kept me paralyzed.

"Colby!"

I jerked, and tears started streaming down my face. I met Jared's eyes over Colby's shoulder. He looked angrier than I had ever seen. A whole tropical storm brewed on his face.

Colby swiped at a tear with his thumb, and then dropped his hand from where he had traced my jaw. He turned to face Jared, and my legs gave out. I slid down the tree.

The rest was a blur: Jared yelled about leaving me alone; Colby said something about Jared not owning me. Jared shoved Colby away from me and crouched down. He brushed away more tears. There was an endless supply of tears. But then he was pushed sideways, and Colby was on top of him with a manic look in his eye. He was possessed; I had never heard the sound of fists hitting flesh before.

I grew up with a physically peaceful family. Sure, Dad yelled, and Mom was... herself. But even when Jared lived with us, he behaved. I didn't see the wild side of him. I knew there was a piece of him that was scarred from the fire. He was irrevocable changed, but only sometimes. Only in the dark, or when the darkness came out of him.

Colby and Jared rolled on the ground, each trying to get on the upper hand. Finally, Jared landed on top. He straddled Colby and hit him once, twice, three times.

"Jared," I whispered. I said it again, louder, on repeat until

I was screaming. I didn't realize I was standing over him until I was close enough to grab onto his arm. "Stop," I sobbed.

"He can't *fucking* touch you, Charlie," he said. Colby glared up at him, blood trickling down his nose. One of his eyes was swelling. Jared got up and put his arm around my shoulder. "I'll bring you home."

A week later, Jared's transfer to boarding school was finalized. He appeared at my door, bruises now an ugly green and yellow, and told me goodbye.

Leah didn't react as I finished telling her that story. I had tears in my eyes again, but they didn't fall.

"I wanted Jared to come back so badly," Leah admitted. "All freshman year, I had a huge crush on him. It wasn't until that day at the beach that he even paid attention to me. It was mostly Colby's doing."

I blinked.

She laughed, running a hand through her hair. "It's so stupid. Colby said he had noticed that I was infatuated with Jared. *Infatuated* was actually the word he used. And then he told me that you and him were hiking to a private beach, and we should crash." She shrugged. "It sounded like a good idea. But I didn't see you, and I didn't see Colby follow you into the woods. All I knew was, one minute I was kissing him and the next he was yelling your name. He took off."

I nodded. My story completed hers.

She shook her head. "He didn't say goodbye to any of us. Even Colby. *Especially* Colby. But... I think Colby expected it? All of a sudden, Colby was on top of the world." She sighed. "And he had his sights set on you almost immediately."

I frowned.

Leah looked at me with wide eyes. "I don't mean that to be

insulting."

I wanted to tell her it wasn't insulting, it was just fact. It was part of the fear: Colby only wanted me because Jared said no. Colby only acted this way because he *could*. Because, like that day in the forest, I wouldn't tell him to stop.

My voice was obliterated.

"Please..." I use both hands to wipe at my face. "Take me home."

Chapter 24

THE DAYS ROLL BY, AND I CONTEMPLATE MY life. Am I happy? Do I like Boston?

No, and yes.

For the first time in forever, I buy paints. I feel like a kid with money to spend in a candy store. I only buy the canvases I can carry without damaging on the subway. I only buy small tubes of paint, because I am cautious. I have the rest of my supplies at home.

My ritual has always been: set up the easel, paints, floor cover—in this case, an old table cloth—and music. Once everything is set, I sit and stare out of that window at the endless row of brownstones. I think, *What the hell am I going to paint?*

Eventually, I dip my brush into the paint and just start.

"This is Love" by Air Traffic Controller plays, and I stop. I listen.

I grab my phone and set the song to play on repeat.

It is anger, it is everything Colby had told me, and everything I had told myself. It invokes every feeling of helpless vulnerability that I have ever felt. I stray, more often than not, toward the darker colors. I tap my heel against the stool's bar. *This is love, love, shut up, this is love.* Hadn't Colby said something similar? Hadn't he said, *You love me.* There were no questions.

Every dream, lately, has been a nightmare. Every nightmare wear's Colby's face, and it always ends in sex that I don't want, but can't refuse.

I still cough and gag when I brush my tongue at night. It's too similar to the feeling of him in my mouth, choking me.

I still hate orders.

I still keep silent rather than speak out. Until today, until Avery.

Abruptly, I switch the song. "Survivor" by 2WEI. A cover for a movie trailer.

Avery is better. Avery has been drawn out, exhausting, uplifting. I smile when I think about him—usually.

I listen to this song until my head spins. I alternate between the two songs. Peace and anger. It isn't until the sky starts to lighten again that I realize I have painted all night.

The painting is small; the canvas was only ten inches, square.

I smile, satisfied, and go to bed.

In my dreams, I stand in front of the solar eclipse I painted. It burns me, but I cannot look away. Something comes from the darkness; a person walks toward me slowly, with too much swagger to be anyone I know now.

It isn't until he's close that I recognize Jared. His smirk. His scowl. His face flits between the two expressions too fast to be human. He holds Colby's head in his hand.

I fall backward, screaming.

Avery and I have yet to have sex again. There are things I sense he is keeping hidden from me, and I can't take it anymore.

"Let me in," I beg one day.

I want take his agony away. It is written all over his face when he's not trying to smile at me. I think I do make him happy. But I don't take up all of his thoughts. I am not on his mind when he first wakes up. I'm not on his mind when he stares into his coffee or when his fork hovers between his plate and his lips because he is caught ensnared in something over my shoulder

Another part of me wants him to get it out so he can get over it. When we met in Chicago, a year after New York, he was broken. He admitted it. But then... He said that he was better. He was ready to move on with me. So, which is it? That part of me makes me purse my lips and raise an eyebrow. I try to school my face into something more akin to sympathy... but I'm not always successful. I don't have much sympathy left while I sit in the dark.

Avery frowns, letting the pain show before shuttering it away. I take his hands and pull them onto my lap. He's had a few glasses of whiskey, between here and dinner, and I hope now is the best time to ask. I can't bear the look anymore without knowing how to fix it.

His fingers tighten around mine, and he looks out the

window.

"Her name is Elaina. We dated for a year. We clicked almost immediately." He inhales, nostrils wide. He's transported to a different place. "We had met on a boat. You know I'm originally from San Diego." I nod, although he isn't looking at me. "It was a summer job after college. I moved back home in July... the year we met." He looks guilty for a moment. "I got an internship with the accounting department of a marina, and they had a full-time position open on one of their bigger tour boats a few weeks after I started. From there, I met her dad. He owns a private yacht, and he told me that he liked the look of me. He needed someone to help on his boat, since he was always taking out high-end clients. All he needed was someone to help run the sails and look nice. Maybe be a bartender once they docked at an island or cast the anchor."

He pulls his hands away from mine. The loss of contact has me floundering, but I don't say anything. He's in his own world, and besides: I asked for this.

"So, I did a few gigs for him on my off days. He paid well. And then one day, he needed me for a family trip. He was going to take his daughter—who he told me he wasn't really on good terms with—out to a good fishing and swimming hole. She was stunning—" I hold up my hand, silently passing on those details. He grimaces. "Sorry. We flirted pretty relentlessly, and we kissed before we returned to land while her dad was in the bathroom. From there, it was a fast and furious sort of thing. We moved in together after a few months. But in all that time, she never said she loved me. She just... I don't know. I *think* she loved me, but she couldn't fucking say it." His hands balled into fists. "So, I left. I figured if she couldn't say it, maybe with me gone, she'd realize..."

I wait.

"She didn't. I mean, she said she missed me. She wanted me back. But I asked her if she loved me, and I got a blank stare." He finally meets my eyes. I've always loved his eyes, but the anger and hurt and disappointment in them nearly kills me. "When I got a job offer here in Boston, I didn't ask her to come with me. I just broke up with her, and broke my heart in the process."

I nod, trying to understand.

It makes me think of Jared—not adult Jared, but the one I knew as a child. I never told him I loved him, either, and maybe those words would've made him stay. Maybe those words would've chained him to me for eternity—it sounds like that's what Avery was going for with his ex, at any rate.

Avery left her. I guess a year wasn't enough time for her to digest her feelings, but it was too long for him. "I had a boyfriend who demanded I love him," I tell him. I wince when he meets my eyes and scowls.

"That isn't the same."

I am the disregarded china in the cabinet. My stories are collecting dust.

His words hurt me, although I try not to let him see. Maybe he doesn't see the ramifications of Colby's actions. He doesn't know anything of Colby, after all, of how he altered my perception of love and how I will *struggle* to admit it, ever, just like his ex-girlfriend seemed to. She might have a desperate, dark past that she wasn't willing to admit to him. Or, more likely, that he never asked about.

I shake my head and turn slightly away from him. It's the best that I can do to protect myself further. I cannot ask him what I want to know: *Will you wait for me to be ready?* A small part of me thinks not; he will know when *he* is ready for love, when he is in it, and if I'm not on the same page...

He lifts my hand from my lap and kisses my palm.

It's an apology, although I wish I knew which part he was sorry about.

Avery went home that evening. There needed to be a mourning period, a respectable pause of our relationship for the love they lost—or maybe that was just him, putting words into my head. It feels too close to cheating—talking about her and then sleeping with him.

Liking someone is a finicky thing.

I sit in my window seat—the best part of my apartment— watching the rain. After a while, I pull out my phone. Avery and I are new friends on Facebook, so it should have been easy enough to go back and find pictures of the two of them. There are marina pictures and pictures of him in a white casual uniform at the bow of a big boat. His grin was huge, and he looked... younger. Happier. More like the first time we met, which was pre-Elaina.

But no pictures of her.

Hell, I couldn't even find her last name.

Finally, after jumping from his photos to the marina's page, I find one that he hadn't been tagged in. But she was: Elaina Williams. The picture is half out of focus: the two of posing on the dock next to *Santa Elena*, a giant yacht.

I only hesitate for a second before I click on her name.

Her profile picture is still a picture of her and Avery. I enlarge it and try to ignore the churning in my stomach. They look at each other. His hair is the same length it was when I had first met him: just curling at his collar. Adorable and messy. It is brighter, bleached from the sun. They both wear goofy grins. She is petite—it shocks me how small she seems compared to him. I am not *huge*, but I am not doll-sized, either. The top of her head comes up to his shoulder, so I probably have at least three inches on her. She has big brown eyes, thick dark brown hair that could've been used in a shampoo commercial, and tanned, olive skin.

She was stunning. Avery's words bounce around in my head. Like a madwoman, I swipe through the rest of her pictures. There are so many of her, some of them with an older guy, tan though decidedly white, but with similar features; I have to assume he's her dad. Avery's boss. They look like they were so *happy*. Until... they weren't.

Pictures with friends, pictures of the water, of life with a dad who owned a boat, of a dog—*I want a dog,* my inner voice whines—of people who look similar enough to be siblings, and an ageless mother. It's the kind of aging my mother tries to achieve through injections, which makes her all the more unlikable.

Enough is enough. Avery and I have only been dating, what, two months? He didn't say when he broke up with her, but enough time had passed for him to uproot his life in San Diego and move to Boston. I count on my fingers back, back, back. I had met him in June before my senior year of college. He was a year ahead of me, so he had just graduated. By the time I saw him more than a year after our first encounter, he was freshly heartbroken. The fact that it's been a solid year since then... well, that would be the anniversary of their relationship and their breakup.

The last thing I click on is a video on her profile, from a year and a half ago. Her face fills the frame. "Ave," she laughs, and

I'm jealous of even that perfect sound, "say it again? For the camera?"

Suddenly his face is squished next to hers. His eyes are wide, and his hair is wet, plastered to his face. He isn't wearing a shirt, but he is wearing a necklace of wooden beads that I haven't seen before.

He turns sideways and plants a kiss on her temple. "I *said*, Elaina Sydney Williams, will you move in with me?"

Her smile is catastrophic.

I close out of the video before I hear her answer.

Chapter 25

PAST

COLBY TEXTED ME AT MIDNIGHT THAT HE was in my backyard. I threw on a sweatshirt over my sleep shirt and snuck outside, wondering why we were doing this on a weekday. When I saw him, he smirked at me. He grabbed my face and kissed me, not unlike the first time. I couldn't move until he released me.

But then his hand slid down and wrapped around my throat. He pushed me back against the side of my house. How could I have not seen the angry glint in his eye when I first walked toward him? A shiver ran up my spine; it was still cold, for the end of March, but that wasn't the cause.

Fear would flay me apart if I let it.

"What did you say?"

I blinked at him. He squeezed my throat, once, and then loosened his grip. A warning? I opened my mouth, but nothing would come out.

Colby leaned into me, his lips at my ear.

"Don't you love me, Charlie?" I shivered again and nodded frantically, as though my body wasn't controlled by my brain anymore. "Say it."

"I love you," I whispered.

"Then tell me what the fuck you told Leah."

What I told Leah? What did I tell Leah?

Something inside me cracked. "Please," I said. "I love you. Please." I couldn't have said what I was even asking for. Tears seeped from my eyes, and all of a sudden I couldn't stop my hands from trembling against my legs. I lifted my arm and touched my fingers to Colby's wrist.

I feared he would hit me.

I feared he would leave me.

I couldn't decide which was worse.

"Son, I'd advise that you take a step back."

Both of our heads whipped toward the back door. My dad stepped out further, triggering the light sensor. He looked scary, the way the light cast harsh shadows on his face. His expression was murderous.

Oh, no.

Colby's hand fell away from my neck, and I glanced back at him. The darkness had hidden the bruise on his temple, an ugly red and purple mark that gave him a ghoulish look. I gasped, unable to fathom how it had gotten there.

"Come here, Charlotte," my father said.

But I couldn't move. My muscles were locked, and the only thing keeping me upright was the side of the house at my back. A step toward my father was a step away from Colby. My lungs weren't working right; I kept inhaling and not getting any air.

Dad came down and pulled me up the steps with him. He tucked me behind him and kept facing Colby. My mother appeared in the doorway with her phone, and she wrapped her arms around my shoulders. I tucked my face into her neck. There were too many emotions in me, but I didn't want to sort them out. I just wanted to go back to bed and pretend they didn't catch me outside with Colby.

"Colby," my dad said. This was it: they were going to forbid me from seeing him. They realized that he had been a bad influence on me, or something. I cringed further into my mother. "The police are on their way."

"You called the police?" My voice was hoarse, but my mom heard me.

"No, honey, they called us."

I risked lifting my head and glancing at Colby. He had sunk to his knees in the grass. He pulled at his hair and looked ready to scream.

"He assaulted your friend," Mom continued. "The one you're always with. Leah."

Leah. *Tell me what the fuck you told Leah.*

The one you're always with—well, that wasn't true. The one I used as a scapegoat, more often than not.

"I told her everything," I said to Colby. He glared at me, but my fear was lessened with my father between us. I couldn't imagine what he did to her, but I felt every shred of guilt.

"You bitch," Colby muttered.

My dad growled. "Take her inside, Lydia," he ordered.

Mom started pulling me inside. I struggled, because there was a piece of me that needed to see this through. I needed to see what would happen. "What did you do to Leah?"

He just shook his head and smirked at me. "I fucked your daughter," Colby said to my dad. "She took so much fucking shit from me. She loves me, though." He grinned at me, craned around my dad. "Sleep well, baby."

My heart stopped, then picked up a much more frantic pace.

"You're never going to see her again," Dad said.

My mom had managed to drag me into the house, then—all the way to the front door. She swung it open and let two officers in, and it clicked that they were arresting Colby. I started screaming as they passed, choking on sobs that burst out of my chest.

But my dad was there, pressing me into his chest and half carrying me up the stairs. He put me on my bed and closed the door; I heard him lock it from the outside.

"A lock?" Mom asked. Her voice carried through the door, skeptical.

"She'd run away—you know it, and I do, too. We're keeping her safe."

I got up from the bed and tried to see what was happening outside of my window, but I had a terrible view. The red and blue lights were gone. *Sleep well, baby*, Colby had said. Immediately, I dove for my dresser. Tucked into an old pair of socks was a small baggie of pills. Xanax, I remembered, because Colby was harassing me for freaking out too much. *Chill pills*, he called them. I put five in my mouth, but then—

My phone started ringing, buzzing and dancing on the nightstand.

I picked it up without saying hello.

"Charlie, oh my god—"

Leah.

She was still talking a mile a minute, "—Colby is insane. Don't go near him, okay? He just—I mean—Charlie, I have your best interest at heart, you know that, right?" She exhaled sharply into the phone.

I spat the pills back into my palm, half-dissolved.

"God, I am so sorry. I'm pressing charges this time. I just wanted you to know. I'm so sorry."

I set the phone down without hanging up, because the guilt that I felt earlier was gone. I had become a black hole. There were tears on my face, and I could hear Leah still talking: her tinny voice was nearly indistinguishable.

I'm sorry, on repeat.

Finally, she hung up. In the silence, I realized that I needed to get this on paper. All of it. It was now almost one in the morning. By dawn, my memory would be fuzzy. I would doubt what I said, what Colby said, what Leah said.

I found the notebook in my closet and started writing.

"I OWE YOU AN APOLOGY," AVERY SAYS.

We are sitting on my couch, watching a movie, when he pauses it and turns to me.

"You do?"

We've been officially dating for two months, even though it feels like just yesterday he was asking me out. Things haven't been going as smoothly as I would've imagined. I feel like we've only been on... ten dates, at most. I think I've cried more in the past eight weeks than I have in the past two years. That seems like a tiny warning sign, but it's nothing compared to the red flag of Colby. I put that little siren at the back of my mind.

"I've been a mess. I thought I was healing and getting better, but I think there's a learning curve. You aren't her, and you're not going to do things the same, or react in the same way."

I nod. "That's realistic. It takes time to know someone."

He reaches over and takes my hand. "I want to know you. I really like you, Charlotte."

Avery makes a point of saying my name a *lot*. It reminds me of my mother, although I don't tell him that. He doesn't say it in a mean way.

He kisses the back of my hand and tells me a story about his childhood. He tells me about when he was sixteen and his best friend—whose name is also Charlie—talked him into "borrowing" a boat and taking it for a joy ride. He laughs until he has tears in his eyes.

"When we got back to the dock, there were police waiting for us. Instead of fessing up to it, we jumped into the harbor and swam under docks until we got to the end of the marina. Charlie's dad was right there when we pulled ourselves out of the water, and he was livid. He grabbed us by the back of our necks and dragged us to his car." He laughs again. "We stunk of beer, cheap whiskey that had been stashed on the boat, and slimy algae. I thought for sure he was going to turn us over to the police. But he just drove us home and hosed the grime off of us in the backyard." He suddenly stops laughing. "Later that month, we found out Charlie's dad had pancreatic cancer. He was dead three months after that."

I blink.

"Wow, oh my god."

Smooth, Char.

"Yeah. I miss him."

"Are you still friends with Charlie?"

He wears a smile that feels fake. "Yes, of course. He's in Ireland, though, so I don't get to see him too much."

I nod.

"Have you been out of the country?"

I nod. "Yeah, we went to Switzerland once. It was a work

thing for my dad, but Mom and I got to sightsee." My voice sounds funny in my own ears. Maybe talking about death has me rattled because I ask, "Do you believe in heaven?"

Avery chuckles. "You're going for the tough questions, huh?"

"Hey, you brought up death first."

He leans back into the couch, eyes on the paused television screen.

"I do." His eyes flicker to mine and back to the movie. "Do you?"

"Nope." I say it just to get a reaction out of him. In truth, I don't know.

His head whips toward me. "You don't?" He looks wild and saddened by this.

"No. I can't wrap my head around it."

He presses his lips together as if he disapproves, then asks, "Popcorn or chips?"

I touch my chin. "No one in my life has died. Except my grandparents on my dad's side, but they both died when I was young."

He groans, elbowing me lightly in the side. "I don't want to talk about this anymore."

"Why?"

"Why don't I want to talk about it?"

I give an exaggerated nod.

"Because death is fucking depressing. And I'd like to think that there's somewhere better that we'll end up." I can't help but think that he's adorable when he's uncomfortable.

"Hmm," I say.

"What?"

"What if *this* is heaven? What if you've already died and this is the best it's going to be?"

A flush creeps up his neck.

We stare at each other for a minute, and the red crawls higher and higher up his face. It's the only indication that he's upset, until: "Fuck, you're annoying."

I jerk back. "Excuse me?"

He inhales and exhales twice, chewing on his lips and on his words. I, however, am having trouble breathing. My lungs stutter. That hurt much more than I would've anticipated.

"I didn't mean that, Charlotte. I'm sorry... it just came out."

I watch through squinted eyes as Avery leans over and cups my cheek. My stomach does a weird dance, a mix of anger and thrill.

"Seriously, I apologize. You riled me."

I cock my head. "I barely did anything."

Avery nods and traces my lower lip with his thumb.

I lean into his touch, unable to help myself. He smiles slightly, leaning forward and kissing me. His tongue invades my mouth, and I can't help the small noise I make.

It's only moments later that he pulls back. "Can we finish the movie, now?"

"Sure," I say.

An hour later, the movie is over and I am in Avery's lap. My shirt is somewhere behind the couch, and his pants are unbuttoned. Our lips are glued together.

"Should we move to your bedroom," he mumbles against my lips.

I lean away. "Are you going to be a dick afterward?"

His eyes widen, like he's innocent. "No, I won't."

I narrow my focus to his face. He has a tell when he lies, I can *feel* it, but I haven't yet been able to prove it.

He smirks. "I'm sure my dick will be too tired to influence how I act."

"It's not funny, Avery. I don't want to let you in again if you're just going to fuck me, fuck *with* me, and leave."

I watch him grow more serious.

"I apologized for that. I won't do it again."

When I don't drop my stare, he sighs. "You're being a tease."

He nudges me until I climb off of him. I abandon him on the couch and sashay to the best of my ability toward my bedroom. As I go, I feel his eyes on me. I reach behind me and unclasp my bra, letting it fall to the floor.

It only takes a minute for him to scramble up behind me. He gives chase and pins me to my bed, kissing his way down my body. The rest, as they say, is history.

"Can I stay the night?" he asks into my back. He follows that with a kiss to my shoulder blade, and then one on my spine. If I was worried—and, *okay*, I was—about how he would act after the last time, he is doing everything in his power to prove me wrong.

"Do you need a toothbrush?" I blurt out. I want to groan, but there's no use trying to get those words out of the air.

He chuckles, continuing his path of kisses from one shoulder to another. He pauses to suck on my neck, making me inhale sharply, before moving on. "I have one in my coat pocket," he whispers.

I roll over and look at him. "What?"

"I came prepared," he says. He keeps laughing, like this is funny, like I've done this before and I'm okay with it.

"We haven't had a sleepover yet," I say. Uncertainty makes my voice waver. "What if I snore?"

"I'm sure you don't snore," Avery says with confidence.

"I hope you're a deep sleeper," I joke.

He trails a finger over my lips, down my chest and between my breasts. His eyes follow, his tongue poking out over his lower lip. Finally, he meets my eyes. "Can we sleep naked?"

I giggle and nod.

"Good," he says in my ear, pressing me back into the pillows. He reaches over me and clicks off the light. "Goodnight," he whispers.

I nod again in the dark, although I can barely see him, and roll onto my side. He fits against my back, slipping one arm under my neck and the other over my hips. It's a puzzle that is finally coming together.

Chapter 27

"GOOD MORNING, DEAR," MY MOTHER SAYS.

I yawn, swiping at dried drool on my cheek. Light has barely begun to filter into my room. It *cannot* be an appropriate time for a phone call.

"Not awake enough to talk?"

I grunt, and then peek over my shoulder at Avery. He faces away from me, on his side, breathing heavily. With some effort, I make myself get out of bed and head to the couch. Once I'm swaddled in blankets, I say, "To what do I owe this early pleasure?"

"Ah, there you are. I was wondering how long it would take."

I wait, because she usually has a purpose if she's calling before the sun has fully risen. Maybe this will be a quick conversation, and I can slip back into bed with Avery when she's done.

"I just talked to Julianne—" Jared's mom, formally known as Mrs. Brown, "—and she told me Jared was in an accident."

I nearly drop my phone. I see it as clearly as if I were standing in front of him: Jared in a hospital bed, tubes protruding from his arms. Jared in a body cast. A crying woman—Marcy, had he said?—holding a toddler. Surely, the kid would be a toddler by now.

"Why are you telling me?"

My mother sighs. Her keyboard clicks, faintly, which means she's multitasking.

"You used to be friends with him, Charlotte Harper, and should I not give you news of your old friend? Especially since you refused to talk to him much at all at our Labor Day party." She sighs again. I imagine she rolls her eyes, too.

"He... he brought a date and you wanted me to flirt with him?"

"Of course not. He was a stable part of your childhood is all."

This time *I* roll my eyes. "And I'm not stable?"

"Of course you are," she answers. "Now, at any rate."

"I don't even want to unpack that statement," I mutter.

The truth is, she's right. I'm stable now—for the most part—but Colby shattered me when he left. It had taken almost three years to recover. To want to kiss a boy again. To smile, fully, without flinching after it.

"*Anyway*," my mother says. "I thought maybe, you know, you'd want to give Jared a call."

I frown. "And say what?"

"I don't know, honey, whatever you want to say to him. Julianne said he would be stuck there for at least a week."

I rub at my face. It's too early to think of all of this. It's too early to think of Jared in a hospital bed for a week. I glance back toward my bedroom door, where Avery is sleeping. Avery's arm stayed around me until he fell asleep, and then he twisted onto his back, mouth open. I couldn't sleep. It felt too peaceful, too quiet. There is another shoe about to drop, but I can't let go of the breath I'm holding.

"I don't know," I finally tell her. "What about that girl that he got pregnant? Why isn't she by his side?"

"She very well may be, but that doesn't give you the right to ignore your proper upbringing and pretend this conversation didn't happen. Just imagine how bored he'll be, all alone..."

Jared isn't my problem anymore. Besides, she wouldn't be encouraging this if she knew I had a boy in my bed. A *boyfriend* in my bed. "I'm going back to bed now."

"He's at the George Washington University Hospital in D.C.," she adds.

I grunt and hang up to my mother laughing at me.

I fold the blanket and toss it on the back of the couch, taking my time sneaking back into the bedroom. Avery is still as I left him. When I slide in behind him, he doesn't even stir.

I wrap my hand around him, taking a small thrill in being the big spoon. My chest presses against his warm back, and we share the same pillow. It's a lot easier to fall back asleep.

When I wake up, Avery is gone.

The momentary panic flashes hot through me, before I register the sound of the shower running. When the adrenaline fades away, a smile cracks my face open. *Wow*, I tell myself, *you almost overreacted big time.*

The water stops, and he appears in the doorway with one of my towels wrapped around his waist. "Hi," he says. He smiles at me.

"Good morning," I whisper, ducking my face into the pillow to hide my happiness.

"I thought you were going to sleep forever."

My smile widens. "I wouldn't have!"

Avery shakes his head. "I'm glad you're awake now."

I raise my eyebrows, and he drops the towel to show me just how glad he is.

Avery and I spent the day walking around Boston. We got brunch at a cute cafe-slash-bookstore on Newbury Street, and walked down toward the Commons. It was sunny, mild, and a perfect day for a spontaneous picnic. We finished with an early dinner, and he walked me home.

I drop my purse on the kitchen counter, looking forward to a glass of wine and a bath. My feet are sore, and my legs ache in a way that shouldn't surprise me, but does. And then, I remember.

I remember Jared, as I hadn't remembered all day.

Tears fill my eyes, because I am selfish.

Before I can chicken out, I look up the number of the hospital and dial. I wait, and then ask for Jared's room.

"Hello?"

His voice sounds the same. *Oh, god, he sounds the same.*

"Jared, it's—"

"Charlie." I can hear the smile through the phone. "Heard of my epic demise, huh?"

"Demise?" I shake my head. "She just said you were in an accident—"

He laughs. It fills me with this warm feeling that I haven't felt since I was a child. "I'm going to guess it was our mothers?"

Can I bottle your voice to savor on a rainy day?

"Of course," I say. "They love to meddle. What's going on, Jared?"

"Oh, nothing."

I snort. "Yeah, right."

He coughs. It's wet and violent, and it takes him several moments to catch his breath. Quietly, he says, "I won't be leaving the hospital for quite some time."

"Just speak straight for once," I demand. "I don't know why I called..."

Jared grunts. After another beat of silence, he says, "I'm a firefighter, Charlie. Did you know?"

"No," I whisper. "My mother knew?" My body-cast imagery seems like it might be accurate. The sight of his house, burning, comes to mind. Of embracing him in his front lawn while his whole world sputtered to a stop.

He laughs, once. It's hollow. "I wouldn't doubt that she does. My high school therapist saw it coming a mile away. Even my parents weren't surprised by my decision."

I shake my head. It makes sense, if he was looking to conquer his fear. If he was looking to tame an obsession. He had a therapist in high school?

"We got a call for a structural fire—a house in the suburbs. It was routine, clear the rooms before it gets too bad... We got everyone out, but then the kid, from the ambulance, starts sobbing about his dog. I started to—"

"No—" I squeeze my eyes shut.

"The roof collapsed in front of me. On me?" He coughs again. "The next thing I knew was feeling like..." *I was on fire.*

It was a nightmare that he'd had for weeks when we were younger. I cringe for him.

"And then I woke up in the hospital."

I take a deep breath. "How badly are you burned?"

"I have burns on most of my lower half. They had to amputate my leg."

My breath whooshes out. "Oh, my god. Which leg?"

"*Which leg*?" He starts laughing. I have to pull the phone away from my ear because his laughter is so loud. I envision it bouncing around the hospital room. "Jesus, Charlie."

I try to hold back my apologies because he's *still* laughing at me. It morphs into a cough, until he eventually says, "The left one is gone, about six inches above the knee. I think you're the only person who would think to ask."

"I was trying to picture it... And it kept switching. I'm sorry."

Jared sighs. "I think that's the first time I've laughed since it happened."

I dare to smile. "I'm glad I could help."

"Can we do this again?" He sounds so much more tentative than I remember. "Can we talk?"

"Later?"

"Yeah, the nurses are going to be coming in a few minutes to change my bandages. And my parents are coming to bring me dinner..."

I swallow. "Of course. I'm sorry it's late—"

"Charlie."

"Yeah?"

"I'm really glad you called."

I nod to myself. Yes, I'm glad I called, too.

Chapter 28

WAKE UP, CHARLOTTE.

I feel the heat, insistent, pushing at me.

Wake up, Charlotte.

It's so hot, my skin starts to blister. It is unbearable agony.

Wake up. Wake up.

I arch my back, trying to get away. The flames eat up my legs, over my torso—an ironclad force holding me down. I squeeze my eyes closed and turn my head to the side. I suck in a lungful of air, ready to scream, but my breath singes in my throat. There is deep, deep pain. I can't control my muscles as they spasm.

Charlotte, Charlotte, "Charlotte!"

I jerk, snapping my eyes open. Avery hovers over me, hands on my shoulders, and I lose it. It still feels like I'm burning. "Get off," I say. My voice is hoarse, cracked. He doesn't move. "Get off, Avery," I try again. He's blurry, and he leans away but I still feel him. *"Get off of me,"* I yell. I roll to the side of the bed and off of it, heaving.

Oh, god, I'm going to throw up. I start patting myself, feeling smooth skin. I keep going, touching my legs, making sure I'm still whole.

"What... What happened?"

I can't even look at him, my heart is beating so fast.

What *was* that?

"Charlotte," he says. He kneels on the bed, facing me. His hands are out in front of him like I'm a wild animal.

At this point, I do feel feral.

This isn't how ladies act, my mother whispers.

"I'm sorry," I say. My voice cracks halfway through *sorry,* and I feel sick that I can't even make it through an apology. I don't even know what I'm apologizing for.

"You were moaning," he says gently. "And not in a good way."

I shake my head, still bent over. I can't seem to catch my breath. Vaguely, I'm aware of the tears pouring down my face. I want to douse myself in ice.

He climbs out of bed and kneels before me. It's *then* that I realize we're naked, and I need clothes. There is way too much vulnerability in this room.

"I'm sorry," I say again. It's too forceful. I edge around him, grabbing a t-shirt out of my dresser.

"Are you okay?"

I can practically feel my mother's glare. Admitting to anything other than perfection is a cardinal sin. I'm not sure why her etiquette is rearing its ugly head now, of all times. Her presence is so thick in my mind, I can almost envision her in my room. Sitting in the chair by the closet, eyes raised, waiting for me to fuck up.

That was the way of it growing up.

Sixth grade, my first crush told me I was fat. I cried on the bus; I cried when I got home. She sat there and watched me, and then said, "Tears don't help you. Cry if you must, but do it in the privacy of your own home, and then move on. Better yourself." She folded her arms. "Fat? Do you think you're fat?" I shook my head, paused at her expression, and then nodded. "We'll get you a gym membership, then." Like a good daughter, I nodded again. *Yes, mother, a gym membership will solve all of my problems. Thank you.*

I blink, and she vanishes.

I'm losing my mind.

"I'm sorry," I say.

"That's the third time you've said you're sorry," Avery says. "What... was it a bad dream?"

I gulp and block out what it felt like. The dream has evaporated, but phantom fire traces my skin. "A nightmare." Inhale, exhale. I shiver, and rub my arms against the sudden goosebumps. "I just need water. You should go back to sleep."

He stares at me for a second, before crossing the distance and wrapping me in a hug.

We haven't hugged in a while, although we've done... everything else. It feels like being wrapped in a warm blanket. It reminds me that I'm still here. "Charlotte, I wouldn't do that to you. I've got you, okay, babe?"

I nod against his chest. When we do climb back into bed, I keep my face pressed into his chest. We're so close, it's hard to breathe, and my breath gets stuck in my lungs until I roll away and let him spoon me. I close my eyes, but I know sleep will be a long way off.

For as long as I can remember, I have had intermittent nightmares. I can go months without a nightmare, and then one week I'll have four or five. They all make me feel like I need to scrub out my brain to forget the way they make me feel: helpless. Alone. Terrified.

The last time it happened was almost a year ago. They had been about someone breaking into my house and tying me up while they ransacked my house. I hadn't even *lived* in a house, then, but my crazy mind had me living in a huge house filled with jewels that the robber took his time sifting through. Each night, it was the same and yet different: the robber wore pajamas in one. I tried to run away in another. The robber beat me senseless in another.

After that one, I woke up with a bloody nose.

Early morning light filters in through my blinds when I finally give up on sleep. I let Avery's arm fall off of me. It's too early for him to be stirring, and he rolls away from me. I watch his peacefulness for a minute; I count the spaces between his inhales and exhales. I feel the press of a headache against my eyes. In all this time, I've never dreamed of being on fire, like Jared used to dream. It feels like a line in my imagination has been crossed, from uneasy to frantic.

I slide out of bed and walk into the bathroom. I turn the shower on and shuck off my clothes. Once I'm under the coldest water that I can handle, I wait. I feel the choking, closing of my throat that precedes the tears. So many tears, so little time. Who knew a girl could cry so much?

I cough, remembering the burning feeling on my legs. This dream scarred Jared for *years*. I would wake up to his screams when he lived in our house. For some reason, I was always the first one there. I would grip his hand as he panted, paralyzed flat on his back, until he could move. He would be covered in sweat, practically dripping with it, his bed soaked, too. I had no problem, at such a young age, inviting my best friend to sleep in my bed. We would fall asleep on opposite sides of my bed, an ocean of space between us, except for our interlocked fingers.

"It was just a dream," I say out loud. I need to hear the words bounce back at me.

Out of the shower, my skin is too pink. I get halfway into my work clothes before I realize that it is Saturday, and I groan inside the closet. Avery watches me from the bed, awake now, with a curious look on his face.

"Do you want to talk about it?" His voice is low.

"Nope."

He nods. He understands, maybe, that I am not trying to push him away. I just can't replay it one more time in my head. I've started to lock it away with the rest of the nightmares.

"Breakfast, then?"

"Please," I say. I'm grateful that he lets it go so easily. He gets out of bed and kisses me—the first time he's done so without going to the bathroom, first. I lean into him, opening my mouth, when I smell and taste what he's been hiding: the worst morning breath in the history of bad breath.

I force myself to smile at him when we pull away. He says something about meeting me in the kitchen, and he disappears into the bathroom. *Bad breath*, I muse. *I suppose I can deal with that.*

"What are your plans for the day?" Avery asks as he walks into the kitchen.

I look him over. He changed from sleep shorts into sweatpants, and graces me with a sexy smile. "I'm not sure," I say.

He hums. A deviant look gleams in his eye. "We can figure something out."

Chapter 29

THINGS ARE SURPRISINGLY EASY.

Yes, we bicker a bit. Yes, his morning breath continues to irritate me.

But beyond that, we mesh well together. We like most of the same foods and understand the same jokes. It feels comfortable. It's easy to sink into a routine around him. We make plans for our future: dates, sleepovers. He even asks me if I'll go to a Halloween party with him, which is weeks away. It makes me feel safer. I've been curled into a protective ball for so long, it's nice to stretch my wings a bit.

Three nights after my nightmare, I have the dream again. It's worse, though, because I can't wake up until my hair starts to burn. Avery isn't there, and I throw up in the toilet before stepping into the shower—in my pajamas—and forcing myself to stand in the cold water until I can't stop shivering.

Once I'm back in bed, I pick up my phone, dial, and then

squeeze my eyes shut until I hear his voice.

"Charlie?"

I bite down on my lip before I say, "How did you know it was me?"

"My mother would never call at two in the morning," Jared says.

I pull back and look at the time on my phone. I'm an idiot. "Did I wake you up?"

"No. I don't sleep too much these days. They were just changing my bandages. Again."

"Someone else wouldn't call you at two a.m.?" *Like your girlfriend?*

"A lot of friends have jumped ship in the past few months."

I cock my head, even though he can't see me. "You act like it happened months ago."

Jared pauses. "Did your mom not tell you—"

"Tell me what?"

"The accident happened two weeks ago. I have a lot of burns, but it was manageable. But then, my leg got infected on top of bronchitis. We decided to amputate when they couldn't get the infection under control."

My heart is galloping out of control. "Fuck," I mutter. I didn't mean to swear—it slipped out—but it felt freeing to let out my anger. "My fucking mother." It made me want to throw something. He'd been alone, this whole time, injured? Not that I would've *wanted* to call him a month ago, or even when my mother first suggested it. But she had made it seem so... immediate. Devastating.

It was devastating.

"Sorry, Jared."

He chuckles. "No, it's okay. It might not have been a priority for my parents to tell your mom. I, for one, didn't want everyone in the old neighborhood to know."

"You wouldn't have wanted me to know?"

"Not you, Charlie. You're the exception." He audibly swallows. "The last time we talked, you were so quiet."

"Yeah, well...." I don't want to tell him that Colby had a lasting impact on my silence. As far as I know, he doesn't know Colby and I ever interacted beyond that time Jared almost beat his face in.

"Charlie."

I jerk. "Yes?"

"I'm assuming there's a reason you called?"

Oh. I pull my damp hair to one side, twisting it around my fingers. "Do you remember those dreams you used to have? Of being..."

"On fire?"

I whisper, "Yes."

He sighs. "Yes, of course I remember." *They became my reality*, he doesn't say.

My face burns. "How did you get them to stop?" I am such a wuss. Jared endured *years* of those dreams. I had two and am ready to call it quits.

We're both silent for a minute, remembering our past.

"It took some time. Eventually, I realized that the fire wasn't just... fire. It was fear that was eating me alive. So, in the dream, I became my own hero. My own firefighter." And then he became an actual firefighter.

I nod, because it makes sense. In a dream, no one can save you except yourself.

"Why are you asking?"

Now, I don't want to tell him. I don't want to admit that I can't seem to save myself from his horrors.

"You're not having those dreams, are you?"

174

I blow air through my lips. Jared used to do this thing where he'd ask me a tough question, and when I refused to answer, he wouldn't talk. He would just... kill me with silence. Young me, who couldn't seem to shut up around him, hated it. He does it now. I can hear his steady breathing, but neither of us says anything for a full minute and a half.

"Fine, yes," I admit. "I've only had two. But I've had nightmares for so long, off and on."

"You never used to have nightmares."

It started because of the pills, I think. That's what my parents blamed it on, after Colby was arrested and my stash was found. I went through a wicked withdrawal, and that was when the nightmares started. The therapist I saw throughout high school and part way into college only moderately helped. Nothing fixed it except riding it out. I would hate to think that I'm back to that... to letting my fears take over.

"They started in high school. After—" I can't force the words out. I'm not sure how this went from me asking for help, to me... being vulnerable.

I don't like being vulnerable.

"This conversation is going downhill," Jared says. "You don't have to tell me. I just—I wish I had gotten out of my own ass when we were younger. I regret losing our friendship."

I close my eyes. *This* is why I shouldn't have called in the middle of the night. Now, we have all these emotions that are going to come out of the woodwork. I can't judge, in this moment, how I feel. Talking to Jared is reminiscent of a past life that doesn't quite fit. I hate that his voice is a balm against the memory of fire.

"Jared... I was a mess in high school. Capital M."

"Why? You weren't a mess before I left..."

"I don't really want to talk about this," I bite out.

His silence reminds me that we aren't friends anymore. I've struck him speechless. And then, "I'm just glad that I've talked to you twice in a week, Charlie."

"Me, too."

When I was younger, I blamed everything surrounding Colby on Jared moving away. The notebook holding my letters to Jared pops into my head; I thought that, by putting the words down on paper, Jared would realize I needed his help. It was my mistake, though, because he wasn't a superhero. I shouldn't have attached unrealistic expectations to him, especially at fifteen. When I left for college, my parents cleaned up my room and made it suitable for guests. They took most of my stuff—clothes, trinkets, the like—and boxed it up, to be stored in a closet in the basement. I'm sure that notebook is tucked into one of those boxes, and if I read it now, I don't think I'd recognize the girl who left herself between those pages.

"I wish things were different," he says in my ear. "But we can talk about that another time."

I glance at the clock, surprised that we have been talking for more than a half hour.

"You're right," I say. All at once, I'm afraid to close my eyes again. My past nightmares suddenly seem easy, compared to burning alive. I shiver. "I'll let you go."

"Are you going to be okay?"

I choke on a laugh. "Me? You're the one missing half a limb, Jared, not me. I'm peachy by comparison."

He is silent for a second. I wonder if I've crossed a line. But then, "It isn't a competition, Charlie. You're allowed to not be okay, even if *my* being not okay happens to be a thousand times worse than yours." I imagine he would then wink at me to lessen the blow of his words. It still hurts to hear.

"Goodnight, Jared."

Chapter 30

I STARE OUT AT THE SEA OF PEOPLE AND SWALLOW. I am not a costume person. Hell, I'm not really much of a holiday person, in general.

Avery stands next to me, and maybe he's shocked into silence because he loosely holds my hand and keeps his mouth closed. The club, which his friend Steve insisted that we go to instead of the party Avery originally invited me to, is packed. Orange and black lights flicker over the dancing crowd from the DJ booth. I feel the pulse of music in my ribcage, threatening to take over my heartbeat. It makes me long for the quiet of my apartment, the safety of my bed.

"Danny Zuko! Looking good, dude!"

Avery turns, and Steve pushes through a group of zombies with a girl following close behind him. The guys do some sort of weird guy greeting—back slapping, fist bumping—while the girl and I stand watching them.

Steve grins at me. "And this is your Sandy, huh?"

"Charlie," I supply, at the same time that Avery says, "Charlotte."

Steve raises his eyebrows. "Okay, yeah. Cool. This is my girl, Larissa." She steps forward and shakes my hand and Avery's. She is dressed as Wonder Woman—the old red-white-and-blue version—and her long black hair falls to the small of her back. Steve has on a white dress shirt and black rimmed glasses. At my confused look, he pulls apart his shirt to reveal the blue, red, and gold emblem of Superman.

"Nice," I say. Avery nods.

It was my idea to go as Danny and Sandy from *Grease*. I opted for pre-transformation Sandy. It was easier, and I already had most of the parts—a white blouse, sweater, and I found a long, pale yellow skirt at a thrift store. But now that we're here, I'm hot. The fabric feels heavy on my skin; the end of October in Boston isn't as chilly as I had hoped it would be. With bodies pressing in on us, the temperature is warm and humid.

We follow the couple into the depths of the club. Steve has a friend who owns the club, and he managed to reserve us a table. As soon as we sit, girls start approaching the two men with their cleavage bared. It's like Larissa and I have turned invisible, although she holds her poker face better than I can.

"I'll be your dangerous Sandy," one girl—dressed as a vampire—croons to Avery from behind us. She leans in dangerously close over the back of the booth. I can smell her cheap, fruity perfume.

He makes a face, says, "No, thanks," and wraps an arm around me. It only takes a second for the vampire girl to register his rejection. She glares at me before spinning away.

Larissa—Wonder Woman—leans across the table. "So, how did you and Avery meet?"

I glance at Avery. "We met in New York a few year ago," I say. She makes me repeat it, louder, and then she nods.

"That's cute! So you guys are boyfriend and girlfriend?"

I catch Steve nudging Larissa with his elbow. "Seriously?" She laughs. "Just harmless questions! Stevie and I met here, at this club! I'm a waitress here most weekends." She watches us with eyes that are a little too sharp for comfort, and I don't answer her.

In truth, I can see how she would be able to work here and be good at it. Her body is alluring: small waist, big breasts, and curved, flared hips. She has yet to stop flipping her hair around. I wonder how tangled it must get, how often she has to tell Steve to get off of it. I feel like a nun compared to her. While she has barely any clothing on, I have a full skirt and blouse. *Lame.*

In my ear, Avery asks, "Want to dance?"

No, I think. But he managed to get me into a costume and to agree to come to a club. I may as well make the best of it. I nod, and he grins.

"See you guys later," he shouts to Steve and Larissa. They're already turning into each other, and they look like they're about to devour one another.

Once on the dance floor, I try to let the music overtake me. I shake out my limbs, move my hips, but I feel awkward. Avery looks at me for a second, already dancing, before he steps forward and wraps his arms around me. He pulls me tightly to him, our whole bodies touching, and he moves us slowly. I wrap my arms around his neck and let him lead.

It only takes a few minutes for me to become lost in the feel of us moving together. The song changes to sometimes with a better beat, and Avery spins me out and back to him. We laugh together, and the rest of the night blurs together.

The next morning, it hurts to open my eyes. I cover my face with my hands, groaning. Avery rolls into me, burying his face into my neck.

"What happened last night?" I ask. My voice is hoarse and scratchy. I remember dancing, and Steve handing me a drink—some sort of vodka concoction—and the rest is a blur. How we got home is a mystery.

"We drank too much," Avery groans. "Dancing. Lots of dancing. Did we have sex?"

He lifts his head and looks at me. Most of the blankets are on the floor, and we're completely naked. I look further down and... "You're still wearing a condom," I giggle.

"Oh, shit," he says. He laughs, then groans, and rolls onto his back. "Does your head hurt? My head is killing me."

I start to nod, but that exacerbates the issue. "Yeah. We're not eighteen anymore."

"You were getting drunk at eighteen?"

No, I think. I was in therapy trying to stay off of pills. Instead, I say, "Weren't you?"

"More like sixteen, remember?" He nudges me.

"Oh, of course. Getting drunk on a stolen boat." I roll my eyes. "Not many girls in high school wanted to be my friend."

He turns to look at me. "Why was that?"

"I was the outcast. Through middle school and most of high school, I was good at school, sat in the front row, sucked up to the teachers. It was practically beaten into me that I had to do well in school in order to get into a good college," I say. Mom and Dad would pick over my reports, tests, every grade my freshman year. By sophomore year, I was skipping classes and getting high after school with Colby. Somehow, I still scraped by with honors.

"That must've been tough." He picks up my hand and kisses my palm. "I'm glad for it, though."

I make a face, because I am not glad for my past, for Colby, for losing my best friend, for my parents. I close my eyes again before I respond. It has been getting brighter in here, and the pulsing behind my eyes eases, slightly, when I duck my head back into the pillow. My voice is muffled when I ask, "Why's that?"

"It made you who you are, and I love who you are."

"You..." I open my eyes and he is way too serious for the hour.

"I love you, Charlotte."

I lean forward and kiss him; bad breath be damned. For once, I don't mind. I examine my feelings for him, holding onto this feeling of being so happy around him I want to cry. And when I am sure, I say, "I love you, too."

Chapter 31

GETTING IN THE CAR WAS EASY. TALKING WITH Avery through the two-hour drive to my parents' house for Thanksgiving was easy.

It was getting out of the car that was not easy.

I knew the scrutiny that waited for Avery inside that house. To make myself feel better, I told more and more stories—good ones—about my parents. I told him about how we went to Maine every other year for the winter holidays, and how it was the one place my parents seemed to be at peace. I told Avery about how I became associated in high school with Jared's friends, and then when Colby took over, I remained in the group. But they weren't *my* friends. They were secondhand friends. I told Avery to avoid the subjects of kids and marriage and *where will you be in ten years?* It was hard because the holidays tended to bring out the worst in my family. I knew this going in. I knew this three weeks ago, when Avery mentioned that he was staying in Boston for Thanksgiving and I immediately invited him home.

I couldn't figure out why I had invited him home. We hadn't spoke about meeting parents or siblings or aunts and uncles. We hadn't really talked about the future. As soon as the words came out of my mouth, I wanted to pluck them out of the air. He had blinked at me, slowly, making sure he heard me correctly, and then he smiled.

Unfortunately, that meant I had to call my mother and explain that, one, I had a new boyfriend and, two, he was coming home for Thanksgiving dinner. She hadn't taken the surprise very well. It had gone something along the lines of, *Charlotte Harper, are you seriously telling me you kept a secret boyfriend for almost three months?* She made me admit my shame. *Yes, Mother, I have a boyfriend and we're going steady. I'm sorry I didn't tell you and Dad.*

So maybe it's natural that, when we pull up in front of my parents' house, I can't move. Avery says my name a few times, the concern sweet but also annoying because *no, I'm not okay, shut up and let me panic.*

I am already sinking into the etiquette that has been instilled into me since I was young. One by one, the rules start to resurface. I want to flinch as each one rolls back into me. *Yes, not yeah, are you dumb?* and *Stand up straight, Charlotte, only hags and homeless people slouch,* and *What are you wearing, young lady? Are you auditioning for a position at the local strip club?*

Avery shakes my shoulder, until I *do* flinch, wickedly, and knock some sense back into my skull via the passenger window. "Oh, my god, are you okay?"

I rub my temple, which took the brunt of the hit. "I've had worse," I say. I smile at him, making sure my eyes crease just a tiny bit. It is the perfected skill of a faker, and he buys it. He smiles back before he leans over and kisses my cheek. It should make me cringe: affection after pain. I'm numb to that.

"You've got this," he tells me.

I nod, and we approach my house.

"Hi, honey! We missed you!" Mom speed-walks toward me as we shrug out of our coats in the foyer. She wraps me in a tight hug, angling so she can analyze Avery. "Not bad," she whispers.

I turn red, shaking my head slightly at her.

"We were having a wonderful autumn, but it got mighty chilly the past few days!" She releases me, turning to my boyfriend.

"Mom, this is Avery—"

"Nice to meet you, Mrs. Galston," Avery interjects. He steps forward and shakes her hand. Maybe a normal parent would've said, *No, by all means, call me Lydia*, but not my mom. She thrives on the formal speech. "You have a lovely home."

My tough, graceful, socially adept mother blushes. She, Queen of the Poker Faces, *blushes*. At a comment that probably wasn't the sincerest, seeing as how he's seen one outside wall and one room inside. I wink at Avery, making sure Mom can't see it, before turning and going to hunt down Dad. It would only make matters worse to linger and let him come to us, thus putting him in an annoyed mood.

"Hi, Dad," I say. He's in his office, typing on his computer, with glasses perched at the end of his nose. When did he get glasses? It dredges up a wash of guilt; I live so close and hardly visit. Not that I *want* to visit, because of their unpleasant interrogations every time I do, but because they're my parents. They're getting *old*.

"Ah, Charlotte. I thought I heard you come in." He looks happy to see me, which means we may survive dinner, yet.

Unfortunately, his pleased face also makes him look constipated. I try to hide my smile as best as possible. He stands and crosses the study space, patting my shoulder. "Brought a boy with you, have you?"

I nod, scrambling to keep up with his long strides as he seems to fly through the house. We come upon Mom and Avery in the kitchen, where Mom has the beginnings of a feast in the works. "Wow, Mom, this looks great."

"Thank you, dear. Avery, would you like to give me a hand?"

"I'll be right back," I say as Avery moves to stand next to my mother by the sink. He nods at me; my parents don't react. I slip out of the room and head to the basement. Once down there, I open up the closet that holds all of the things I left behind: sweaters and jackets I have long since grown out of, boxes holding trinkets and shoes, formal dresses that my mother didn't want to part with, and there, at the back, a smaller box on which I had written, *Private!!!*

Inside are pictures of Jared and I, and Colby and I, and three notebooks. Most of high school after Colby was arrested is a giant blur. There were the side effects to deal with: a massive detox of pills that landed me in the hospital for a weeklong stay. My "friends" were sympathetic, then mean, then distant. I expected a boomerang effect. I thought, surely, they'd come back.

They didn't.

Even Leah, whose *bravery* for standing up to Colby made her instantly more popular than she used to be, slowly withdrew her conversation, her smiles, her eye contact.

I'm tempted to throw away those pictures of Colby, of the lot of us on a lake beach somewhere, of Leah and me. I stare at them, barely recognizing the girl I used to be. There was a stark difference between fifteen and sixteen-year-old me. I had lost weight rapidly; in one picture with Jared, my freshman year, we looked happy and healthy. A year later, I was forty pounds lighter. My eyes were sunken. I looked *miserable*. How had my parents missed that?

I keep one of the pictures with Colby in it. We're standing by the door of his parents' house, and I know that he had given me something. I don't even remember taking that picture. He was supporting most of my weight, his hand tightly bunching my shirt at my waist. My arm was around his back, too, but loose. Hair dirty, eyes impossibly wide, I wore something closer to a grimace than a smile.

I keep it to remember.

I keep one of Jared, too, because I need to remember the happy times in my childhood.

My mom's voice drifts down as I stare at all of these memorabilia.

"So. Avery." Mom draws out his name into three syllables: aye-ver-ee. "Did you grow up in Boston?"

"No, ma'am." I'll bet my mother *loves* the ma'am. "I grew up in San Diego, actually."

"Oh, how interesting. Do you have plans to introduce Charlotte to your family? I'm sure she'd love to see California." She's sneaky, I'll give her that.

Their voices fade as they must move into a different room, farther away. I can hear their tones, but the words are indecipherable.

I find the right notebook. Finally. It's black, and the spine is worn from being bent in half. I flip through, just to make sure, and the words jump out at me: *Please come home. I'm sorry.* Sliding the two pictures—*evidence*, I think—into the notebook, I hurry up the stairs and tuck it away in my purse. When I return to the kitchen, Avery is talking about work.

"I know accounting is boring, but it makes money. There are hobbies I enjoy that are expensive and require a decent job."

My mother nods. "Interesting. And yet, you didn't want to make a hobby into a job?"

"No," he says, "because then it wouldn't be fun. It would be work."

"They can't be one and the same?" Dad interjects. This family loves a good, healthy debate above all else. Dad would play devil's advocate to the end.

Avery shrugs one shoulder. "They might, but I don't think it would happen for me. I tried it and failed." We settle in at the dining room table.

"And how's your job, Charlotte?" asks my mother.

We are suspended, for a minute, in awe of the feast Mom has prepared for us. She comes to the table, at the head, and starts passing dishes to her left.

"We never hear anything from you," says my dad.

"What do you do, Mr. Galston?" Avery asks.

"We pray," Mom reminds us. We bow our heads, say Grace, and dig into our plates.

"Pass the butter, Charlotte," Dad mutters. "I work for an insurance company," he says to Avery. "It allows us to live in this wonderful neighborhood."

I smile while handing Dad the butter dish. "It also allows him to play golf whenever he likes."

"Charlotte," my mother admonishes.

"You've cooked a delicious meal, Mrs. Galston."

Dad says, "She spent all day working on it."

Mom says, "Thank you, Avery, that's very kind," and blushes again. "Okay, now, what are we all thankful for this year?"

Avery's palm finds my thigh under the table. I put my hand

on top of his and smile at him.

Dad clears his throat, indicating he will go first. Of course, he's always first. "I'm thankful we managed to elect a Republican as our Governor."

I groan.

My mother eyes me. We've been going around the table clockwise, which means that I will be last. I've been known to say, in her words, *silly* things. "I would like to congratulate my daughter on a successful move to Boston, and say that I'm thankful to be her mother." My heart stops. I have almost no recollection of my mother being proud of me. Maybe once, when I was in middle school and got a "Most Valuable Player" trophy from my basketball coach, although she was quick to point out that I couldn't rely on athletics. "I'm proud of you, Charlotte," she says to me. I feel every muscle inside my body tense and then relax when a "but" doesn't follow her words.

"Thanks, Mom," I whisper.

Avery squeezes my leg again. His turn. "I'm thankful that Charlotte came into my life again. The first two times were luck, but the third was fate. And I'm so grateful." He leans over and presses a kiss to my temple, lingering for a minute.

"What are you thankful for, dear?" Mom asks me.

One may think that I would have been contemplating this as we went around the table.

I take stock of the year behind us: I had been relatively new to working with Tom; I had lived with Georgia; I made the move to Boston and survived alone in the city—I didn't automatically have a network of friends. I found Rose and Eve, even if that was a temperamental and unstable relationship. I found Avery again, and love. I had managed two successful conversations with Jared.

"I'm thankful for the trials I've had," I finally say. "And that they have made me a stronger person." Everyone is quiet. Maybe they're remembering those trials of mine and are looking at me with pity, or annoyance.

My thoughts snag on talking to Jared. When was our last conversation—a month and a half ago? How selfish of me, to ask him for help with my stupid dreams and then fade away from him. What would he be thankful for? Not dying? That's a shitty year, to be thankful for that.

My father catches my eye. "Are you enjoying work, Charlie?"

I shrug. Do I enjoy work? I want to say, *At this point, not really. I pick up dry cleaning and run errands and am Tom's scheduler and email-answerer. He appreciates me, but it's menial work, and my brain is dying.* Instead, I say, "It's nice to be useful and keep busy."

Dad nods. "Well, this is just a stepping stone."

I glance at Mom, who is way too invested in my response. "What do you mean?"

"You were meant for greater things than a *personal assistant.*"

My face turns red.

"There's nothing wrong with being a personal assistant," I say. "There isn't."

Dad grunts. "Of course not. The world doesn't go around without them. God knows that I need mine more than anything." I feel a sudden wave of shame, that I would be a lowly servant my father would employ. "But we didn't raise you to do that."

What was I meant for? Corporate America? Wall Street, like where I suspected Avery was headed? The thought of moving to New York City with him—I don't know. I don't like it. I don't want that much change.

It only occurs to me later, as I am merging onto the pike on the way home, that Avery didn't try to defend me. When I glance over at him, he is absorbed in his phone. We have been sitting in silence since we left my parents' driveway.

"What did you think?" I ask.

He looks up, watching the cars in front of us for a second. "You have a nice family," he says.

I snort.

"You don't think?"

I say, "I think they can be brutal. And tough. And hard to please."

He shakes his head. "But you told me those nice stories about them. They honestly seemed pretty nice."

"I should've scared you off with horror stories?"

I wasted my horror stories on previous flings, and they didn't last. Colby wasn't afraid of them, either.

"No."

"Okay," I say.

He shakes his head at me.

"What, now?"

Avery puts his hand on my thigh. "It's just, I don't know."

"You don't know?"

"Why would you want to tell me horror stories?" He withdraws his hand. "Why don't you want me to like your family?"

"That's not what I'm saying," I say. I try to keep my voice even. "I didn't say that."

"You literally said that. You said you should've scared me off with horror stories."

I say, slowly, "No." Because that's not what I said. "I didn't say it like that. You think they're nice."

"And?"

"And that's *wrong*."

"How is that wrong? They were nice to me. Your dad and I talked about the economy, the Patriots, and San Diego. Your mother enjoyed my compliments and wanted to know more about my family—"

"Just stop," I cut in.

He shakes his head again. If he keeps shaking it, it's going to fall off of his neck.

I grip the steering wheel tighter.

"You're wrong that they're nice. They're not nice to *me*. Doesn't that matter?"

I sigh at his silence.

"You're not going to answer me?"

Still, nothing.

When I glance at him again, he has his head ducked, eyes glued to his phone.

"Seriously, Avery? It's Thanksgiving. Who is texting you?"

"My sister," he says quietly.

That shuts me up.

"You didn't defend me," I say after almost ten minutes of quiet.

"Huh?"

"When my dad was attacking me for being a personal assistant, you didn't say anything."

"Attacking is a harsh word." I look over at him again.

He looks so handsome today: like he really tried. A nice button down, sports jacket, and black jeans. His hair was freshly cut to my favorite length: where it curls just above his collar. He had shaved, too. He wore pristine black converse, as if to say, *I'm vintage.* It also said, *I don't get dirty.* Which was true. He wasn't the outdoorsy type. He was a loafers-on-a-yacht boy; he was a suit-to-work-everyday guy.

And I never, ever would've guessed he would take my father's side over my own.

The feeling of utter abandonment makes my heart pick up speed.

"Why?"

"Why what, Charlotte?"

"Why didn't you say anything?" There were notes of hurt in my voice; there was a lump in my throat. Why was I getting emotional about this?

Because his opinion matters?

He exhales sharply and looks out the window.

We don't say anything for the rest of the car ride.

When I pull up in front of his apartment instead of parking, he looks like I caught him off guard. "Are you coming up?"

I swallow and say, "Nope."

"Charlotte."

"I don't want to hear it," I say.

"Charlotte!"

"Get out of my car, Avery."

He groans, leaning his head back. "Stop it." His hands tug through his hair. "You don't—you *shouldn't* settle for being a personal assistant. You have a good degree from a great school. Not many people get into the University of Chicago. You've got all this potential, and you're wasting it on doing the dude's dry cleaning?"

"Seriously?" I blink at him and feel my face flushing bright red.

"Yes, of course. I have a high opinion of you, Charlotte, and so does your family."

The waves of incredulity washing through me are quickly turning back to anger.

"Seriously, Avery? That's not even the fucking *point*." It's my turn to shake my head at him. "You're supposed to be on my side and not let my dad steamroll me without backup. Now get out of my car."

"You know what, Charlotte? You're being a brat right now."

I pop the trunk. "You're being a jerk!"

He jumps out of the car, slamming the passenger door. A second later, he yanks his bag from the trunk. "Call me when you cool down," he yells through the glass.

I flip him off and drive away.

What just happened?

Chapter 32

ROSE SHOWS UP AT SEVEN O'CLOCK SHARP. WHEN I open my door, she holds up a bottle of tequila and a bag that smells like Chinese.

"Welcome," I say, waving her inside.

It's been two days since Avery and I fought. I'm surprised that he hasn't called me. I'm a little hurt, too. Although... I did flip him off. Maybe he's trying to come up with the best way to break up with me.

"Happy Thanksgiving," Rose says as she passes me. She sets the bag and bottle on the counter and turns toward me. I had filled her in a little bit about our argument—thus the tequila—and she now looks at me with pity. "Please tell me you've talked to him since we spoke?"

"Nope." I sigh. "It's just as well. I'm still pissed at him."

"I can't believe he implied... what, exactly?"

"He actually said that I was not living up to my potential.

That I was wasting my time."

She shrugs. "I've learned a few things since our companies merged. Would you like to hear them now or after I pour you a shot?"

"After," I say with a smile. "Definitely after."

My buzzer sounds again. "Oh," she says. "I invited Eve."

"Oh, goodie," I grumble. I hit the button to let her up and unlock the door. "Shot glasses are in the cabinet above the microwave," I tell Rose.

Eve knocks on the door a minute later, and I pull it open. "Hey," she greets me. I motion for her to enter. "Happy Thanksgiving, ladies." She pulls a bag out of her giant purse. "I brought cookie dough."

"Perfect," Rose says. She hands me a shot glass full of the clear liquid. "We're giving Charlotte a dose of tequila before the hard truth." She hands Eve the other glass, then picks up the third from the counter. "Ready?"

"If you say so."

We clink our glasses together, and Rose watches as I throw back the shot. It burns a path down my throat and heats in my belly. She and Eve quickly follow suit.

"Okay," she says. Eve and Rose lead me to the couch and sit. They pat the space between them. "Don't get all weird, okay?"

"Yeah, sure." I want to roll my eyes, but I don't. I do laugh, nervously, and say, "This feels like an intervention."

"Hon," Eve says as she pats my knee, "we think you may have been a little unfair."

My eyes nearly bug out of my head. "Excuse me?"

Rose smiles gently and lifts my hand. "You said that your dad was trying to get you to agree that this job wasn't going to be forever. Right?"

I shift. "Uh, yeah."

"Well. Do you see yourself doing this in five years?"

Eve snorts, and Rose glares at her. Finally, I answer, "I don't think so. No. I... I don't know." A small tremor of fear runs through me. I watch my hands, curled in my lap, and whisper, "I don't think I know anything else."

Eve pats my back. "Girl, you're young. You can do anything you set your heart on. After watching the temp girl brought to tears by your boss yesterday, I'd say you would be able to earn a very good recommendation from him."

"Thank you, Eve," I say. And, to my surprise, I mean it. I don't know for sure how Tom would react to me giving notice, but her words give me strength. When the time comes, I'm sure I'll be able to handle it.

"Okay, Charlie, listen to me," Rose says. I look back at her. "You reacted to me in a calm, reasonable manner. How was it different with Avery? Did he not say much of the same?"

I close my eyes. The feeling of shame is familiar, and it makes me want to run.

"He should be on my side, though, shouldn't he?"

Eve cocks her head to the side. "Can you clarify?"

"I mean..." I stop and take a breath. "He's my person. Supposedly. I love him, and I thought he loved me. All I wanted was someone to stick up for me when I couldn't do it myself."

"Aw, honey," Eve says. She puts her arm around my shoulders. "I think he does love you because he wants you to be the best version of yourself. Don't you think?"

The thought rankles, but it makes sense.

"I get it."

Rose smiles. "Great. Time for food?"

Once Rose and Eve leave, I pick up my phone and call Avery.

"Yes?" It's how he always answers his phone.

"Avery," I say.

"Charlotte? Are you okay? It's after midnight."

"I'm sorry." I can only hear his breathing as I walk around my apartment, turning off lights. "I was cruel." I crawl into bed, pulling the covers up to my ears. "I didn't understand. But you were saying those things because you love me, right?"

"Yes, Charlotte. Of course I love you."

"Okay." I yawn.

"Are you drunk?"

"No," I say. "Just tired. And maybe tipsy." I don't bother telling him that I don't get drunk anymore. "I'll let you get back to sleep."

"Okay," he whispers.

And since the jury is still out on if it's been a good night or not, I settle for, "Night, Avery."

Chapter 33

TWO DAYS LATER, AVERY MEETS ME FOR DINNER. Even though I apologized, there is a weight pressing on my chest. I haven't seen him; we haven't even really spoken too much, beyond the midnight phone call. It isn't until I see him and my heart starts beating out of control that I realize I've been more anxious than anything. I've missed him. I've been afraid of losing him.

The North End has so many fantastic Italian restaurants. The one *slight* downside is that most of their streets were built with cobblestones, and the narrow sidewalks are always swarmed with people. It takes me a few minutes to find the place and locate Avery. I catch a glimpse of the side of his face. He is leaning against the brick, but straightens when he sees me. When I reach him, he pulls me close and kisses my forehead. "I'm sorry," he whispers.

"Me, too," I say into his chest. We stay like that for a

moment, in a bubble, and I let the weight lift off of me.

He threads his hand into mine as we walk into the restaurant. "How have you been?"

I laugh because it hurts. Boy, I didn't expect it to hurt, to see him, to feel awkward. We lost our groove, just as we were sliding into it. "I'm okay. And you?"

He shrugs.

He *shrugs*.

I stare at him, feeling this desperate urge for his words. I haven't felt so recklessly desperate since... Colby. That makes me tense, and a lump forms in my throat.

I grab his hand, squeezing, and demand, "Talk to me."

Avery meets my glare. "What are you doing, Charlotte? Do you even know?"

"What?"

He sighs. It sounds *so* condescending, I might pull out my hair and scream. As it is, I slowly pull my hand away. My fingers tremble on my lap, twisting together. He says, "What have you done about our argument?"

I'm still confused, and also now getting a little angry. "What have I done about our argument? In what way?" I keep my voice level.

"I was trying to help you. You started it out of nowhere, and then flipped me off. To apologize, you got buzzed first. What kind of apology is that?"

My mouth drops open. He's right, but he's also so wrong.

"I told you it wasn't about you *helping* me. I wanted your support!"

"So if you were arguing the sky was green, you'd expect me to back you up then, too?"

I roll my eyes. "Don't be dramatic. I'm not an idiot."

He points at me from across the table. "Exactly, Charlotte.

You're not an idiot. Why are you doing a job anyone else could do?"

I jerk my head back. I do *not* think anyone could do my job; I think maybe a lot of the population could figure it out, and it doesn't require a college degree, but to work with Tom? He is as difficult as they come. I know this, but it burns worse when it comes from Avery's lips.

In college, I had all this passion. I wanted to save the world with art. I wanted to paint the world into a better place and make people happy. It breaks my heart, now, to remember that passion. It somehow dissipated like smoke, so slowly that I didn't even feel it leave. But now that I'm looking for it, I can't find it.

Tears fill my eyes.

"I have to go," I tell Avery. I feel like an idiot. I feel like he's just like my family, and I'm letting him walk over me. When I stand, he catches my wrist. I stare down at his fingers, pressing into my skin, and wonder how we got here so quickly.

This instant loathing is wrong, but it's so easy to lean into it.

"Charlotte," he says. His voice is soft. "I love you. I tell you these things because I love you."

I snatch my wrist away. His hand drops back to the table. "Well, Avery, you should be able to tell that it's a sensitive subject."

He exhales. "Just, sit. I've missed you." When I do sit, he says, "I can help you."

"I swear to God, Avery..."

He shakes his head, his eyes skating around the restaurant, before meeting mine again. I'm always taken away by the beauty in his eyes, but today it doesn't distract me from how he's acting. "Okay, Charlotte. I'll stop talking about it." *For now.*

The rest of the dinner is awkward. I want to slink away, to hide and lick my wounds. Part of me is wholly disappointed with myself. The other is completely devastated by Avery's opinion of me. We part ways at the door, and I go home alone. Why do I keep going home alone?

Once in my apartment, I decide to research jobs. Any jobs. In any city. *I'll move there alone, start all over,* I think. An hour later, I am having no luck. Everything requires experience that I don't have. I growl and contemplate throwing my computer against the wall. Before I can get that far, though, my phone rings from an unknown number.

"Hi," I mumble. I'm hoping it's a telemarketer or anyone other than my mother.

His voice is warm as butter when he says, "Hi, Charlie."

Jared doesn't introduce himself. There's no need. I could recognize his voice anywhere. I don't know how that happened. Had those two phone calls really cemented his voice in my head?

"How are you?" There is so much guilt sitting in my stomach, suddenly, that I don't know why I didn't bother to call him again. I only had two more dreams of burning, a few days after I talked to him the second time. Each time, I had woken up in a panic and rushed into the shower. I had been alone both times.

"They sent me home a week ago," he says. "Just in time for the holidays."

"Home?" I wonder if he means some apartment in a city somewhere far away. If he means with his girlfriend, or wife, or whatever she is. With the baby—a toddler by now, right?

He coughs. "Yeah, you're familiar with it, Charlie. You watched it be built, after all."

I almost drop my phone. He's back in Massachusetts? He

was *across the street* at Thanksgiving? "I—I was—"

"I know," he says. Mind reader. "He's quite the looker."

I can't help the blush that makes my face feel too hot. "You spied on me?"

"I am stuck on the first floor of my parents' house with nothing to do," he answers.

I pause, quiet. "I'm sorry." How can I apologize so easily to him, and not to Avery?

Jared says, "I should've called sooner."

I bite my lip. "Same," I answer.

"We suck," he says. "But... I wanted to see if you were okay. I missed your voice."

My ability to breathe leaves me. Where did my lungs go?

Finally, I manage, "Are you, Jared Wyatt Brown, admitting to missing me?"

"Yes," he laughs. "Don't let it go to your head."

Too late.

He asks, "What's his name?"

"Whose?" I pretend to be ignorant. He just stays silent, until I answer, "Avery. What do you want to know about him?"

"I want to know why you sound like you're wrinkling your nose when you say his name," Jared replies.

It's true. I did wrinkle my nose. "He's just..." How on earth do I say this nicely? "I work as a personal assistant. It isn't glamorous. It isn't my end-goal job. But I like it. That's okay, right?" I hold my breath, waiting for Jared to inadvertently take the side of Avery and my parents.

"It's your life, Charlie. Where are you going with this?"

So, I tell him about Dad's comments, and how Avery didn't even pretend to be on my side. And then I tell him, in perhaps too much detail, about my ongoing argument with my boyfriend. I end with, "I don't even *care* that you caught me job-hunting. It's that they seem to be ashamed of my job."

Jared is quiet. He's always had this ability to see things from multiple angles. "Listen, Charlie." I roll my eyes, and I think he knows it because he says, "I'm on your side. Okay? I get it—that you wanted your boyfriend to be different than your pissy father."

I crack a smile.

"But maybe he's being supportive in a way that you don't quite see. It's hard to leave something once you get comfortable. I know you, Charlie. At least, I used to know you. You like comfort, and not a lot of change, and then you get stuck. When we were nine? I thought you were going to have a meltdown about moving your bedroom down the hall."

I remember that. It also makes me think of later in my life, and how *getting stuck* has been a real trend. And I remember something else he said. "You saw a therapist in high school?"

"Are you changing the subject?"

"No, it made me think of something."

He hums. "Okay, I'll let this clear diversion slide... Yes, I saw a therapist after my parents sent me away."

"You shouldn't have beat up Colby." I immediately regret bringing him up—I want to snatch the words out of the air. I guess we're going to talk about this now.

He inhales, coughs, and grinds out, "Oh?"

The animosity in my voice surprises me when I say, "Yeah, because then you were forced to leave, and I got stuck with him."

"What does *that* mean?"

I try to remember how it went: how Colby took over my life. "Colby wouldn't leave me alone. Not at school, after school, nowhere. He manipulated my mother into letting him take me out. She was excited, because—"

"She's your mother," he cuts in. "I know how she is."

"Right," I agree. "But then it just got... weird. I don't know what happened. One minute, I didn't want anything to do with him. The next, I was taking whatever pills or alcohol he gave me, doing whatever he said, and who I was as a person... disappeared."

There is so much shame hanging around me, now, that I'm not surprised by the lump that appears in my throat and how my eyes slowly fill with tears.

"Oh, Charlie," he whispers. His voice has so much grit to it, I feel it scrape against my soul. "So the nightmares—"

"They started after he was arrested."

"He was *arrested*?" I pull the phone away from my ear, wondering if he's going to wake up his parents. I swipe at the liquid seeping from my eyes. "Did he hurt you?"

"He was on probation for a while because he beat up Leah. Broke her nose, fractured a rib. She called the cops. Honestly, he never did anything like that to me... Just, different sort of stuff."

"Charlie..."

The tears flow down my cheeks faster and faster. "I'm sorry, Jared."

"What?" He groans. "Don't apologize. I should be the one saying sorry."

"No," I immediately say. "I put too much faith in you coming back to save me. Eventually, I figured out that only I could save myself."

"I'm going to kill him."

I sigh. No one knows that I've kept track of Colby over the years. I figured, if I knew where he was, I would know how to avoid him. "Don't bother, Jared. He raped a girl *on camera* a year ago. He's in jail in California." His parole is coming up, though. The law takes it easy on rich white boys.

Jared makes a noise in his throat, like he's in pain.

"Is your leg hurting—"

"Charlie, did he rape you?"

My stomach feels like it's on a rollercoaster. I don't want to think about Colby's hand on my throat. I don't want to think of him telling me what to do, never asking. A freaking lightbulb clicks, then, that *none* of my relationship with him was fully consensual. How did I let him get away with that? "Jared..."

"Oh, my god, Charlie." He stops talking, then, and I realize he is crying. The choking noises he makes break my heart. "I'm so sorry. I'm sorry I left you with him. I'm sorry I made you seem like a prize to him. I just wanted to keep you safe, I didn't think—"

"Stop." I'm crying, too. "It isn't your fault, Jared."

"I should've known he was going to go after you. He was fucking obsessed—"

I keep saying his name until he stops talking. Until he listens to me. Lightly, I say, "I'm okay now. Right? I sound okay?"

"You sound like you're doing okay, Charlie," he murmurs. "Your boyfriend is good to you?"

I hesitate, but I don't know why. "Yeah. Yeah, he's good."

"Good. Good, Charlie, that's good." I think he's searching for a way to change the subject. I am curious about his child, and why he hasn't mentioned it, but I hold my tongue. My heart rate is slow and steady again by the time Jared asks, "Why did you ask about my therapist?"

I rub at my eyes and suppress a yawn. It's nearly eleven. "I saw one, too, is all. I'm kind of surprised, since you were so put together."

He has so many different laughs; I could spend a lifetime cataloging them. This one rings false. "Oh, Charlie, you have no idea. But I think we're both too tired for this conversation."

"Yeah," I agree.

"Do me a favor?"

I nod, realize he can't see me, and say that I will.

"Forgive your boyfriend for trying to help you out of your rut."

Coming from him, it sounds doable. A mountain, but a manageable one.

"I will," I promise. "Thanks for calling."

"Anytime."

Chapter 34

PAST

I SAT IN THE CAR WITH MY DAD, GLARING AT THE building he expected me to go into by myself. I should not be surprised that he *still* had ridiculous expectations, even after everything. I felt like shit; I had only been discharged from the hospital two days ago.

"Come on, Charlie," my father said. He didn't usually call me anything except Charlotte. I constantly wondered if he'd let go of his anger over my lies, over Colby, or if he pushed it so far down I couldn't detect it. "This is the first step in moving forward. Talk to someone."

See, the thing was, I had gotten so used to silence. I had become accustomed to not having a voice. He wanted me to talk to a therapist? I didn't have any words to give. I turned my glare on him, but he just raised his eyebrows. He was used to this new attitude of mine, and he wasn't putting up with it. He just ignored it. "Go," he said. "Talk. Take your *life* back."

Take your life back.

Colby had really done a number.

I had this dark, ugly part of me that yearned for the drugs he had fed me. I wanted to be that numb again. I wanted to be that... far away from reality. It was only when I woke up sober, after a terrible time in a private hospital, detoxing, that I realized how medicated I had been. That scared me to no end. The police took a statement from me—in which, out of fear, I barely said anything. Colby going away or Colby coming back sent me into a panic. I didn't like either option, because didn't I love him? Didn't love mean forever?

I didn't want to love Colby forever.

"Kid," Dad said, and I nearly jumped out of my skin, because he hadn't called me that since I was seven, "you let him mess with your head. Go fix it."

I took a deep breath. I supposed I could go in and sit for an hour; I could kill sixty minutes. I could pretend, for Dad, that I was okay. I didn't want to lose this supportive side of him; it so rarely emerged. In my imagination, I leaned over and hugged him. I hadn't been able to tolerate touch since the night the police took Colby away, but I desperately wished I could show my dad the appreciation he deserved. The idea of his arms around me locked up my muscles.

I settled for grimacing at him. I got out of the car.

Chapter 35

SINCE THE THANKSGIVING FIASCO AND ENSUING arguments, I've done my best to be extra nice to Avery. I apologized and conceded that I might be *in a rut*, to use Jared's words. We eventually got back on track, but it took just long enough that Avery made plans to go home to California without me.

In a perverse, self-sabotaging sort of way, it was relieving to know that I wouldn't have to impress his family. He had charmed mine so readily; I didn't, and still don't, have faith in myself to do the same. Why should his parents like me? Sometimes I'm not even sure if Avery likes me. We just pick at each other until one of us bleeds.

Why do I only know love associated with pain?

Someday, maybe Avery and I will be celebrating our first Christmas together. A cozy apartment, Christmas lights and ornaments on a tree, sharing a meal and thoughtful presents...

Do I want that? At what point do you decide you'd rather spend the holiday with the person you're dating over your family? At what point do you claim, *He's my family, now,* and relegate your parents to those who you'll visit later in the day, or later in the week? Taking *that* plunge is commitment. Celebrating a holiday with someone you not only love, but are in love with, is a whole new adventure.

Avery and I aren't there yet. Rationally, I know this. But I picture all the Christmases we will have in front of us, and a lump forms in my throat. I want to start now. I want to grab our future and make it a solid road ahead of us. I only wish I had realized that before I got in my own way. Holidays bring out the worst in me.

Georgia is my savior.

"Come visit me," she told me one night on the phone.

I missed my best friend, I missed Chicago, and the plane tickets weren't too outrageous. I was moving apartments at the beginning of January, but I was already mostly packed. It was decided. I called my parents from the airport; they thought I had to work most of the holiday week and wouldn't be able to spare time to visit my father's brothers in Florida. There was a heated phone call debate between my dad and I; he insisted that if I was feeling left out, I should just come to them for a few days. And then my mother had taken the phone from him and tried to guilt trip me.

"Mom," I said, just yesterday morning, "the ticket is bought. Georgia is really looking forward to seeing me."

"*We* would look forward to seeing you!" she cried.

"I'm sorry," I told her.

But I was also relieved to escape.

On the plane, a kid turned around in his seat and looked at me with huge eyes. He smiled a nearly-toothless grin, and I felt nothing. As a female, automatically enrolled in the destiny of having kids, I realized *right then* that I didn't really like them. I tried to shake off that feeling. It unsettled me too much. There was so much expectation riding on me. I didn't usually feel the brunt of it: marry a good guy, have 2.5 babies, be the perfect wife, have a perfect job. Staring at this child made me want to run away and never return.

When did that happen? When did I suddenly decide that this life wasn't for me?

An overwhelming urge to scream washed over me, a bubbling inferno in my belly. There is a lot in life that we don't get to choose: we don't get to pick our parents or how they raise us. We don't get to choose who harms us, who loves us, or where life eventually takes us. As a kid, I went with the flow. Jared led; I followed. My parents ordered; I complied. Colby demanded; I shut my eyes and gave him whatever he wanted. Now that I'm growing a backbone, people don't like it. I just need to wait for the perfect time to make a decision about who to be. Right now, I can't do anything besides tell myself: *I don't want kids.*

That alone is liberating until I remember that I'll have to break that news to my parents.

I close my eyes and sleep the whole way to Chicago.

Georgia and I spent Christmas Eve wandering around our old Chicago favorites. We took pictures in front of the giant Christmas tree, and drank cocoa overlooking the river. There was no one else except us in our universe.

"How's Henry?" I asked at one point.

She smiled, her eyes glossing over in happiness. I grinned. It warmed my heart to see her that way. "He's going to come over tomorrow afternoon," she answered. "I wanted you two to spend some time together, since..."

"Since it's getting serious?"

She blushed. "Yes."

I grabbed her hand. "I'm looking forward to it."

We wake up to a white Christmas. Swaddled in blankets, Georgia and I exchange presents and sip coffee. For the first time in a while, I feel an acute sense of homesickness. When Georgia stands up to make breakfast, I call my parents.

"I'm sorry I didn't come down," I whisper to my mom. It's the first time we haven't been together for Christmas. "I miss you."

"Oh, Charlotte," she says. "We miss you, too! We'll see you soon. Just stay safe, yes?"

"Yes," I answer.

"Charlotte," my father says. Mom must've passed off the phone to him. "Merry Christmas."

"You, too."

"We'll see you for dinner in a few weeks, if the weather allows."

I exhale a shaky breath. That eases the ache: I'll see them soon. "I love you."

"Love you, too, girl."

Georgia delivers me Mickey Mouse pancakes with a chocolate chip smile. "Are you okay?" she asks as she sits next to me. "Your cheeks are all blotchy."

"I'm good." I look at her closer. "How do you feel? This isn't the first Christmas you've spent away from home. Does it get easier?"

She grimaces. "No. It sucks. But that just means I'm extra happy that you're here."

The rest of the morning passes quickly. I break open the new sketch pad and charcoal pencils Georgia gave me, practicing with a focus that I haven't felt in a long time. I get lost in it until my best friend says, "You better shower. Henry will be here in an hour."

I put on nicer clothes and fidget in the entryway to the kitchen. Georgia has been preparing dinner for an hour. Her cooking skills are undeniably delicious, but it's making me nervous. "I've already met him," I say. "So I shouldn't feel anxious about this."

Georgia shoots me a smile. "He's nervous, too."

I blink. "Why?"

She laughs. "Because he wants to make a good impression. You're my forever, dummy. He knows that."

My eyes fill with tears. I've been Niagara Falls with how much I've cried this year. "Wow," I mutter. "Thanks for ruining my eye makeup."

She comes over and pats my shoulder. "You okay?"

"I just have something in my eye. A tree branch, maybe."

"That's an outdated joke," she tells me.

I chuckle.

"See? You'll be okay."

My life would be drastically different without Georgia. She found me toward the middle of our first semester of college, when I was nearly drowning under the weight of peer pressure. In college, it's easy to find drugs and alcohol. I had promised my parents and Dr. Sayer that I would stay clean. To them, I was something akin to a drug addict: a wild girl with a wicked impulse for drugs. I suppose that they were right. It took so much energy to concentrate on things other than pills and alcohol. I knew that I didn't want to end up in a state that would leave me vulnerable. I didn't ever want what happened with Colby to happen again. For that reason, I isolated myself. I was terrified of letting a guy into my life, and I was having shit luck making friends. Everyone wanted to party. No one wanted to watch movies and binge on popcorn and milk duds on a Friday night.

One night, Georgia stumbled upon me in the dorm bathroom. Someone had left a bottle of vodka on a shelf near the showers, and I was staring at it. I willed myself to move away, but a desperate part of me wanted to forget everything for a night. I wasn't settling in; I had no friends and it was already the middle of October.

She walked in and ignored me at first, but on her way out she stopped and looked at me.

"You okay?" she asked.

I managed to nod. She could probably see the sweat on my forehead.

"I'm Georgia. My roommate is at some party, and I was just about to watch a movie." She smiled when I met her eyes. "Want to join?"

I nodded again.

The following Monday, she sat next to me in one of my classes. I hadn't noticed that she was in it. She gave me a small smile and said, "Never would've imagined myself sitting in the front like you. Do you have to avoid eye contact so the professor doesn't call on you?"

After that, I wasn't quite alone. I had successfully made my first friend.

I learned that she was just as lonely as me. Her parents were both alumni of the university, so it was practically written in stone that she would be accepted and attending. But just because her parents came before her didn't mean that she was guaranteed success—the opposite, in fact. Students sneered at her for being a legacy, and professors didn't want to show favoritism, so they were harder on her. That night in the bathroom, she was just as desperate for someone to save her as I was.

That made me feel a little better.

Over the course of the next four years, I told her my life story. She was horrified over Colby and miserable for me about Jared. She slowly glued me back together. In turn, I got her story: she was the forgotten middle child of three growing up, until her older brother was hit by a car and broke his back. Suddenly, with her brother in a coma, her parents looked to her to be the "perfect" child to carry on their legacy. Maybe they didn't mean for that to be so cold, but that's what it was.

We were more similar than we originally knew. When I told Georgia that she saved me from picking up that vodka bottle and drinking myself into a stupor that night—upending years of therapy—she cried. She admitted that she had been contemplating dropping out of school, running away to work in Texas or California.

"He's here," Georgia tells me now. She sets down her phone and moves to the door to let him in. "Breathe, Charlie."

I smile at her.

He looks just as I remember, except a smidgen older. A little more comfortable. He's always been pretty, with his Ken-doll hair and jawline. He grins at me. "Nice to see you again, Charlie."

I let myself relax. "Nice to see you, too." We shake hands, which feels awkward. We laugh. Way back when they first started dating—when Georgia and I lived together—I would watch out the window as Georgia would meet him on the street. They were cute; he would smile shyly, and she would light up. It's the same now: he looks at her like he's never seen anything so beautiful, and she only has eyes for him.

That's what love is supposed to look like.

"Merry Christmas, baby," Georgia says. She kisses him, and I look away. "Ignore her uncomfortable face," she whispers to him.

I snort. "I didn't have an uncomfortable face."

Henry shakes his head. "Sorry, Charlie. You kind of look ready to combust."

It's easier to walk away than to tell them, *I haven't looked at Avery that way in months.* So I do walk away. I allow myself a momentary time out in the bathroom to gather my thoughts. When I come back out, everything feels more comfortable.

After dinner, we sit on the floor around her coffee table and play card games. "I'm happy for you guys," I tell them. "Henry, I'm glad you came into Georgia's life."

Georgia swipes at a tear. "Shut up, Charlie."

Henry nudges her. "I just got a compliment out of the Ice Queen—no offense, Charlie—and you want her to stop talking?" He grins at me. "I was convinced you hated me."

In the space of time when Georgia and I lived together and they dated, Henry and I hadn't had much interaction. His nickname makes me shake my head. "Me? I'm the Ice Queen? I mean... I'm not that cold, am I?" I can't tell how I feel about it. I take a sip of my wine and purse my lips.

Georgia starts laughing. "He mentioned the Ice Queen once but I had no idea who he was talking about. You were talking about *Charlie?*"

He shrugs. "Sorry! It was a nickname that just stuck. But I

never meant it in a bad way, Charlie. It was just a good way to describe your personality to my friends."

I nod. "Yeah, that's fine. It's kind of badass."

Georgia snorts.

"So, what are you two ladies going to do tomorrow? It's your last day, right?"

I nod. "I don't know what we're going to do, but I leave the day after."

"Have you heard from Avery?" Georgia asks. I don't know why she brings it up, but my face falls. "Oh," she mutters.

"I emailed him this morning," I tell her. "But..." *Nothing.*

His silence shouldn't surprise me. As the day went on, I made up excuse after excuse: he's spending the day with his family, not attached to his phone. He might've broke his phone, or saw it and forgot to reply. Maybe his message got stuck in the outbox of his email. He could've forgot to hit send. Maybe—

I shake my head to stop the thoughts. "I don't know what's going on with him. We're just... figuring it out still, you know?"

"You've only been dating for six months?"

I blink. "Has it been that short? It feels like more than a year," I say with a laugh.

Georgia and Henry exchange a glance. "A *good* year? Or a..."

I scowl at her. "It's been a fine six months."

"With a lot of arguments." Henry frowns at Georgia's tone. She adds, "And a lot of tears."

"Stop."

She puts her hands up in surrender. "It's the truth. You just need to keep hearing it..."

Perhaps Henry senses my mood darkening, because he lays down his hand of cards and says, "Let's have dessert."

Chapter 36

PAST

"CHARLOTTE?"

I jerked my attention away from the window. Instead of answering her, my eyes slid over her. She was a tall, giant woman. Her hair was always impressive, and I imagined that it was a source of pride for her. Today, it was in beautiful, thick curls that bounced around her neck and on her shoulders. She always wore wonderfully bright, silky shirts that complimented her dark skin tone. Maybe she was trying to inspire happiness through her clothes, through her smile, through her tone.

"Do you feel like talking today?"

This day was like every day. Except, maybe not. For the first time, I wanted to open my mouth to answer her. I wanted to say, *I do feel like talking, thank you, Dr. Sayer.*

Instead, I pressed my lips tighter together.

"I was thinking that we should have your parents come in,"

she said.

"No," I whispered. It was out of my mouth before I could lock it inside. Once that magic floodgate was broken, my words flowed out like a waterfall. "Dad's coddling is weird. Mom is avoiding me. I just want everything to go back to normal."

Dr. Sayer nodded, like she was just waiting for this moment. "Okay, Charlotte. Let me help you find a new normal. Sound good?"

I scratched at my arm. I didn't consider myself a drug addict—not really—but I knew that I was acting irrational. The fact that I had been acting irrational because of *Colby* pissed me off. "Can you call me Charlie?"

She nodded again. "What's the last happy memory you remember?"

It took me a while to think of an answer. We sat in silence again as I filtered backwards through the last six months. "My best friend and I were running through the woods..." I told her about the day Jared and I went to the private beach on the backside of the lake. I told her how, up until everyone else showed up—until *Colby* showed up—it was perfect.

I thought she knew enough from my parents, and my hospital file, that she would know Colby's name. Instead, she quirked an eyebrow and asked, "Who is Colby?"

Something in the depths of my mind was screaming. It had cracked me wide open, a yawning gap into the shattered psyche of Charlotte Harper Galston. I had a brief moment where I thought I should minimize it or lie. Or, better yet, stay silent.

Instead, I told her everything.

Chapter 37

"MERRY CHRISTMAS!" I SAY INTO MY phone. Christmas is barely hanging on: there's only ten minutes left. I'd been wondering if Avery was going to call me. Hell, I would've settled for a text at this point. I don't know why I'm still awake; Georgia and Henry went to bed long ago.

"Merry Christmas, Charlie."

My knees buckle at Jared's voice.

"Hi," I squeak.

He laughs, and it soothes some of the ache inside of me: missing my parents, hurting from Avery's cold shoulder, wishing I had something as special as Georgia and Henry. Jared and I used to sneak up to my treehouse once it was dark, even in the middle of winter—*especially* on Christmas—with a candle, blankets, and warm cookies while my parents hosted a party. We would stay out there until our parents hollered for us from my back porch. Even in our hiding spot, we were never out of place.

"I just wanted to see how you are doing," he says.

"Me?"

One of the floorboards in the hallway creaks. Georgia might be eavesdropping. She's always had *good thoughts* about Jared, even if she didn't like that he left without a backward glance. On the other hand, she sneers at any mention of Avery. She holds my grudges for me.

When Jared doesn't answer, I say, "I'm good."

"Are you home?" Jared asks.

"No, I'm actually in Chicago." I don't bother to mention with who; he wouldn't know Georgia by name, anyway.

"That's a far way to go for Christmas. You didn't want to be with your parents?"

I start to roll my eyes, but then I wonder if he's at his parents' house. "They went down to visit family. My boss..."

"Ah, him again."

I grunt. "He can't survive without me."

"As long as it isn't the other way around," he says lightly. "How's the boyfriend?"

I remember how he watched Avery and me out of the downstairs window in his house and never said anything until we had left. I wonder if he's doing that now, if he's still staring at my empty house, wondering if I'm coming home.

Jesus, Charlie, stop that idiotic talk.

"Charlie," he mutters. "Chill."

"I didn't say anything."

"I feel like I lost you for a minute."

I chew on my lip. He lost me for a lot longer than that.

"He's in San Diego."

"With his family?"

"That, supposedly, he wanted me to meet over the holidays." I roll my eyes. It makes me feel better, even if he can't see me do it. "I thought he meant *these* holidays, but I was wrong, I guess? I don't know."

"Well, you're still together," he says.

That's helpful, and I tell him so.

He laughs again. "It sucks that you're not home."

"Would you have actually said something? Asked to see me?"

He doesn't say anything. I wonder if he's only calling *because* my parents' house is dark.

"How's the leg?"

He grunts. "It's great."

"How's the side without a leg?"

He laughs. "Wow."

"I heard you can get phantom pains. It still hurts, even if it's not there?" I sigh. "Our brains are fucked up." He makes some sound of agreement, so I continue, "I mean, my brain, for example. I send Avery a nice Merry Christmas email, and he doesn't reply. So, of course, I'm thinking the worst of him right now."

"I do seem to catch you when you're feeling down."

There's that damn lump in my throat again. It's hard to swallow around, threatening to choke me up. "Jared..."

He sighs. "I wish I had said something about Thanksgiving, while you were home."

I do, too.

"It would've been nice to see my old friend," I manage. "Can I ask you something personal?"

His voice holds his smile when he answers, "I owe you a personal detail or two by now, Charlie."

"Why are you calling me? I mean—aren't you with your

parents? Or..." *Or your child?*

"Charlie, who do you think I should be with, besides my parents?"

"Seriously, Jared?" I snap.

Inhale.

Exhale.

"I have to go." *That came out nicely.* And then, "But, seriously, don't pretend we both don't know about your girl and the baby."

"*Macie?*"

I grunt affirmation, and he doesn't respond.

"Merry Christmas, Jared."

I hang up.

And then burst into tears.

Chapter 38

PAST

"HOW DO YOU DEAL WITH ANGER?" I ASKED.

Dr. Sayer tipped her head to the side. She did that when she really had to *think* about a question. I had so many questions, and for most of them, she had a ready answer. But for some, we would sit in silence for a few minutes, her head tilted like the Leaning Tower of Pisa, while I stared out the window. Eventually, she would give me something close to an answer.

Outside, it was snowing. It was a weird April: almost halfway through, we were still getting flurries. The clouds were moving quickly, too. Birds shrieked and chattered at each other, probably cursing the sky and Mother Nature. I was still wearing coats and scarves. Dr. Sayer explained that until I was back up to a healthier weight, the temperature would feel colder than normal.

"I've got it," she said. She smiled at me. "But first, tell me, how does anger feel?"

I picked at my fingernails. "It makes me feel sick. Like everything has twisted up inside of me. I can't breathe. I just want to scream or run or hit somebody."

She nodded. "That's a good way to describe it. Some people have difficulty voicing how anger feels, and how it affects them. The first step is to recognize it. Saying, 'I am angry' can help. Figure out why you're angry. In your case, think, 'Is this making me angry because it reminds me of Colby?'"

That made sense—to figure out the root cause of my anger. "I always take it out on the wrong people."

"If you're in the heat of the moment, Charlie, you need to remember to breathe. Think about what you're going to say, and how it's going to come across. Don't be blinded." She wrote something down on her notepad. "I'm going to give you a homework assignment. I have a stack of journals in my desk. Take one, and I want you to carry it around with you. When you're angry, write in it. Don't think, just write. We'll go over it next week."

"Okay," I said. "Write in it. Sure."

Chapter 39

I SQUIRM IN MY SEAT, UNABLE TO KEEP STILL. THE plane is taking forever to unload. As soon as the wheels touched down, time slowed down. Avery is picking me up, and after barely a week away for the holidays, I miss him so much my heart is going to explode. The older woman next to me pats my hand. I blurted our whole story to her with the help of a glass of wine. I left out the unsavory details.

When it's our turn to go, she steps into the aisle and forces the man behind her to take a step backwards. "After you, dear Charlie," she says.

I grin, scrambling up. "Let me get your bag for you?" She points to the one above my head, and I drag it down for her. "Happy New Year," I wish her, and then I'm off.

I'm here, I text Avery. His plane was scheduled to land a few hours before mine.

I get my suitcase and head to the curb. My phone has been

radio silent. Did he forget? I'm tempted to call him, but he never texts and drives. He could be on the way already and not able to respond. The air is freezing, although it hasn't started to snow yet. I duck back inside, standing so close to the glass that my breath makes a fogged circle.

After ten minutes, I start pacing in circles around my suitcase. Every red car that flashes by makes me whip around, trying to see the driver. *Where are you?* I text him.

He had replied to my Christmas email the next day, when I was out with Georgia. It was short, and he apologized for the lateness of his message, and said that he was eager to get home and see me. *Home.* I had been so relieved to hear him call Boston his home. In that way, I felt like my mind was warped. Was there some part of me that thought he'd go home and run back to his ex-fiancée? Our arguing, his choice of not inviting me to San Diego for Christmas, the melancholy that fills the holes of our relationship, were all tiny red flags that all seemed to flash before my eyes. I was cranky because I hadn't talked to him—because he hadn't reached out to me. Perhaps *distance makes the heart grow fonder* doesn't apply to Avery and me.

After thirty minutes without a response, I start to worry. Did something happen to Avery's plane? I force myself to sit as I track his flight. It landed on time three hours ago. His phone goes directly to voicemail, like it's off. I hang up without leaving a message. Shoulders slumped, I head toward the T's Silver Line to get myself home.

Meekness is not in my character anymore.

When I get home, an hour later—public transportation in Boston is a joke—and when I am finally safe, I am angry. I stewed the entire time I sat on the bus, and my anger grew when I transferred to the train, and then to another train. I temper the desire to smash something, curling my hands into fists. A few of my knuckles pop. I wish I could release the tension building in me as easily as that: *pop*, and it's gone. Most of my things are in boxes; almost everything breakable is wrapped in newspapers and bubble wrap. There's not much to smash if I were to give into the urge.

"Screaming is probably inadvisable," I force myself to say aloud. I look out the window. Something twinges in me when I don't see Avery or his car.

My phone rings from my kitchen counter.

"Hey, baby," Avery says after I answer. I wait for him to keep talking. "I'm so sorry I wasn't there. I missed my flight, so I had to catch the next one. By the time I remembered to text you about not being able to pick you up, the flight attendant was yelling at me to turn my phone off...." He sighs. "I just landed. I'm going to come see you, okay?"

"Okay," I say. Hurt swirls around me, as well as white hot anger. They flicker back and forth, beating out all other emotions. I stay at the kitchen counter, leaning on it, wondering if I need to start writing my anger down again. But, no. I've learned that writing helps me let go of anger that I cannot justify. However, this *is* justified, and I deserve an apology.

In no time at all, Avery knocks on my door. He gives me a small, tentative smile. "Hi," he whispers, coming closer. I am tense, but my legs tremble. He wraps his arms around me. It's the last thing I want, and yet I instantly relax against him. I don't hug him back. I rest my cheek against his chest, the roughness of his coat scratching my skin.

228

Together, we breathe.

"I am so sorry," he says again. He's still speaking softly. Am I a wild animal that needs taming? Something that may run away at loud noises? His apology is better in person. He runs his hands up and down the length of my torso, and it ignites my nerves. After a minute, I tilt my head up to look him in the face. I watch his eyes, and then his lips.

When we kiss, he shows me he is sorry. He is gentle, but he is solidly there, everywhere, invading my senses. I don't want sorry. I want fire. One of my hands stays at my side, while my other touches the back of his neck. My fingers slide into his hair and fist there, nails scraping against his scalp. He makes a small noise in the back of his throat as I pull on his short hair. I capture his lower lip in my teeth, tugging, until he gasps and leans into me, kissing me harder.

Avery walks us toward the bedroom and pushes me onto the bed. He has a wicked look in his eye that I don't get to see very often, and he doesn't waste time pulling off my shoes, and then my pants. I can see the outline of his erection through his jeans. I shiver with anticipation.

He makes quick work getting out of his clothes and climbs over me. He nuzzles into my neck, inhaling. When his tongue flickers against my earlobe, I can't stop the moan that slips out. I hook my legs around his hips, drawing him closer. He kisses me again, his tongue taking over my mouth. At the same time, he slides inside me, eliciting a gasp. We meet eyes, paused momentarily, until I nod. He pulls almost all the way out and slams back into me. I groan, biting my lip. The sound spurs him on, and soon we're both sweating. Finally, after we both finish, he flops down next to me. The wetness between my legs is...

Unexpected. We had the talk about not using condoms a month ago, but so far he had been unwilling to go without. I hadn't had a problem with the idea. Avery and I are both clean, and I had an IUD inserted right after college. I didn't expect the emotional impact—feeling so close to him. It's a true step up in intimacy.

I turn my head, looking at him through half-closed eyes.

He stares at the ceiling, one arm bend behind his head. The other traces lazy circles on my arm. "A picture would last longer," he chuckles.

I blink, and find myself turning red. I watch him a lot. He should be used to it. "I should go clean up..." I wish *this* had been my first time without a condom. I wish Colby didn't ruin my sixteenth birthday with a romantic gesture—the candles, the dinner—and then stealing my first time having sex without protection. And then he ruined the romance, too.

When I come back from the bathroom, Avery is in the same position. He pats the bed next to him. "Come snuggle," he says. I curl into his side, resting my head in the perfect hollow of his shoulder. The room smells of sex and sweat, but under my head, his scent is a deliciously masculine musk. It fills my nose, and I don't ever want to exhale.

"Did I tell you how sorry I was?"

I roll onto my stomach so I can look him in the eye. "You did," I say. "I was worried. And angry. And panicked. And..." I focus on the wall behind his head until he touches my chin.

"Charlotte, you can tell me."

Taking a deep breath, I say, "I thought you had forgotten. Let your phone die, or set it down and just... forgot about me." My fears from Christmas sneak out.

His eyes soften, and he leans forward, placing a sweet kiss on the corner of my lips. "I could not forget about you, Charlotte. Ever. You're magical, beautiful, powerful, and..." he smirks, "great in bed." *Much different than the first time*, I remind myself.

He succeeds in making me laugh, but I still feel the pinch of unease in my stomach. Dropping the smile, I whisper, "It just seems really easy to believe that you're not totally invested. I know it's still kind of a new relationship. We haven't discussed where we want to be in a year, or five, or ten—"

"I want to be with you." Right now, he *sees* me. All of me. My nerves and insecurities and everything I've been trying to hide. We sit up, facing each other. We're naked, literally and figuratively, and a small part of me appreciates the irony. "I want to be with you now, a year from now, hopefully five years from now... Charlotte. Did you doubt that I was serious?"

Tears prick my eyes. "Well, yeah, I ...kind of doubted it. You never said anything!"

He laughs, but it isn't comforting. It beats against me like a dull roar. Oh, how the cliff side must ache as the ocean pounds against it every day. "I never *said* anything? Are you serious? Charlotte, I don't try to fucking coax you into romantic dinners and shit for nothing. I'm in love with you. I've said that before, and I meant it. I mean it now. I fucking love you. God," he exhales, and it feels like a slap.

Instead of crying, I blink it away. I smile, although I know my lips wobble at first. "I'm sorry." I hate that I am the one apologizing now. "I know. It's just," I try to think, but I can't, because I'm talking over the lump in my throat that threatens to choke me. "I love you, too." Even that feels kind of lame, a throwaway line that I half-mean. It's meant to placate him—I recognize it because I would do the same thing to Colby.

Avery's face lights up, fast enough that I could've imagined any other emotion except for love. I forget my negative feelings and focus on the happiness. He kisses me hard, bruising my lips. This whole visit has been a rollercoaster of emotions. Is he happy? Upset with me?

"I was planning on waiting, but with your lease coming up..."

I raise my eyebrows.

"Charlotte Harper Galston, will you move in with me?"

It isn't until later that the sense of déjà vu clicks. On my phone in the bathroom, I pull up a video I once watched on repeat. *Ave, say it again for the camera?* His face appears. He kisses her temple. *I said, Elaina Sydney Williams, will you move in with me?*

Should I be hurt he used the exact same... wording? Full name. Happiness. And when I said yes, surrounded by an impersonal room filled with boxes that I had already packed, he kissed my forehead. We had sex again after that, slow and passionate and probably more aptly described as *love making*. In rewind, it feels cheapened.

I am his do-over girl.

I brush away the tear that tracks down my cheek. It snuck up on me, and I don't generally cry. I close the app and pocket my phone, creeping back into the bedroom. Avery stirs as I slide under the covers, rolling closer to me before I'm fully settled. I don't get a chance to turn on my side before he has his arm over me, palming my hip and pinning me to the bed. His leg twines with mine, immobilizing me.

After twenty minutes of counting Avery's slow breaths, I wiggle out from underneath him. I tiptoe to the kitchen, pour myself a glass of water, and tuck myself up on the couch.

A million thoughts course through my head:

Am I okay being a do-over girl?

Does he even realize he did it?

Does he close his eyes and see her instead of me?

I fall asleep on the couch.

Avery finds me at three in the morning.

"I found a place already, Avery. I put down the deposit already," I say as I follow him back into the bedroom.

He blinks at me, bleary-eyed. "You want to discuss this now?"

"I..."

"Jesus, Charlotte. Go to sleep."

I say, "Avery."

He grunts, already climbing back into bed.

I say again, "Avery."

"Charlotte," he answers back, mocking.

We are mean as we orbit each other, with sleep still in our eyes. Every word that comes out of our mouths is barbed. And still, we push forward.

"There are things we need to talk about," I say. The urge to shake him comes to mind. I smooth my palms along my thighs as I stand at the foot of the bed.

"Tomorrow," he mutters. "Lunchtime. Now, sleep."

I sigh, hoping he remembers this in the morning. And then I do as he asks: I crawl into bed with him and sleep.

Chapter 40

GEORGIA'S NAME POPS UP ON MY PHONE AS I'm walking to work.

It's funny how spending time with someone invokes the feeling of missing them. Although it's only been a few days, I miss her voice. Sudden worry fills me at the sight of her name. She is *never* awake before eight o'clock on purpose.

"Guess what!" she says when I answer. Her voice is cheery for such an early hour. Relief floods me, easing my adrenaline rush.

"What's up?"

"I just accepted a new job!"

"Oh my god, congratulations! Details!" I can't help but shriek the last part, causing some heads to turn on the sidewalk ahead of me.

"It's with a marketing firm in Seattle!" She had mentioned applying for new jobs when I was with her, but she hadn't heard from any of them. "It's a really good company, Charlie. I'm excited to finally put my marketing skills to good use. They work with a nonprofit out there that pairs caregivers with disabled people. How cool is that?" I roll my eyes. She has such a giving heart, it's sickening sometimes. "Seriously," she says. "Where I'm at now is so... snobby."

"That's what you get in Chicago," I tell her.

"And..."

"There's more good news?"

Her voice is hushed. "I asked Henry to come with me."

I squeal. "Excuse me? Are you real?"

I pull the phone away from my face and stare at her name. Flashes of us in college, neither of us able to keep a solid boyfriend, spring to mind. Late nights soothing each other's breakups with chocolate and rocky road ice cream and *The Notebook...*

She laughs in my ear. "He said yes," she says. She sounds happy. Really, really *happy.*

"You're moving with your boyfriend to a city across the country!"

I picture her boyfriend: tall, averagely built, a nerd. They had been dating for almost a year before I moved to Boston. He dotes on her, loves her. I had been surprised they hadn't moved in together before then. When I brought it up, just a few weeks after I moved from Chicago, she had told me, *I wouldn't do that to you.* It still hadn't happened, even though I left for Boston six months ago.

I had been mildly insulted. Was she implying that I couldn't live alone?

I love living with you, goober, she had added. But now that I am living alone, I realize: she was right. I loved living with her, too. I had sowed my 'wild' oats, and now I was agreeing to live with Avery. Speaking of which...

"Avery asked me to move in with him," I blurt.

"Really?"

"I'm sorry—I don't mean to steal your thunder. It just came out." She makes a noise of disagreement. I lower my voice and say, "He said it in the same way that he asked his ex."

"How...?" I filled in her unspoken questions: *How do you know? How did he ask?*

"I found a video a while back on her Facebook page. In it, he was all, *Full name— will you move in with me?* And then two days ago, he said, *Charlotte Harper Galston, will you move in with me?* The similarities kind of... suck."

"Oh, what an ass. Did you kick him to the curb?"

I roll my eyes and wish she could see me. "No, but, Georgia... I don't know how to feel," I whisper. "I don't..." I realize I'm outside of work already, so I sit down on the bench facing the street. "I already have a place. I put down the deposit a few weeks ago. I'm set to move in a few *days* from now. My parents are coming to help me move, and..."

"And you're thinking, 'Why is he springing this on me now?'"

"Yes. Exactly."

"Charlie?" Tom's voice cuts through the cold morning. "What are you doing out here?"

I turn, and he is poised at the entrance to the building. One gloved hand is at the door. "I'm just finishing a personal call, Tom," I say. He nods and disappears into the building.

Georgia laughs into my ear. "You going to be late?"

"It's okay," I say. "He's gotten used to me being late." I tug my hat down further on my head. It's going to take forever for my butt to warm up; the freezing metal bench has numbed my lower half.

"Do you want my unbiased opinion?"

"Can you do unbiased?"

She coughs to cover a laugh. "Ask yourself if you want him in your life, and if you see yourself with him in a few years. If it's a yes, then, hell. Move in with him. If it's a no? You know how it has to go. This guy has put you through some shit, Charlie."

"I know you don't like him because of what happened more than a year ago—"

"It's not just that!"

"What is it then?"

"He has strung you along for a while. Hot and cold. It just..." She pauses, and exhales. "Look. I just don't want you to get hurt, okay?"

"Same," I say. "I have to go."

"Love you," she says.

"Love you, too."

Avery shows up at my office at 12:30.

"Hey, babe," he says as he knocks on my door. Rose is a few feet behind him, looking pissed. I imagine that he probably ignored her and the receptionist. I give her an apologetic smile, and she turns on her heel.

"What are you doing here?"

He holds up a bag. "I figured you wouldn't want to go out in this weather. It just started snowing a few hours ago." He tilts his head in the direction of the windows, which are slanted closed. Tom has been in a conference call since nine; the door has been firmly closed with a *do not disturb* instruction left for me.

"We can eat here," I offer. Tom would kill me if I left my post and someone went into his office. Avery nods, and I catch myself staring at his lips a beat too long. I point to the couch, and we both take a seat. "So, how's your day?"

"You said you wanted to talk, remember?"

I nod, now recalling his gruff dismissal in the middle of the night. "I'm sorry I brought it up so late—early—"

He holds up his hand. "It's okay. Now that I'm conscious, though, I wanted to talk to you about all your worries and whatever else was keeping you awake."

"Thank you," I say. "I just... Why spring it on me now? I went through all the work of finding a place and paid the deposit. Do you expect me to drop it?"

"No, babe, of course not. While I was home, I had some pretty serious talks with my parents. Individually and together, they told me about how they progressed their relationship. It was a conversation that I really needed in order to learn. Grow." He takes my hands in his. "You already know that I love you, even if I don't show it how you want it." That makes me smile a little. "I just realized that it was time to get more serious. We've been dating for a long time, and I want to come home to you. I want to wake up with you. Every morning."

I'm waiting for him to answer my other questions, and so I just squeeze his fingers and keep my mouth closed.

"We looked at your new apartment together, right? Well..."

It clicks. "You want to move into the new place with me?"

He looks into my eyes, searches my face, and smiles. "Is that acceptable?"

I throw my arms around his neck, pressing my lips to his neck. "Yes," I say against his skin. "Definitely acceptable."

Chapter 41

PAST

I'M ANGRY AT MY MOM. SHE WON'T LEAVE ME alone. *All I want is some peace, right? No, she gives orders and expects me to jump up and obey. Guess what, Mom, I'm not an effing robot! I can't wait until I can get away from her. Away from this stupid house. Orders. I don't like orders. Colby used to order me around. I used to do whatever he freaking wanted. 'Open your mouth, Charlie.' 'Drink this.' 'Tell me you love me.'*

Gah. No wonder I have issues.

You know what would fix it? A nice little pill that mellows me out. One that makes me forget the world. One that makes me happy. One that makes me float.

Colby had a never-ending supply of little pills that made me feel all sorts of things. But then, I never was able to fend him off. He ordered me to take the pills, and then did whatever he wanted because I'd be so high, I didn't care.

Not caring was nice.

Now? Sober me cares a lot. Sober me wants to erase his fingerprints from my skin. There aren't enough showers in the world to get the memory of his hands off of me. Out of me. I still hear his voice in my dreams. Okay, they're nightmares. I still hear him, laughing, telling me what to do, to calm down, to kiss him, to love him.

I wish he was rotting in jail. (He isn't. He got out on parole and his parents sent him back to California.)

Oh, but how I miss him.

That's what I'm angry about today, journal. Not my helicopter mother—she needs to back off, though. I'm angry at myself for missing Colby.

Ugh.

This stupid journal isn't working. I don't feel better. I feel about 10 times worse.

Chapter 42

DOES GOING HOME TO AVERY MAKE ME nervous?

It's not like I'm walking into an unknown. We've lived together for two whopping weeks—and the first ten days were bliss. We had sex every night, made dinner together, *talked* about stuff. But suddenly, I've started working later and later, and Avery has started going to work earlier and earlier. Just last night, I crawled into bed at ten, and he was already asleep. I kissed his cheek, and he rolled away from me.

When someone knocks on my office door, my heart nearly stops.

Eve pokes her head into my office, smiling at bit at the expression on my face. "Hey, sorry to startle you," she says. "Why are you still here?"

"Because I'm avoiding going home," I say. It feels good to be honest.

"We could get a drink," Eve suggests.

I think about it for a split second. "Yes, please."

We end up at the bar where we met a few months ago. The bartender leers at our chests, and we dutifully ignore him until he comes over to take our order. "Wine for the lady," Eve says with a nod in my direction, "and whiskey for me."

"So," I say once our drinks are in front of us. I'm not sure what to say. Besides Georgia, with whom I faithfully FaceTime with every weekend, I have never had many friends who are girls.

"Why are you avoiding going home?"

I take a big swallow of my wine. "Two weeks ago, I moved in with my boyfriend."

Eve looks at me like I'm crazy. "That's not supposed to be a bad thing."

I say, "No." I think, *It may be.* "We're... not coping well, I think. We may kill each other from neglect." I force myself to laugh, because the alternative is to cry.

"It's been two weeks, Charlie. It's going to take some time. You're young. Both of you still have a lot of growing up to do." Eve leans back on her stool. "When I was in college, I lived with three roommates. I fell in love with one of them, and we had this secret relationship until we graduated." She smiles a little, but it's sad. "Rachel and I were too similar in some instances, and polar opposites in others. We fought constantly. At first, it was something we did to keep the charade up that we were *just friends.* People would think, 'Oh, they don't even really like each other that much as friends.' And then we'd sneak into the bathroom or a bedroom and fuck. It was fueled by those arguments, and the adrenaline." She shakes her head, now, and I have a feeling she's cursing herself. "When the arguments fizzled out, and the adrenaline wore off, we realized we had nothing to talk about."

I grimace. "That sounds...."

"It was messy," she says. "Especially when we both realized it." She holds up her hand, pausing my question before I've even begun to ask. "The thing is, we still had to live with each other for the rest of the summer. We were still convinced we were in the middle of this white-hot romance. We agreed that it was passion that made us argue, and passion that made us compatible."

I wait, breathless. I wish I hadn't put off friendship so long with Eve. I know she's telling me this for a reason, to make a point, but her life sounds *interesting*.

"She realized before I did that we weren't going to work. I realized it only after I caught her sleeping with our other roommate."

I jerk back. "She cheated on you?"

Eve lets out a hollow laugh. "I can't even say I was surprised. Rachel and Mike had this weird, epic friendship. I envied them."

"She cheated on you with a guy?"

"She's bi." Eve raises one eyebrow at me, and I feel disappointed in myself. Snap judgements don't help anyone. I can't make any assumptions about who people love. "And yes, they're actually married."

"He... they..." I shake my head, at a loss. "What?"

She watches me. "I found out later, from my third roommate, that Rachel and Mike had a long, sordid history. I was just a speed bump in Rachel's path." She exhales. "I just wish I had known beforehand. We weren't as subtle in our own apartment, and I'm sure Mike suspected, if he didn't outright know."

I shake my head. "That wasn't fair to you."

Eve makes a face, as if she doesn't believe me.

"No, it wasn't fair. Listen to me. Mike didn't tell you about Rachel and him. The other roommate didn't tell you. *Rachel*, who you *dated*, didn't tell you that you two were both living under the same roof as her ex-boyfriend. That's messed up."

"I read this book once, and it reminded me too much of my situation," Eve says. "The main character, a girl, was in a relationship with a guy. And, for some reason that I don't remember, they broke up. How they pined for each other was devastating. The girl finally found him again, reached out, and the guy had someone else. A fiancée."

I shake my head, because I don't understand how this relates to her.

"I'm the fiancée in the story. I'm the one who tore the main character's world in half, because when she was brave enough to go after her man, I wasn't supposed to be there."

"How did the book end?"

She smiles, and it in itself is heartbreaking. "Well, someone was crushed."

"Probably not the main character," I guess.

"No," she agrees.

I reach over and take her hand. She squeezes my fingers. I fear we're both overcome with this emotion that I can't name. It is despair's cousin, and sadness's child, and anger's sister.

After a minute of silence, Eve excuses herself to the restroom. "One more round," I tell the bartender. His eyes still skip from my eyes to my chest and back, as if a damn tennis match is happening on my skin. "House red. Whiskey straight." He looks like he needs the reminder. He grunts and pours, but it's like I have magnets on my breasts. "For god's sake," I mutter. This is a tame shirt, a wide scoop neck sweater that doesn't show a hint of cleavage, and that makes me madder. "I'm not even showing that much skin!"

He flinches.

"Did you think we wouldn't notice? You're like a fucking bull in a china shop," I say. Now, he can't look at me. In fact, his face is so red, he may implode. "Just give us our drinks." He slides them toward me, still concentrating on the far wall.

I jump when Eve puts her hand on my shoulder. "That was fun," she whispers. "Do you usually blow up at sleazy bartenders?"

"Just the ones who deserve it," I say. In truth, the answer is, *no way in hell.*

"It's getting late," she says. "How about we down our drinks and head home?"

"Deal." I try to look at all of her—not just what she's presenting to strangers. She looks strong, and steady once more. I can't believe she shared something so personal with me. "Eve," I say, and turn toward her. She takes a sip of her drink and faces me. "Thank you for sharing that with me."

"Hopefully you can learn from my mistakes."

Chapter 43

AT THE BEGINNING OF FEBRUARY, SOMETHING clicks. Maybe it was the discussion I forced us to have. We both agreed to try harder. Living together didn't mean that we could slack on the effort in our relationship.

Those were the words of my therapist, who I ended up calling and crying to one day. Dr. Sayer was glad to hear from me. I had dropped off the face of the earth once I started my second year of college. I had Georgia, I had a handle on feeling the need for a pill to make me feel better, and I had a life that I was happy about. It seemed natural to me, then, to end our sessions. When I talked to her a few days ago, she was so glad to hear that I was doing well. And, the most important thing, she talked me through my relationship and made me see a path to fix it.

By the time Avery gets home, I've been here for twenty minutes. Most of our dinner is prepared and ready to be cooked.

My skills in the kitchen are not the best—Avery far outshines me in that area—but I am a great sous chef. He comes over and kisses me like he missed me.

A whimper slips out of me, and he pulls back long enough to grin. "I wish we could skip the movie," he whispers. "And just spend the night naked."

I cock my head. "You want to cancel our date?"

"If it means having sex, then, yes."

I laugh and touch his cheek. "That's cute. It's Friday, we have all night."

He rubs at the back of his neck, grimacing. "Well, Steve invited me to play golf tomorrow morning."

My smile fades. "So, you don't have all night."

"Right."

I look at his chest because I can't meet his eyes anymore. I was looking forward to this movie. Instead of saying that, though, I start to undo the buttons of his jacket. He watches me push it off his shoulder and let it fall to the ground. He watches me undo his belt buckle. When my knuckles graze against the skin just above his waistband, he sucks in a sharp breath.

"Dinner can wait?" he breathes.

I nod, taking a step toward our bedroom.

It can all wait a little while.

Chapter 44

I SMOOTH MY PALMS ALONG MY THIGHS WHEN I realize that I've discovered something that was probably not meant for me to find.

A ring.

I silently berate myself as I stare at the opened box, nestled between two pairs of Avery's underwear. If I didn't have such a *stupid* compulsion to organize things when I get stressed, I wouldn't have been folding his underwear, and I wouldn't have been sorting them by color, and trying to tuck the dark grey ones between the black and the white pair—where the velvet box sits.

Bad habits die hard, I guess. With organizing comes snooping, of the unintentional variety.

Are you ready to marry him?

I shake my head, clearing away any doubts. If he's all in, I can be all in. Simple. I tuck the ring away and close his drawer. There is a certain finality to the motion.

It's Valentine's Day, and we have reservations at a fancy restaurant. I've been firm that we will *not* be distracted by sex— which has happened three times this month. We just wind up in bed when we had other plans for a movie, dinner, or meeting friends.

I originally came into the bedroom to find my phone; I hadn't received any texts from him. That led to an acute sense of paranoia, which led to anxiety, which had led to the organizing, and then my find.

Oh, god, I might throw up.

How is he going to do it? He knows that I'm not a fan of romance, as annoyed as that makes him. Will we go on a road trip, and he'll propose somewhere with a good view? Or maybe it will happen at dinner one night, just out of the blue, or when we go up to my parents' house later this year. Or maybe it'll be when we fly to his parents' house for Easter, which we briefly discussed a few days ago. Hopefully he won't make a spectacle of it. But then, we'd have to find time to sit down to discuss the wedding, and that would turn into an argument itself.

My phone buzzes in my hand.

Meet me in the lobby? Be there in 10.

I put my shoes on and head down the stairs. I'm still nervous about the ring. I want to run back and double check if I closed the drawer all the way, or if I left the box exactly as it was. I force myself not to turn around. It's probably fine.

Avery is already in the lobby when I get down there. I guess he overestimated how quickly he would arrive? I see that he's not alone. He's talking to a girl who looks vaguely familiar. Something about her hair and the way she's standing...

I shake my head. I must be imagining things.

The girl touches his arm once, briefly, and then leaves. She looks like grace incarnate, walking with a floating stride. He stares after her for a long moment. I have half a mind to be jealous, but then Avery turns and he smiles when he sees me. His eyes are troubled, although he tries to hide it.

"Are you okay?" I touch his arm where I can picture her handprint branded into his clothes. He smiles larger and tries to hide the barest of flinches. It takes a lot of effort to keep from making a face at him, but I don't. I'm curious, although I doubt he'd give me any answers. He is a locked box sometimes, and I never have the right key.

"I'm fine! Sorry I'm so late. We had a meeting, and then my boss wanted to talk to me about a possible promotion. Steve is leaving, so..."

As he trails off, I nod like I don't notice anything amiss. "A promotion would be exciting," I manage.

He takes my hand, pressing a kiss to my palm. I run my fingers down his cheek. His stubble is almost too much. If he is as predictable as I think he is, he'll shave tomorrow morning. It's too bad—he looks good with the five o'clock shadow.

We head back out onto the street. "You don't have to go get anything from the apartment?"

I'm a half step behind him, so I watch his profile and the back of his head as he shakes it. "No, I would've asked you to bring it down if I did. I have an Uber waiting for us."

Right.

We get into the car.

A ring. The design wasn't exactly my style, but it wasn't ugly. It looked like it was passed down in his family: one big diamond front and center with a gold band, and four gold prongs hold the diamond in place. It could be his grandmother's ring, for all I know.

You're supposed to not care about the ring. It's just the person. But you wear the ring for the rest of your life, practically.

No, if I was picking, it would've been something drastically different.

It doesn't matter, I tell myself again. Love is supposed to outshine any diamond.

I watch the city flash by our car windows and marvel at such a thing as two people being joined together forever. Avery's hand is heavy on my thigh, his thumb rubbing in small circles that drives me crazy. Sometimes good crazy, like *yes, touch me more* and sometimes, *please for the love of god that irritates me, stop.* Which crazy is this?

Right now, I can't decide.

Chapter 45

"YOU HAVE THE WORST TIMING," I TELL Jared. The phone is pinched between my ear and shoulder as I put on my jeans. I'm supposed to meet Avery at the Museum of Fine Arts—the MFA—for lunch.

"Hello, Charlie," Jared's mother says.

I drop the phone. It thumps on the carpet, and I dive after it. "Sorry, Mrs. Brown... Uh..."

I'm stumped. I have no idea why she's calling me from Jared's cell.

"I'm sorry to catch you unaware." She's always been so nice. So different from my own mother. When it came down to it, though, Julianne was a tough-love mother. "Jared is at physical therapy, and he left his phone in the car." She sighs like she can't believe he would do something so forgetful. "How are you, dear?"

"Are you just calling to check up on me?"

"Perhaps that isn't my only motive. Jared mentioned a few weeks ago that he had talked to you a few times. As a concerned mother, I wanted to check and see... what exactly was happening."

I scowl as I finish getting dressed. She's calling to snoop? That's a new one.

"I'm not sure what you want me to tell you, Mrs. Brown," I say.

"Charlie, dear, you're old enough to call me Julianne." Her voice goes hoarse when she says, "He doesn't talk to us. I just wanted to see if you knew... how he was doing?" She sniffles.

I think back on our conversations. "Mrs. Brown—Julianne—I'm... I'm sorry. We..." Dang, it's hard to admit that I suddenly had an epiphany about how selfish I am. "I'm afraid we mostly talked about me."

She chuckles. "I wasn't expecting different."

That makes me wince, because, *ouch.*

"Not—I'm not saying you're a selfish person, dear. Jared just has a way of deflecting. He learned it at a young age."

No, he couldn't have. He never deflected with me. I knew his darkest secrets—I pried them out of him—and he knew mine, in return. Maybe she means he learned it in therapy. Dr. Sayer, my therapist, is a great deflector.

"I'm sorry." I don't know why I feel the need to apologize, but I do. "Our last call... I was upset with him. I haven't talked to him in over a month."

"Oh, Charlie, I'm sorry to hear that."

"Thanks. I was actually just pissed that he never brought up Macie." I squeeze the bridge of my nose. Why am I telling her this? "It isn't like I don't know she's around with a baby. My mom told me at our party two years ago that she was pregnant. He made it sound like he was all alone, but he only called me at night. What about her?"

"Oh, Charlotte," Julianne says on another sigh. "You should really talk to Jared again. It isn't my place to share his secrets. He's an adult, you know."

I don't like secrets, even though I have plenty of my own. I glance toward Avery's dresser.

"I'll take that under advisement," I tell her. "I have to go."

"Of course," she answers. "I'm sorry to bother you."

My mind whirls as I head toward the museum. I knew that Jared wasn't telling me much. I hadn't really bothered to ask, besides about his health. It makes my stomach flip. Maybe I *should* call Jared.

When I see Avery, I try to smile.

"What's wrong?" he asks. He kisses my cheek, and I pull him into a hug.

"Oh, nothing," I sigh. He snorts. "You don't believe me?"

"You're a shit liar, Charlotte."

"An old friend called me a few months ago. They were in a bad accident, and the recovery has been really slow going. And just now, I got a phone call from their mom." I realize, belatedly, that I'm using pronouns as to not give away Jared's gender.

Avery looks sympathetic. His eyebrows dip together. "Maybe you should go visit her."

"Yeah." I swallow my guilt. "I'll think about it. Work is busy and all."

But then, I do think about it. I think about going home, seeing my parents, getting away from Avery and the ring that seems to suck the air out of our bedroom whenever I remember it. Sometimes, I remember the ring in the middle of the night. My eyes shoot open, and I can't breathe for a second. Other times, I remember it while we're eating dinner, or when we're having sex. It sparks some fear. It alights some feeling of relief that I won't be alone forever. A ring, superglued to my finger for eternity. It will follow me into death.

That is both thrilling and terrifying.

So, after we get lunch at the MFA and wander around the exhibits, I tell Avery, "I think I am going to go home next weekend."

"Okay," he says. He kisses my temple. "To see your friend?"

I nod. "Yeah, and to see my parents."

"Are you going to tell them about the jobs you're applying for?"

I hide my wince with a cough. No, I won't, because I've been procrastinating actually applying. I don't tell Avery that. Instead, I force a smile and say, "Probably!"

"Good," he says. "Ready to go home?"

"Absolutely."

We walk hand in hand, enjoying the unusually warm weather. In my experience, we still have at least two more snowstorms before spring officially starts.

"Are you all set for getting the time off for Easter?" he asks me. It seems like it's been a while since we talked about flying to California to visit his parents. "I need to book our tickets."

"I can let you know tomorrow," I offer. I straighten my shirt. "They'll like me, right?"

He grins. "Of course they will, Charlotte. They'll be excited to see where your life is heading, too."

A stone drops into my belly.

It always comes back to my imperfections, doesn't it?

Chapter 46

PAST

THE THERAPIST FROM HELL, DR. SUSAN SAYER, asked me to read from my journal. I had been dutifully scribbling in it for the past two weeks with more and more frequency. I dug it out of my backpack and flipped to the most recent page.

"Where do you want me to start?" I asked. Most recently, my voice had lost all of its inflection. I was robotizing myself. It made me feel like I had a speck of control over my situation.

Dr. Sayer blinked at me. "Wherever you think you should."

I scowled and opened to the one I had written two days ago.

I read, "I am angry at myself for digging through my mom's purse for Advil. I'm angry that I snuck into their bathroom searching for something stronger than Advil. I hate that they don't trust me, and that my mother caught me with my hand in her purse. I lied and told her I was looking for money. She automatically assumed it was for drugs, anyway.

"This limbo I'm in sucks. It sucks. It SUCKS." I stopped and sighed. I had written it in all capital letters, nearly ripping the paper in my haste to underline it. I didn't give away that anger now, though. I held it tight and remembered. I continued, "It humiliated me—the way she looked at me like I had kicked a puppy. I hate having to write this because I'd rather not. I hate this journal, I hate Dr. Sayer for making me write this," —I winced— "and I hate myself for what I've turned into."

Dr. Sayer didn't react to my insult. Instead, she smiled.

"Why are you smiling?"

"I noticed that you showed empathy for some statements you had written. For example, you sounded guilty when you talked about your mother. You physically winced when you mentioned me."

I shrugged. Sometimes, there was so much guilt inside of me that I didn't know what to do with it all. I knew I would eventually drown under it. It was buried under layers of anger. When my mother saw me, her face fell. We weren't in a place that we once lived in; we didn't know how to find our way back to a comfortable way of coexisting. Instead, my parents tiptoed around me. Because I had been sent to the hospital, there was now a large sign marked *fragile* following me.

Don't say the bad thing, you'll send Charlotte on a bender.

Don't criticize her Physics grade, she'll relapse or run away.

Don't mention Colby, or else she'll seek out the next available destructive boy.

"There's hope, Charlie, don't you see? We work through the anger, and then the world will look bright for you again."

Chapter 47

THE CAR IS THE BEST PLACE TO THINK, BECAUSE it is isolating. Everyone on the road is in their own little bubble, their own world. Mine has music playing: "Don't Wanna Be Your Girl" by Wet. I find myself humming along and sympathizing with the singer. Sometimes I wish Avery and I lived on different planets. I still crave his touch. I still want him to kiss me. I just can't help that I change my mind at the last minute. We were so struck by each other in the beginning. It was the perfect set up to believe that fate played a part in our relationship. I can't separate the threads of my emotions. When I look at it, I try to pick out those feelings of love. I can't help but think I'm getting it confused with contentment. Complacency. Comfort.

Did I ever love Avery?

Or, like Colby, did he trick my emotions?

I shake my head. *No*, he wasn't like Colby. Comparing him

to Colby would be doing a disservice to Avery's whole being. Avery is good. Avery is kind. It isn't his fault if I misinterpreted how I feel.

When my music switches to "Wait" by Maroon 5, it makes me think of Jared.

Jared.

The very person I'm driving to see. I need to apologize to him, just as Adam Levine sings.

God, the last time I saw him was almost two years ago. More than two years ago? It was at the party in September, right after I met Avery in New York City. I do the math in my head, and realize it was two and a half years ago. Macie—her name is burned into my head from our last phone conversation—wasn't even showing her pregnancy. It isn't the kind of thing I would have immediately noticed; maybe she was showing and I missed it.

Now, I'm headed back to my parents' house, and Jared will be living across the street. Burned. It could've been the way we turned out when we were nine. He could've been in the house when it was on fire; he could've been hurt. Then, maybe his nightmares—and mine—would've been more justified. Our friendship was everything to me. *He* was everything to me, from the time I was nine years old up until he left for boarding school when I was fifteen. Heck, he was my only friend!

I glance at the notebook sitting next to my purse on the passenger's seat. That thing carried me through high school. I filled it, first with letters to Jared, and then journal entries for therapy. Dr. Sayer had me fill two more after that, too, which I subsequently filed away and never dreamed of looking at again. The first pages of my first journal spell out my desperation for Jared. I don't know if I'll show him, but I am betting on needing it to clear my head. It will remind me of who I thought he used to be.

In no time at all, I am home.

My mother meets me in the driveway, her purse and keys in her hands. "Charlotte, honey!" she calls. I hug her, and for once, I mean it enough to give her a good squeeze. "Oh, honey," she whispers. She squeezes back.

"I missed you," I say.

She inhales and takes a step back, then pats my cheek. "I've missed you, too. I'm glad you've decided to visit your poor old family."

I can't help turning and glancing in the direction of Jared's parents' house.

When I look back at my mother, she has a knowing smile on her face. "Your father is out golfing with his friends. I believe Rick is with him." Rick is Jared's dad. I shake my head at her when she adds, "And Julianne is meeting me for lunch in a little while, after her manicure."

"Did you set this up?" I ask.

My mother sheepishly shrugs. "I always regretted what happened between you two. I'm just doing my part to make things right. As right as they can be, anyway." She leans forward and kisses my cheek. "You have a key to the house?"

I tell her yes, and she waves goodbye, getting in her car and pulling out of the driveway. Within seconds, she's gone.

I look toward Jared's house again. Fourteen-year-old me would have never hesitated.

Then again, I didn't view him as a stranger, either.

I suck in a big breath as I walk across the street. There's a spotlight on me—a million eyes that are screaming their judgements. My face is hot when I knock on his door, and I can't seem to kick the slight tremor that runs up my body.

"Coming!" he yells from somewhere in his house.

I wonder how long it takes him to maneuver his house. Is he on crutches? A prosthetic? Is he still wheelchair bound?

When he opens the door, he simply gapes at me.

"Hi," I say after a notable silence.

"What are you doing here?"

He's standing. Crutches hold him upright. Where his left leg should be, there is only empty air. I can't see other burns, but I imagine they're under his sweatpants and loose white t-shirt. He had rolled up the sweatpants of his left leg, so the fabric swings just below where his leg ended. Or, that's what I'm guessing.

I try not to stare.

Jared looks haunted, the same way Avery looked when I found him in Chicago a year and a half ago. His eyes are the same, yet harder. Different than the last time I saw him. He's lost weight, too. I remember how he looked two and a half years ago. I had pictured how he should look now: strong. He is not strong. He tries, though his face is gaunt, and his waist is too tapered. He has such a death grip on those crutches, it must hurt to be standing here.

"Oh, Jared," I whisper. "Can I come in?"

He grunts and steps out of the doorway.

The Browns' house is eerily similar to the last time I was here. I think I went over with eggs for Jared's mom when I was seventeen. She had grilled me about everything happening in my life. I was angry at her, and her husband, for taking away my best friend. Maybe that's why I told her everything. In the end, we sat at her kitchen table—the one by the large windows that overlooks their big, sloping yard—and she passed me tissues as I cried.

I wander toward the kitchen, unsure, and pause when I see the same table. When she told me on the phone that she wouldn't tell her son's secrets, I knew that she had never told him about our conversation.

I turn back to look at Jared, but he's gone.

"Jared?"

I follow his voice, a string of curses floating toward me, into what used to be his dad's office. It's now his bedroom, and he sits on the bed, glaring at me.

"Charlotte, I asked why you're here."

I flinch. My toes curl in my shoes. I hate apologizing. I hate admitting when I am wrong. I never have, and I don't think I ever will. It's clearly been a point of contention between Avery and me.

And yet, this was my first friend. My dearest friend.

If anyone deserves to hear me beg for forgiveness, it's him.

"Have you come to stare?"

I swallow. I've stared too much. "No, Jared."

I wonder what he sees when he looks at me. Someone weak? Someone strong?

There's a chair in the corner of the room, but it's too far from him. Instead, I take a few steps forward until I'm directly in front of him. He just watches me, teeth clenched, as I sit down next to him. I pick his uninjured side, because I don't want to hurt him.

"I'm so sorry, Jared. That's why I'm here. I came to apologize."

He just looks at me.

"We talked, and I accused you of—" I shake my head. "It wasn't fair. I should've asked you, and I know that my, uh, outburst must've hurt." I roll my eyes, because I've become good at self-deprecation. "I never even asked about you, beyond your leg. How selfish am I?"

He puts his hand on mine. Tiny sparks zap through my

body, and I'm so relieved that he is here, that he's touching me, and that he hasn't kicked me out of his house yet. "We can talk about it, Charlie."

I'm back to being Charlie.

I inhale my first breath in nine years.

"Okay," I say. "Tell me everything."

He does.

His story starts four months before the Labor Day party at my house, two and a half years ago, in Washington D.C. This was the end of his college career, just a month before graduation. At this point, he knew he wanted to be a firefighter. He had already been part of a local volunteer firefighter unit for the better part of three years, and his degree in Fire Science made him a shoe-in for a paid position... somewhere. His ultimate goal was to become a smokejumper or hotshot out west. They were the real tough ones, Jared told me, who battled the front lines of wildfires. But first, he had to work his way up the ranks.

He met Macie at a bar in D.C., and he was enamored by how she acted: as if the world didn't matter outside of her friends. He watched guys approach her and be rebuffed. When he sent her a drink, and the bartender pointed him out, she smiled and raised the glass in a silent cheers. He approached her after that, and it was instant attraction.

There was more than just looks that drew them together. They actually had more in common than they knew at first. She was from a small town west of Springfield—maybe only forty minutes from Jared's house. She lived with her mom; her dad was an attorney in Boston, whom she occasionally visited. They had both experienced house fires as children. It inspired Macie to be a nurse, to help burn victims. She was still a junior, like me at that point, but eager to get out and explore the world.

They started dating right around the beginning of May, and their romance carried them back to Massachusetts for the summer. They got to the point of spending weekends at each other's' houses, talking seriously of living together the following year—if Jared got a job in D.C., that was.

The weekend of the Labor Day party, Jared had planned on travelling down with Macie to D.C. and moving into their apartment. He had accepted a part-time job working the reception desk of the D.C. Fire Department's main hub, which would cover his half of their expenses, and he also remained on the volunteer team to get in more structural fire experience.

But then, Macie freaked out on him. She said she had to go home, that they could move the following weekend, and she essentially disappeared on him three days before they were supposed to leave. Jared's room, upstairs in his parents' house, had been packed away in boxes. Suddenly, he was thrust into limbo—something with which I was familiar.

His mother, Julianne, insisted he make an appearance at the party. "The Galstons were so disappointed when I told them you wouldn't be able to make it. Don't you want to see Charlie again?"

Jared went to the party, fully intent on just making an appearance, when Macie showed up looking worse than he had ever seen her. She was a wreck, and she blurted out that she was pregnant. Luckily, Jared had been talking to Nathan, and Nathan swept them up to his bedroom and left them to their privacy. There, Macie told him how she had missed a period, and had gone home to see her doctor to confirm her suspicions.

"I reacted badly," he tells me. "I asked her, 'How the fuck did that happen?' and she immediately started crying. That's pretty much when you saw her trying to leave."

"Okay," I say. For Jared, I can be strong. "It's okay. What

happened next?"

"I ended up following her after we talked. I drove to her parents' house, I begged her to talk to me. It took hours, but she opened the door. Let me in. I told her we could make it work. I said something about figuring it out." He laughs, but it's hollow. "I told her we could get married."

My stomach drops, and I find myself looking at his fingers for a ring.

"We didn't, Charlie," he murmurs.

They went back to D.C. and moved in together. She continued at school and held job, and he continued work and volunteering. He came home one day, three months into her pregnancy, and found her in the bathroom. Her legs and the floor were covered in blood. She was sobbing.

I can see this story like flash cards thrown up against my eyes every time I blink.

The tears.

The grief.

The anger.

Oh, I know all about anger.

He says, "After that... it was different. We were just orbiting around each other. There was the arguing, and she..." He shakes his head, dislodging the words from his throat. "She hated me. She told me that more than once. Engaged and estranged," he muttered. "I moved out shortly after that, and got a job out west."

Here, he smiles. It changes his face, and I suddenly recognize who he used to be.

"I started working on wildfires. I worked with the hotshots in Washington until I fell off a cliff and tore my ACL." My mouth drops open. "Don't worry, it was my left one," he jokes.

I stare at him, and then at his left leg –what remains of it, anyway.

I start laughing. "You joke?"

"It's amazing how I still have a sense of humor, right?"

It's easy to nod. To put my hand on his.

Touching like this should be forbidden. His hand wakes up every last nerve in my body, and that makes me feel guilty. Avery thinks I'm visiting a girl. Is this cheating? Is touching Jared's hand, talking to him, lessening my guilt, actually something sinister?

"Do you forgive me?"

He nods and traces my jaw with his free hand. It's too intimate, but I have to stop myself from leaning into his fingers.

"I just—" I swallow, "I'm sorry I didn't know your story. I didn't want to know, because I didn't want to think you were talking to me in the middle of the night when you had someone—a wife—and a baby..."

"Charlie. Stop. If anything, I felt bad calling you when I knew you had a boyfriend."

I straighten my shoulders. "It's okay, Jared. It isn't like we were flirting."

He leans backwards, slightly, and rolls his eyes. His smirk looks the same—plus a five o'clock shadow, which fifteen-year-old Jared most certainly did not have. "We're not flirting?"

"No!"

Right?

"Okay," he laughs. "Just checking. God, I missed you."

My eyes fill up with tears. Bam. Just like that.

"Oh, no..."

"Jared—"

"Charlie Harper, do *not* start crying."

I stand up. It feels good to have some of this energy come out. "You *missed* me? When? When did you start missing me?

When did you decide to come back into my life? Because I sure as hell could've used a phone call when I was sixteen. Or, I don't know, a reply to *my* phone calls?"

Jared's cheeks turn red. "I told you, that was a mistake."

I flinch when I hear Jared's mother's voice call, "Jared, we're home!" Her voice gets closer when she says, "Did Charlie visit? Her mother mentioned... Oh! Hello, Charlie!"

I pretend we didn't *just* talk on the phone. "Mrs. Brown, nice to see you." The last time I saw her, I was seventeen and miserable. Do I look different? Am I twenty-three and miserable? "I should get going," I say, scooting toward the door. "I'll... uh..."

"Maybe Jared would like to visit you in Boston sometime?"

My eyes widen. I should've figured this level of meddling from our parents. I can only guess whose idea that would've been: Julianne's or my mother's.

Jared tilts his head. "That might be a little awkward, Mom, since Charlie lives with her boyfriend."

"Oh! Well, surely he wouldn't mind an old friend visiting..."

I hold back a smile at Jared's mortified expression.

"Mom," he hisses, "you can't just invite me to spend the weekend with Charlie and her boyfriend."

Julianne smirks. She has the same mouth as her son, the same straight white teeth and lips. "Oh, hush. You have an elevator, don't you, Charlie?"

I manage to nod, biting my lip. Not smiling is getting more and more difficult.

"Your father and I have discussed it," she says to Jared. "We think it's time that you start leaving the house more."

"I leave the house," he mutters.

"To go to physical therapy appointments."

I blurt out, "That's it?"

He scowls at me. "Don't pity me."

"It seems you've been doing that enough," I reply.

Julianne laughs. "Oh, Charlie, we've missed you."

I look down at my feet. "I've missed you guys, too."

After Julianne tells us about her day, I manage to excuse myself. I practically run back across the street to my parents' house. My mother is home, and she smiles to herself when I shoot a glare in her direction. *Ugh, meddling parents.*

Even so, it's nice to be home and to spend some time with my parents as an adult. This is the first time I've been home of my own volition alone, for no occasion other than seeing them— and Jared. I talk with my mother about real things. Now that I'm an adult, we can have real conversations. We're almost friends. Maybe that's the way it happens when kids grow up. Parents are obligated to love them, and maybe they'll like them, too. But then, the kids get older and develop a personality that's completely separate from their parents. It's shaped by their life experiences: how their friends treat them, how their bullies treat them, and how they choose to react.

Hopefully, my mother likes the version of me that I've become. I hope she doesn't look at me and think: this girl is a mess. Hopefully she wants to be my friend.

For kids, we grow up and we realize our parents aren't all sunshine and roses. They have flaws, and they make mistakes, and sometimes they don't know what they're doing, either. Even my mother, who is the queen of put-together, sometimes just doesn't want to deal with any of it. There were days as a kid— rarely—that she'd let me stay home from school. We'd do at-home facials and eat popcorn and watch TV shows like *Cheers* and *Golden Girls* that played through the day. I forget about those days, because the bad sometimes outnumbers the good.

Dad talks about the stock market and my 401k, and I try to

keep up. In fact, I can contribute something to the conversation because of my Economics background. He smiles at me as I talk.

Mom and I talk about cooking and the weird people we run into in gas stations or grocery stores. We trade recipes. I tell her about Rose and Eve. Mom describes the new women at the country club who started a book club with her.

After dinner, I wander around outside with my dad.

We go down the porch stairs together, and he puts a hand on my shoulder. "That night..." I immediately know the one he's talking about. The night Colby got arrested. "It was the most scared I had ever been."

I swallow. I wish I could say, *Me, too.* Instead, I just shake my head and look toward the setting sun. The sky is streaked with oranges and pinks. This is the therapy session Dr. Sayer had tried to push on me when I first started seeing her: talking to my parents about my ordeal.

I never managed to open up to them. Not fully, anyway.

"Not for me, Dad," I whisper. I think, *Holy shit, I'm doing it.*

He looks at me, eyebrows raised, but something about his expression is open. It reminds me of when we sat outside of Dr. Sayer's office for the first time, and he told me to get on track to fix myself. "What is the most scared you've been?"

I tell myself to keep breathing. "The day Jared beat up Colby."

He hums. "You never said a word about why it happened. You never even said you were *there*. We suspected, but..."

I force a laugh. We're by the tree in the back, where that platform still stands. The tree has grown, and the planks the construction workers had built to help me get to the first branch are now almost out of reach. It's funny how life moves on when you aren't looking.

"I was there. I was always with Jared."

He grumbles, "That boy covered for you about something?"

"No, I decided to come home alone." I shake my head, because I used to always come back and tell him about Jared's and my epic adventure, no matter how small. "Our adventure was interrupted by Colby and all of their popular friends. It was too much. But." *Breathe.* "Colby followed me. I-I don't know what he was going to do, but he touched my face—"

Dad's face is thunder. "Jared intervened?" he asks. His voice is so low.

He used to intimidate me. Sometimes, he still does. The way he holds onto his anger. It's so black. When he would get angry at me, it was an endless sea of darkness. Part of growing up, I think, is learning that your parents do crazy things because they love you. Right now, I want to hug him because I know he's not mad at me. He's angry *for* me.

"Jared was suddenly there, and he told Colby to back off...."

He rubs at his face. He's older, I realize. More gray, more wrinkled, and even though it looks good on him, he isn't the same as he was when I was fourteen. "That boy is damn lucky he's still in jail."

I shiver, and it has nothing to do with the weather.

He turns to go back to the house, and I stay by the tree. I touch the bark. This tree holds most of my secrets. "Dad," I call. He turns around. "Thank you."

"For what?"

"Everything," I say. It's the most honesty I'm allowed in one word.

He nods. "I had someone look at that platform up there the other week. It's still in fine condition. Although, you may catch a cold if you go up there tonight. I doubt Jared could manage to climb in his condition."

My mouth drops open. "You know we used to...?"

"At ten years old, Charlie? You weren't subtle. Not even a little bit."

I tip my head back and laugh. It is so refreshing to laugh, to know that they paid attention and let me do it anyway because it was harmless. He chuckles and starts toward the house again. "Goodnight, Charlie."

"Night, Dad."

Chapter 48

"CHARLIE," JARED WHISPERS. "WHAT ARE you doing?"

He hadn't answered my text, and so I snuck across the street and tapped on his window until he slid it open. I grin at him. "What do you think I'm doing? Sneaking you out."

He smiles. "Oh?"

"Yeah. It's not that far of a drop. Pass me your wheelchair, grandma."

I have missed his laugh.

"I am not throwing my wheelchair out the window. I can manage on my crutches," he says. "Depending on how far we're going."

I shrug. It's been awhile since I've done anything spontaneous. My life has been carefully drawn out in ink for as long as I can remember. For tonight, the whole canvas is blank.

"Not far," I say.

He grunts. "I'll meet you by my car." He closes his window and disappears. It takes him ten minutes to open the front door and meet me in the driveway.

Wordlessly, I turn and start toward my backyard. "Grass okay?"

"Should be able to manage," he answers. "Probably not a tree, though."

I look back at him and wink. "I've got that under control." Before we get into view of our tree, I glance at him and joke, "How do you feel about a pulley system?"

Jared stops and glares at me.

My poker face fails me, and I start laughing so hard I double over. "Oh, my god," I wheeze. "That was a joke. But your face—"

He finally starts laughing, too, and I give into the urge to hug him.

I'm on him in two strides. He doesn't flinch when I wrap my arms around his waist. I spread my legs, stabilizing both of us, just as he drops his crutches and hugs me back. I rest my chin on his shoulder and try not to bury my face into his neck.

"I thought, since I was burned—"

"That I wouldn't—"

"Yeah."

"I'm not afraid of you, Jared. I never have been. I never will be." I crane by head back so I can see his face. His eyes are closed. "Jared."

He opens his eyes, and his arms leave my back, but stay on my shoulders, balancing him. There's an ocean of vulnerability in his eyes one second, and it's shuttered away the next. "Can you get my crutches, Charlie? Please?"

I nod and put my hand on his waist as I pick up one, then

the other.

We continue on as if that didn't happen.

"You're sneaky," Jared says when he sees the blanket spread at the base of the tree. We lay flat and stare up at the sky. After a few minutes, he says, "You haven't mentioned your boyfriend."

"No," I admit.

I haven't thought much of him, either.

"Tell me."

I sigh. "I just... I don't know."

"You don't know?"

"I think I love him, but I'm not sure what that feels like anymore."

He breathes, and it feels like he's breathing for me. "I understand that."

Our hands are laced together. I don't remember the exact moment it happened, but my body flashes hot when his hand squeezes mine. I am thankful that this February is so mild. That the earth isn't frozen solid and covered in snow, that the air is warmer than it has a right to be. I'm thankful that we can be out here, together, in jackets and sweats and that we don't have to worry about catching a chill.

"Did you know my parents knew we snuck out here?"

We meet eyes. "Really?"

"Yeah, Dad said something about it today."

He's quiet for a minute. "Those were some of my favorite memories."

We resume staring at the sky.

Then, "You can visit, you know. I don't care if it was our moms' idea. I'd love to have you."

"Avery would love to have me, too?"

I shrug. "He'd be fine."

"Our moms have been meddling in our lives for a long time."

"You think so?"

He blows air through his lips.

"Macie never tried to get me back," he says. "I told her I was leaving, and I couldn't stop staring at that damn ring I had given her. She just twisted it around and around and didn't say shit." I listen to him breathe for almost a full minute until he adds, "The day I left, she tried to give it back to me. I told her, 'Keep it, pawn it, I don't give a fuck.'" He looks at me. "I should've taken it back."

I don't ask why, because I think I know. It's the same with Avery and the ring in his underwear drawer. That ring sits like a lump in my throat because I am so aware of its existence. It must be unbearable for Jared, to know that he once was in love and it didn't work. That ring, that girl, are somewhere out there.

Eventually, my back starts to get stiff, and I can't feel my toes in my boots. I've yawned approximately six times in the past fifteen minutes. "It's time for bed," Jared says after my seventh yawn. "Your dad would kill me if I let you fall asleep out here."

I nod. "Will I see you tomorrow before I go?"

I climb to my feet and hold out my hand to assist him in regaining his balance. "Thanks," he mutters. We start the walk back to his house. At his door, he says to me, "I have PT tomorrow morning. It lasts a while." He rubs at the back of his neck.

"That's okay. I'm glad we got to..." ...*whatever it is that we did.*

He gives me the ghost of a smile. And then, he steps forward and pulls me into a hug.

"Goodnight, Charlie," he says in my ear.

I can barely breathe. "Goodnight, Jared."

It's harder than I thought it would be to walk away from him.

Chapter 49

FEBRUARY FLIES INTO MARCH, AND BRINGS snowstorm after snowstorm. By the time my birthday rolls around, we have a foot of snow. The wind makes walking to work miserable, and it's making me cranky.

I can't stop thinking about what Jared said: how he and Macie orbited around each other. That is how Avery and I operate. We have developed nearly opposite work schedules, where he rises early and goes to sleep early, and I sleep in until he's gone and stay in my office later than I should. Every night, I watch the clock on the wall tick toward nine o'clock and, every night, I think, *maybe I should go home now.*

I don't.

For my birthday, my parents send flowers. They were supposed to come up to Boston and take me to dinner, but the snow impeded their plans. It was sort of comical: the flower delivery guy showed up on his bike, with a box that had nearly frosted closed. His eyelashes had accumulated ice. Georgia sent a card—which arrived on time, because the postal service never falters—and Rose and Eve both surprised me with little presents at work. Rose got me a picture frame, already filled with a picture of her and me. Eve presented me with a delicious-smelling candle. Tom agreed to let me go home early, which was a gift of its own.

When Jared calls, I'm not surprised.

I'm eager.

"Happy birthday, Charlie," he says after I answer. His voice is deeper than usual, gravellier.

"Thank you. How are you?"

He chuckles. "I'm okay. They fit me for my last prosthetic the other day. Now it's just a matter of learning to walk on it. How are *you*?"

I nod to myself. I'm not ready to go outside and freeze my fingers off. This phone call is a nice way to procrastinate the walk home from work. "That's great to hear."

"Charlie."

"Yes?"

"I asked how you are."

"Oh," I say. "Orbiting."

He sighs.

"Jared?"

"Charlie."

I manage to say, "Thanks for calling."

When I get home, my hair is wet from the snow that collected on it while I walked. Avery, for once, is already home. He blinks when he sees me, as if he's surprised I'm home while the sun is still out, and then he smiles. "I was just making you dinner," he says. "And I picked up a pie."

I laugh. My birthday is March 14. Pi Day. Today, it's easy to slip in next to him and kiss him like I mean it. "Thank you," I tell him.

He responds, "Happy birthday."

And then we go back to orbiting.

We haven't had sex in almost a week, but tonight we slip out of our clothes and make love under the covers. He whispers to me, "I love you," just before he finishes, but I know it's the orgasm talking. We hold each other for a few minutes, until our eyes grow heavy. Only then do I slip away from him.

Avery is asleep and snoring before I even get back from the bathroom.

When his alarm goes off the next morning, he punches the snooze button and rolls toward me. He always looks perfect in the morning.

He kisses me, pressing his closed lips to mine. When he opens our lips, his tongue sweeping into my mouth, I try my hardest not to pull away. God, what foul breath. But this is the most intimacy he's shown in a long time. And while I'm cringing at his breath, I love the way his hands slide up my rib cage. His touch is feather-light, but he stops just under my breasts. His thumb traces back and forth while his tongue explores my mouth in a way that makes me think he's forgotten what I taste like.

Avery stops.

"I have to go," he says against my lips.

I don't breathe for a beat, and then let out a long sigh. I push his hands away from me, out from under my sleep shirt. "Then go," I say. I let out a laugh for good measure. It's a mean laugh that I know he'll interpret as, *I was bored of this, anyway.* I wish I knew where this annoyance was coming from, on both sides. It's a never-ending push and pull that makes me tired.

He tenses, still half over me, before he rolls back away. I see his erection as he goes. He had passed out so quickly last night that he never put his boxers back on, and it hurts that he is choosing to leave for work instead of spending a little extra time in bed.

I'm tempted to ask him if I can pee first, but I'm too proud for that. I can wait until he's up and gone, and then get ready. I roll over and force myself to lay still as he gets up and showers and dresses. Time crawls as he gets ready. He doesn't say anything as he leaves, but I feel his absence.

When the front door of our apartment slams closed, I open my eyes. It's only nearing seven o'clock, which means that Avery left earlier than usual—he doesn't have to be in until eight. I get out of bed, walking around the room and rubbing out the indentations in the rug made by his shoes.

By the time I finish getting ready, it looks like I have enough time to stop and get breakfast and coffee along the way to work. It's finally warm enough to walk a few blocks without freezing, although there's still a good amount of snow on the ground. Putting a pair of flats in my purse and boots on my feet, I leave the apartment and trot down the stairs.

I sail into the café that Avery and I don't go to together. He says the coffee is too strong "for someone who only drinks it black." We met in a coffee shop. It seems only fitting that, with the way our relationship is sliding, we can't agree on where to buy our coffee. Avery is wrong. Their coffee is great with some cream and sugar. After I order, I take a seat near the window and mess around on my phone until something on the street catches my eye.

It's Avery, bundled in a jacket against the cold.

He exits the Starbucks, holding a drink tray with two coffees and a pastry bag. I should text him and tell him I'm not home anymore, so he doesn't have to walk all the way back. But then he's holding the door open with his foot, and a girl walks out behind him. She smiles at him in a way that is *way* too familiar.

He smiles back. I've never seen him smile like that: open and bright. That sunshine smile is quickly replaced with a familiar frown. *I'm disappointed in you*, it says. They walk off down the street, toward his work. They travel close enough that their arms keep brushing.

It feels like I can't breathe for the rest of the day. Avery texts me twice, checking in, but otherwise it's radio silent. I flip between wanting to know and not wanting to know. I flip between rage and tears, and I don't even have conclusive answers, yet. My lungs just won't work right; inhaling is hard.

I tell myself that this is rational, the silence of the day. We don't usually have lengthy texting conversations. This is normal. And yet, I find myself rushing home as soon as Tom leaves. When I get there, Avery is pacing the kitchen. He isn't one to pace or fidget, but it seems he's been doing both of those things.

"Hi," I say from the entryway. I startle him out of his trance, and we meet eyes. "You're home already?" It's still weird to say *home* and refer to the place where we both live.

"Yes," he says. I'm reminded how much my mother likes him: because of his proper use of *yes* opposed to *yeah*, his stable nine to five job, his devotion to everything he does, his desire for kids... "You are, too."

"Yeah," I say, because I can't help it. And then I ask, "Are you okay?" His face is lined with new tension. I see it in the way his mouth is held so tight. What I really want to ask is, *Who's the girl?* or, *Are you cheating on me?*

"We need to talk." Ice shoots through me. The fear must translate through my face, because he holds up his hands as if in surrender. "Nothing terrible."

I follow him to the couch and perch on the edge, facing him as he sits beside me. He leans forward and kisses my cheek, putting his hand on my knee. His eyes look tired. Why haven't I noticed that before now?

Maybe because he is always asleep when I get home.

"Do you remember when I told you about my ex, Elaina?"

The beautiful brunette. With an awful sense of awareness, I realize that she's here. She's in Boston. She got coffee with him this morning and was talking with him *weeks* ago. I should've recognized her, but it never occurred to me that I may see her in person.

I say, "Yeah, I remember that," when I really want to say, *What's that bitch have to do with anything?* And then I ask myself why he didn't tell me when we went to dinner that night, after I practically caught her talking to him in the lobby of our *apartment*. This is our space, isn't it? It shouldn't be something that she can infiltrate.

"I ran into her when I went home for the holidays," he starts.

"You didn't mention that?" My voice squeaks. I meant it more as an accusation than a question.

The look he gives me makes me feel foolish and a little crazy. "I didn't think it was worth mentioning. I ran into her when I was running errands for my mom. Picking up her dry cleaning, actually," he says with a laugh. Ironic, because that's part of *my* job. I get paid for that. I don't laugh. It isn't funny. His chuckles run out after a minute. He keeps looking at me.

I motion for him to continue. "Please, just tell me all of it. Rip off the band aid," I whisper.

He nods. "Right." He squeezes my knee. "I saw her and it was like a punch to the gut. She looked... not great. She asked how I was doing and where I was—I guess she didn't even know that I moved. She probably didn't know who to ask, if she cared enough. I told her I moved here, and about my job, and... I don't know, Charlotte, it was just like catching up with a ghost. It was unnerving."

I feel like there's a side to this story that he isn't telling me. It settles in my bones, the surety of my intuition. I can relate to the feeling of catching up with a ghost. It was how I felt when I first talked to Jared after so long—at that party at my parents' house. It got easier, and those cobwebs were swept away. I don't want that to happen to them, though.

"I only saw her that once while I was home. And then just yesterday, she was waiting for me outside of work."

He's excluding the other time, weeks ago. That's what he won't say.

Last night, *on my birthday*, before we had sex for the first time in a week, was when he saw her? He knew she was in the city? It cheapens the sex. It cheapens my birthday. Me. *Even if it was me he came home to,* the voice in my head says, *did he think about her while making love to me?* The question sits on the tip of my tongue, pressing on my teeth.

"How long is she in town? What did she want?"

He rubs at his face. "She said she felt terrible... Wanted to take me to dinner to talk. I told her I had plans with you... that I had to get home to you. I'm sorry, Charlotte, I didn't really think to mention you to her in California. I didn't want to hurt her more...."

In other words: she came to Boston expecting him to be single.

"And how did she take it last night?"

"About as well as could be expected." He shakes his head. "No, probably worse than that."

I nod. I don't know this girl, but I can picture how she might react. Ugly.

"There's more," he whispers. After a moment, he says, "I think she may have moved here."

My eyebrows shoot up. "Permanently?"

He shakes his head. "She insinuated she'd be around for a while. I don't think she got a job here or anything like that. Her dad has money; she could be at a hotel for who knows how long. I don't know... I'm sorry, Charlotte."

"It's okay," I tell him. "You're okay?"

He blinks. "Why are you asking if I'm okay?"

"She's your ex. You aren't affected because she's here? Trying to see you?"

"Oh, well. Yeah, it's kind of shaken me up a bit." He leans over and kisses my forehead. "Thank you."

I press into his touch for a moment before rocking back. "Why are you thanking me?"

He raises his eyebrows. "For being understanding."

I am only understanding *because* I understand.

Chapter 50

I HAVE A NEW ROUTINE.

After Avery leaves for work, I slide the ring out of its box, sit on the floor, and hold it. I stare at it and twist it so it catches the morning light and memorize every detail. I never put it on, though. That's an experience that a woman should get with her new fiancé: the moment of putting on the engagement ring for the first time. So, while I admire, and I poke my index finger through it to warm the metal on the inside, it never touches my ring finger.

Is it unhealthy?

I ask myself this every single time I peel back his underwear. I pray that it hasn't disappeared. If it were to disappear, I might think I hallucinated the whole thing. While I stare at it, I picture the life ahead of us. I haven't met his parents yet. Is that important to him? It's important to me. I don't want to marry into a family that hates me for chaining him to the east coast. I wonder where we'll live; I wonder how soon my parents will start mentioning kids—and then I realize that's a joke, because they already mention it. Big wedding? Small wedding? My mother doesn't do anything small—that answers that question. I wonder how we'll raise our kids, if he'll push for more than one. I don't necessarily like kids, but maybe I'll like one that comes out of my belly. Will he help me paint the nursery? Will he deal with my mood swings with grace? Will he get me pickles in the middle of the night if I get a craving, or hold my hair in the morning if I have morning sickness?

Stop, I have to tell myself.

And then my thoughts turn to how little I know of Elaina. I've turned into a stalker, really, the amount of times I check her social media. It was a sucker punch when I discovered that they recently became friends with each other on Facebook again, and they also followed each other's Instagram and Twitter accounts.

She showed up like a blazing comet, and Avery was left blinded by her. Me? Just blindsided. I carefully ask about her at dinner, or as we get ready to leave for work in the morning. That's another thing that has changed: my level of effort.

Suddenly, there is a competitor. I've always been competitive in the best sense of the word. It shouldn't be surprising that, given Elaina's arrival, I am suddenly waking up when he does, touching him more, eating breakfast and leaving for work with him. If he has noticed this about-face, he does not mention it. When we part ways in the morning, I sag. I exhale a breath of relief.

"Plans to see Elaina today?" I ask at dinner. Sometimes, "Did you hear from her today?"

His eyes cut to mine, always weighing my misery as a tangible thing. *How thick is this dark cloud surrounding Charlotte today*, he must consider. Sometimes he answers, "I didn't see her today." Sometimes, and increasingly more often, he will tell me, "She was waiting for me outside of work. We walked home together."

I feel her presence like a pulled muscle: a twinge of pain when I move the wrong way. I want to know where she is, how she can be stopped or discouraged, but I don't know how to do this with any degree of subtly. This means that I must resort to bluntness.

"We should invite her for dinner," I say to Avery one day. It has been raining all weekend, and the temperature made a nice transition from cold to chilly. The end of the season snow we got two weeks ago was finally melting away. April, and spring along with it, was finally arriving.

"You want to have dinner with who?"

"With Elaina," I confirm. My stomach does a weird flip. "We can have her over. She can bring someone, if she wants."

His eyes flash. I bite back a question about that bothering him, because it clearly does. The idea of her dating someone else has him tense. "That could be fun," he says.

"Okay," I answer. "When?" It's Sunday morning, but we have the rest of our lives to plan a dinner with his ex-girlfriend.

"Let me call her."

I bite my lip. I didn't know he still had her number, or that they were on a familiar enough basis to call each other. Deep down, I assumed they probably communicated. But I didn't want my imagination to run away from me. Did they snapchat nudes to each other? Did she say, *I wish you were here*, in place of *I love you*? She wasn't able to say those three little words to him before—would she say it now that he wasn't hers?

"Elaina," he greets her. "Charlotte and I were wondering if you'd like to join us for dinner?" He nods as she says something, her voice indecipherable. We meet eyes. "When?" he repeats for me. I shrug. "Sometime this week. When are you free?"

He cups the mouth part of his phone after a moment.

"Does Friday work?"

Five days to mentally prepare. "Yes," I agree.

He nods again and angles his shoulders away from me. "That works for us. No, you don't need to bring anything." And, quieter, "I don't know. Probably not.... I have to go, okay?"

Once he hangs up, he breathes harshly: a sharp inhale and a long, shaky exhale. He turns back to me and hugs me tightly to him. "I know that you don't really want to do this," he says.

"No," I answer. I *really* don't. "But she's here."

He pulls back and meets my eyes. "She's where?"

I tap his temple with my index finger. "She practically lives here, now, and..."

"And you want to know her?"

Something like that.

"What are we going to cook?" My cooking skills can be questionable sometimes.

He perks up. "She likes chicken marsala."

I wrinkle my nose. Doesn't he know I hate mushrooms? "Chicken parm?"

"No, she's lactose intolerant."

I blow out a breath. "Fish?"

He nods. "Yeah, fish would be good. I haven't had any in forever."

Because I suck at cooking fish, I want to say, *and you don't buy it.* Instead, I say, "I'll see what the fresh fish the market has." He can cook the damn fish.

We leave it at that. I step back in the circle of his arms and sigh when he pulls me closer.

"Movie?"

He shakes his head and gently pushes me back. "I have to

go meet Steve," he says. "Actually, I'm already running late."

I follow him into the bedroom. "It's a Sunday. Is this a work thing?"

"Yeah," he says from the closet. "I took some papers home on Friday, but he's leaving for New York at the ass crack of dawn tomorrow. He needs them for a presentation."

I nod. "Okay, well. You'll be home after you meet with him?"

He shrugs. "We may do lunch or something."

I hold back a sigh. "Okay." I look around the room, wondering how much neater it could possibly get. Since stressing about Elaina, I have had a single-minded focus of cleaning *everything*. Avery never said a word about how the place suddenly shined.

"Maybe I'll go see Rose, then," I say.

He says, "That would be fun. Go do that." He comes out wearing a sweater and my favorite pair of his jeans—they're dark, low slung, and hug his butt and thighs in a way that makes my body heat.

Wasn't Steve leaving their company? I can't remember when Avery mentioned it. I almost don't *want* to remember. I don't want to catch Avery in any sort of lie.

I kneel at his dresser and reach for the ring. Once it's in my hands, I call Georgia. It has been too long since I last spoke to my best friend, besides the occasional emails at work and texting. "Charlie, it is seven o'clock in the morning. This better be good," Georgia growls.

I laugh. "I forgot about that damn time change. Sorry, Georgie. I just missed your voice."

I can practically feel her waking up through the phone. "Everything okay?"

"Yeah...." She snorts. "Okay, no," I admit.

"Spill it, sister."

"Before I do, how are you and Henry?"

She makes a dreamy sighing sound. It makes me want to slap her, because I can only imagine the in-love expression on her face. "Oh, Charlie, he's so perfect. I mean, obviously he's not *perfect* by any sense of the word, but he's perfect for me. Do you remember how you and I got along really well, and it was seamless living together?"

"Of course."

"It's better than that because I get to have awesome sex with my handsome boyfriend every day. Usually more than once."

I wince, because... that sounds nice. That sounds like the way it should be: two people, completely compatible and at peace with each other.

I feel broken when I tell her, "I don't have that."

She grunts. "I could've told you that."

I breathe through the lump in my throat. "I found a ring in his underwear drawer. I keep looking at it. I'm holding it right now."

"Fuck," she whispers.

I rub at my forehead. "He made me a pie for my birthday. Or, no, he picked one up from the grocery store and thought I wouldn't notice."

She snorts. "That's original."

"I pretended my parents hadn't done the exact same thing every year of my childhood." All I had wanted was a cake like everyone else. But I let myself smile, because my news kept getting better.

"Oh, and I'm meeting his ex-girlfriend."

"WHAT?"

Georgia is taking this well.

"I know. She showed up from San Diego and apparently will

be in town for a while. She keeps seeking out Avery, so..."

If she were here, she'd be grinning at me. As it is, her voice sounds devious when she agrees, "So you're keeping your friends close, but your enemies closer."

"Maybe she'll back off if Avery and I put on a show of being in love."

"Just don't fake it," she warns.

I run my thumb over the diamond before tucking it back into its box. It doesn't stir excitement—just dread.

"I think I already might be."

Chapter 51

IN TRUTH, I THINK I WAS HOPING I'D BE STRUCK by lightning before Friday rolled around. To my everlasting dismay, that doesn't happen. I leave work early, pick up fresh cod, and bolt home. The apartment is already spotless, but I can't help puttering around until they arrive.

When the buzzer sounds, my heart stops. Avery isn't here yet and she *is*? I double check to make sure it's her, and her voice floats through the speaker. "It's Elaina," she says. Her phantom voice—just her *voice*—feels invasive. I hit the button that will unlock the downstairs door and feel like I'm going to throw up. I want to take it all back. I wish I didn't know she existed, I wish I didn't invite her, I wish I wasn't here without Avery backing me up....

Stop panicking, I order myself. *Channel your mother.*

Elaina knocks on the door, and I swing it open wide. We take each other in; I wish I had not changed out of what I wore to work, because she looks dressed up, comfortable, and pretty. She wears leggings, a long blouse and vest, and shiny boots with knit socks peeking over the top. With that outfit, she fits right into New England. Opposed to her, I wear black jeans, which have a bit of mud on my calf, a t-shirt that I just remember has a hole in the armpit, and fuzzy neon green socks.

While I consider myself pretty average—in height, in my mousy, almost-blonde hair, murky blue eyes, and so on—she is like a petite version of Aphrodite. Olive skin that makes me assume she has a Mediterranean heritage, thick brown hair, and cool brown eyes. More than that, she has this presence that seems to amplify herself. I die a little, because if she is here to reclaim Avery, I don't know how to stop her.

"Please, come in," I say and step aside.

She enters and takes off her boots by the door, next to mine. I allow myself a small smile. I hear her inhale and exhale slowly, and I have to wonder if she's nervous. Once her boots are off, she straightens and holds out her hand. "It's nice to meet you, Charlotte," she says.

I reach forward and take her hand, although it feels like I'm betraying myself by saying, "It's nice to finally meet you, too, Elaina." I wave my hand around the apartment like an idiot. "Please, make yourself comfortable." *But not too comfortable,* I think. "Avery should be back soon." I ignore how her eyes light up at the mention of his name. "Would you like something to drink?"

"No, thank you, Charlotte."

I almost tell her that she can call my Charlie, but we aren't friends.

There's little merit in that, though, because my *boyfriend* doesn't even call me Charlie. And for the first time in a long time, I wonder at his intentions with that. Does he do it to keep separate from me? To hold himself apart?

Regardless, there's nothing I can do about that now. I watch from the doorway as Elaina sweeps through the apartment. She contaminates everything she touches, which is most things. There are new pictures on the walls of Avery and me, blown up photos that my mother had professionally done of the family, shots of his family laughing and posing in front of a campfire. My favorite is the one of him and Charlie, his best friend, clutching each other. It looks like they were high school aged, wearing almost ill-fitting tuxedos with obnoxious boutonnieres. Avery has a smirk that says, *I rule the universe,* and Charlie looks like he'd follow his friend anywhere.

She only lingers on that for a moment. She mirrors Avery's smirk and then giggles. "I was there," she says. "Not, you know, *there.* But I went to his school's prom with another guy." She shakes her head and moves on. "Charlie flirted with me for about two seconds, until my date threatened to punch him in the face."

I don't say anything, because there's nothing to say to that.

She moves on to the painting I *finally* had the courage to hang a few weeks ago. It was one of my most recent works, after the solar eclipse that hangs in our bedroom. I never told Avery what that particular painting meant.

"Where is this city?" Elaina asks me. This painting was of the Chicago skyline in abstract: the sky was a mess of swirling reds, yellows, oranges, warm purples, and browns. The buildings, collectively, were vertical splashes of cooler colors: blues, greens, shades of purple and black.

"Chicago," I answer. *You're coming into your own,* Georgia had said when I sent her a picture of it. *You've got something special.* She had sent me my old paintings—most of them were incomplete—right after I moved to Boston. They sat, still rolled in their cardboard and plastic cylinders, stacked in my closet.

"Who's the artist?"

She is eyeing the painting too intensely, dissecting it. And so I answer, "I think it says Anonymous on the back, under the frame. What do you think?"

"I think it's gorgeous, but unsettling." I tilt my head, trying to see how it unsettles. "It's like the sky is on fire. The end of the world."

"Yes, it could be." The world could end tonight, at dinner, and we'll all go up in a blaze of flames. It would be preferable to the embarrassment that I'm sure is coming.

I hear the door open. Avery calls out, "Hey, babe," before he is fully visible. His eyes swing from the second set of boots, to me, and then to Elaina in the far corner of the room. "You're already here," he says, an octave higher than his regular voice.

She grins, and her eyes clearly say, *I love you*, but she shuffles her feet and folds her arms across her stomach. "I am. I wanted to get to know Charlotte uninfluenced."

He raises one of his eyebrows. "Oh?" He sounds like me.

She smirks.

"How is that going?"

Maybe he knows I can be as tight-lipped as a clam when I want to be.

"I learned a good deal," she says.

Oh?

She glances at me, then back to Avery. Her cheeks turn a rosy pink that I used to wish I had. "She's smart, obviously," she winks at me, "and talented. She knows how to clean, because this place is spotless." Avery looks around, as if just now noticing the lack of disarray. "And she's proving to be a great hostess and a very funny woman."

I hardly breathe, because I was not expecting her to be

genuinely *nice.*

Avery, though, latches onto one thing: "What did she do to prove she's talented?"

Elaina waves her hand around at my entire apartment. "I have to assume you didn't decorate, Avery. I've seen your style."

...And, there goes my good mood.

He smiles. "You're right." We meet eyes, and he gives me a real smile. "You are talented, Charlotte. I'm sorry I didn't notice your cleanliness."

Elaina says, "What did you get us?"

I just now notice the paper bag in his hand. He puts it on the counter and pulls out a six pack. "Sam Adams IPA."

I try not to let the wince cross my face, because, okay, maybe he assumed that I had wine here. Honestly, I almost wish he had bought tequila to make the night more bearable. But then Elaina grins at him, and I know they're sharing some secret memories of drinking those beers somewhere. They had probably followed it with sex.

"Is that what you drink, Elaina?"

"Yeah, any type of IPA is my go to!" She seems to be getting more cheerful by the second; I am getting grumpier.

I rummage in the fridge, whispering, "Hallelujah," when I see a half-drunk bottle of white wine on the door shelf. I pull it out and pour myself a hefty glass.

Avery pops the cap off of a beer and hands it to Elaina, then sets about making dinner. We make small talk until the food is ready. Since she has been quiet, and Avery, in opposition, hasn't been able to stop talking, I figure I should ask her something. "So," I say while Avery is between stories and clear my throat, "Elaina. What do you do for work?"

She gives me a warm smile. Her previous bouts of awkwardness have fled, leaving a calm, confident person in its wake. "I'm a school teacher," she says. "I teach at a public school. Seventh grade."

"Oh, wow," I say. "That must be difficult. What is that, twelve year olds?"

She nods and spins her fork in her fingers. "They're actually on a little field trip with the sixth graders, and when they get back from Sacramento, there are some substitute teachers that will be covering for me." She looks at Avery, swallows, and says, "There are two other teachers from my school in Boston with me. We're taking a class at Harvard about special education, since it's only offered every other year in the spring. It's a pretty prestigious class that's offered to teachers nationwide, and the fact that my school was able to send *three* of us was incredible." I hear an unspoken, *It's more incredible that you're here, too, Avery.* Or maybe I'm just extrapolating.

"That's..." I glance at Avery, and he's... angry. I close my mouth. He trembles, and his lips are pressed into a thin line.

He bites out, "Can I talk to you alone?"

Elaina doesn't look surprised at his temper. Every time it comes out, I draw back. She just glares and says, "Can't it wait until we're done eating?"

"No."

We watch him slam his chair back and disappear into our bedroom.

"I suppose I should follow him," she says, pushing her chair back. I shrug. The door closes behind her. It is such a definitive noise, it makes me wonder if I live here at all. Yes, because there is my favorite decorative pillow, and there is my face spread across ink on the walls next to Avery's, and there is my painting.

Avery's voice echoes through the space, muffled only slightly by the door. "What does *that* mean?" he yells. "*Choose.*"

I keep my eyes on the painting, whose colors and brush

strokes soothe and aggravate me.

"You are here as a fucking *fluke*?" and then, "No, no."

Things get quiet; only the clock on the wall is audible. I imagine them whispering furiously, or shocked into silence, or undressing each other with their eyes—or their hands. I imagine what he would do if she jumped forward and kissed him. Maybe would kiss her back. He would wind his arms around her and fist his hand in her hair and never let her go.

Maybe Elaina was right, and I predicted the end of the world with some acrylic paint and a brush.

As is the way with apocalypses, Avery exits our bedroom first. He looks at me with an apology in his eyes and leans down and kisses the top of my head. "You asked for this," he whispers to me. He straightens, but stays behind my chair.

My heart picks up speed, because the last thing I expected was the blame for this. I haven't even yet defined *this*, and it comes at me in the form of stones cast. My stomach does this weird flip, a form of anxiety, because whatever happened in our bedroom seems to have scared him.

When Elaina reappears, her eyes are bloodshot. She swipes at her nose and looks from me to Avery and back to me. "She's leaving," Avery says.

Elaina says, "Yes," faintly, and although I hate her, I hurt for her. She touches my shoulder as she passes. "You have a beautiful home. I'm sorry for the way it turned out."

I jerk my head up and down. My neck has forgotten how to operate smoothly, and nothing is working tonight. Avery practically vibrates with unshed anger, but he doesn't move. He doesn't speak. She takes forever to put her boots on, and then she opens the door.

I clear my throat and say, "It was nice to meet you, Elaina. Thank you for coming."

When she leaves, I push my chair back. It forces Avery to take a step back, and I scramble up. He is *seething*, and I can't even begin to understand why.

"You cannot blame this one on me," I say.

"Oh, can't I?"

"No!" My voice comes out louder than I intend. "You're the one who dragged your ex into our lives. Not me! How on earth can you blame me for this shit show?"

Avery grabs at his hair. "It is *her* fault, and your fault for inviting her to dinner."

I growl. "I invited her to dinner because you were seeing her every *fucking* day. What else was I supposed to do? Just sit back and be like, 'Okay, this stranger is pretty much stalking my boyfriend, I guess I'll just twiddle my thumbs!' Or, I don't know, put up a fight of keeping you?"

Unexpected tears prick my eyes, and I have the heart of it: I'm so terrified of him leaving.

"Do you think love is a cure-all? Do you think love is *enough* to hold a relationship together?" He scoffs at me. "Come on, Charlotte, you're sabotaging us!"

A sob bursts out of me, the pain of it so acute that I can feel it to my toes.

"I'm not the only one tearing this relationship apart," I howl.

He softens at once and steps forward. I step back, although all I want is him to touch me. He stops following me. He just looks at me, and I see his own sadness, his own heartbreak. He wears it the same way he wore it a year and a half ago.

"I'm so sorry," he says. His voice is hoarse, low, and it seems to reverberate in the sudden quiet. "Charlotte, it was never my intention to make you feel like you aren't enough."

"I know," I whisper, but it's not enough. It's never enough.

Chapter 52

JARED IS COMING.

Yes, it might be retaliation.

Avery didn't react when I told him a friend would be visiting.

In truth, I think he is mourning Elaina. Since dinner, we haven't heard from her. That hasn't stopped me from asking him, tentatively, if she's reached out to him. He always answers with a quick shake of his head, like he can't believe it, either. I try to keep my words like feathers: any more weight than that and they'll break our delicate truce.

Now, I've taken the Friday off of work—exactly three weeks since Elaina visited—and I stand at the door to my building. It has a few stairs in the front—which Jared is aware of—and then an elevator inside that will get us up to my apartment. His father had business in Boston and offered to drive him into the city.

These three weeks have been worse than I could've

imagined. We haven't had sex *at all*. We argue about anything and everything. And through it all, he casts the blame onto me. It's my fault for working late, for picking fights about stupid stuff, for...

I sigh.

And through it all, the weight of that damn ring in his dresser presses on me.

"There she is!" Mr. Brown calls.

I jerk, embarrassed to be caught off guard. Jared climbs out of his dad's car. I'm surprised to see him wearing the prosthetic leg and no crutches. His jeans cover it, and so, besides the slight limp in his gait, it looks like he's whole.

That isn't right.

Missing a leg doesn't make him any less *whole*. Any less of who he was. He just *is*. He's always been himself, even after the accident. Nothing changed, really. Not that I could tell.

"Hi, guys," I say as I come toward them. They meet me on the sidewalk, and I get a hug from both of them.

"Lovely to see you, Charlie. What beautiful weather we're having."

The sun is out, the snow is gone, and it finally feels like the beginning of spring. "Yes, thank goodness. It rained the past week."

"Hi, Charlie," Jared says. He grins at me.

Inexplicably, this situation feels like we're being dropped off at summer camp together. There is so much weight of promise, of excitement, behind this weekend.

"Jared," I respond.

His dad lifts a small duffle bag out of the trunk. "Do you want me to carry this up?" he asks me.

I hold out my hand. "I can take it. Thanks." I pause and look at Jared. "Is that discrimination?"

Jared rolls his eyes at me. "Any excuse not to carry a duffle bag is fine by me."

Mr. Brown nods. "Well, I'm hoping to be on time for my meeting. I've got to get going." He claps Jared on the shoulder. "Call if you need anything. We'll see you Sunday."

They say their goodbyes, and we watch his dad pull out into the street and disappear down the block. "Well," I laugh. "Shall we go up?"

"Yeah."

A weird sense of peace washes over me. I tell him, "You look good."

"Because it looks like I have my left leg?"

I frown at him as we step into the elevator. "No. You just look healthier." I poke at his stomach for emphasis.

He grins again. "I'm excited to be here. I haven't been to Boston in forever." His smile fades when he says, "My therapist made me promise to treat my body better so I could physically handle the trip. Ever since you invited me in February, I've been trying to be better."

My cheeks turn red. "I'm glad I helped?"

He nods. "You did. Don't doubt that."

He's slow on the new leg, but not as slow as the crutches. He sighs once we get to my door. I unlock it and hold it open for him. As he enters, he whistles. "Wow."

"Yeah, it has a good view," I laugh. "It's a lot better than my old place. I was supposed to live here alone, but—"

"Yeah. Your boyfriend decided at the last minute to move in," Jared says.

I press my lips together. Jared continues a slow tour of the place, even peeking into my bedroom and the bathroom. "You have your choice of an air mattress or the couch," I tell him.

He plops down on the couch, sighing, and I move to sit in

the chair adjacent.

"This couch doesn't seem so bad."

I smile. "Is it me, or are we being awkward?"

That gets Jared to laugh. "It's definitely a little weird."

"Okay."

"Did I tell you that our moms got into an argument?"

My eyes widen. "What? When?"

"Just the other day," he says. "Your mom is apparently under the impression that I'm going to break up your relationship."

I roll my eyes. "I'm doing that just fine on my own. You won't be thrown under that bus."

He chuckles. "Yeah, my mom was obviously Team Jared. She said that you and Avery were just a fling."

"A *fling*? We aren't—"

"Relax, Charlie."

"Does your mom think so little of me?" I continued. "Seriously, Jared?"

He just leans back. He used to enjoy our arguments, and him relaxing just seems... like I know him. He isn't predictable by a long shot. But, from what I can tell, the same boy that I grew up with is sitting in front of me. At the same time that it makes me sad—we missed so much of each other's lives—I'm so grateful that we're here. Now.

"Charlie. She loves you. She hasn't met this Avery fellow."

I roll my eyes. "It isn't even like you're competition. We're friends. I love Avery."

He raises an eyebrow, and I scowl.

I say, "I do."

He says, "Okay," like he doesn't believe me.

I scowl again.

"You're single-handedly the most... *bored* in-love person

I've ever met."

That makes me laugh, because he hasn't met Avery yet. Avery would win that competition.

"Avery should be home soon. He said he'd leave a little early and we could go to dinner."

Jared smiles, but it doesn't reach his eyes. Instead, he reaches over and covers my hand with his own. "Charlie, I hope you're happy."

My own smile wavers.

"I can't tell anymore. Sometimes I am." I clear my throat, because talking about this stuff is hard. I haven't put it on anyone except Georgia, who already loathes Avery. But the truth is, I have this feeling of utter exhaustion. At some point, I started treading water and I lost track of the shoreline. I'm stuck. "Can we talk about you?"

We stare at each other for a minute, so long that I can tell he's trying to read my mind. I wonder if he's successful. Eventually he says, "Yeah, we can talk about me."

"How are you?"

"How am I?" He sighs and rubs at his jaw. "Honestly, it's tough. I've been working through it with my therapist, Dr. Sayer—"

My jaw drops. "Shut up."

"Charlie?"

My laugh is bitter. I cannot *believe* that he's talking to someone who... practically already knows him. *Shit.* "Seriously? What, did my mother recommend her?"

"How did you know my therapist is a woman...?" He closes his eyes. "Oh, no."

"Yep. I saw her all through high school. She probably remembers more about your childhood from my perspective than you realize." I am going to kill my mother.

He starts laughing. It's wildfire: uncontrollable, contagious. He's right to laugh. Only fate would be this ironic. I start laughing, too, so hard that my ribs hurt and tears pool in my eyes.

We go on and on, until our giggles subside and he says, "That's... Well, that would explain the expression on her face when I told her about you."

I snort. My hand flies up to my mouth, but I manage to get out, "I'll bet," before we start laughing again.

Jared is the first to sober. "You know what that means. She takes her doctor patient confidentiality seriously—I never would've guessed she knew you."

Well. That makes me feel a little better.

"You were saying how you were," I prompt when he doesn't say anything else.

He grunts. "Yeah, yeah. It's been hard. My whole life changed."

I remember a question that had come to me, randomly, a few days ago. "Hey. You never said how you went from living out west, with a torn ACL, to the hospital in D.C. What happened in the middle," I clarify.

"Right. I moved back to D.C. because they didn't require as much rigorous physical strength. After my ACL was pretty much healed, I started picking up jobs and when I was able, started to go on calls. It was only my second call when the roof collapsed on me." He runs his hand down his right leg, massaging his knee, before stopping on his thigh.

"You were badly burned?" I whisper.

He jerks his head to the side and stares out of my window for a minute. "No, Charlie, compared to how bad it could've been... It was mostly on my left leg. It's a lot better than it was."

I stare at him. The protective part of me wants to strip him down, to see how bad the damage is, and how much he's been minimizing it.

My phone vibrates, making both of us jump.

"Hey," I answer.

Avery answers, "Hey. I just got out of work. Do you want to meet at Legal Seafood in the Pru?" The Prudential Center restaurants, and almost anything on Boylston or Newbury St., are our go-to places. "I can meet you there in fifteen."

I glance at Jared. "Sure," I tell Avery. "We may be a few minutes late."

Avery agrees, and we hang up.

Jared watches me. "Just out of curiosity, how much did you tell him about me?"

I bite my lip. In truth? Nothing. I can't shoulder all the blame; Avery didn't even ask me about him. Our conversation went like this:

Avery, my friend wants to come visit. The one I went home to see a month ago.

He said, *When does she want to come up?*

It was my fault that I ignored the pronoun. *Next weekend. I'm thinking about taking off Friday.*

He pats my leg on his way by me. *Sounds great. She's staying with us?*

If you don't mind, I hedged.

No. That's fine.

So... No. He didn't really know anything, at all.

"Great," Jared mutters.

I call an Uber on my phone. "It'll be fine," I say. I hope.

But really, if it isn't? That's fine, too.

"You're playing with fire."

I cringe.

He eyes me as we make our way out the door and to the

elevator. Once we're in, it's like our world shrinks to just the two of us. "Are you still having those dreams?"

I shrug. "Dreams?"

He just watches me.

Finally, I look up at the mirrored ceiling and whisper, "Sometimes."

"How often?"

"The burning one? Not too often. Thank god. Although I do have dreams about being raped. Those are new." I force myself to laugh. "I don't know which one I would rather have."

He puts his hand on my shoulder. It's too easy, how he pulls me into his embrace. My front hits his side, and I wrap my arms around his waist.

I try not to focus on how good he smells.

Or how his arms feel like home.

No, I don't think about any of that. I just smile into his shoulder and stay there until the doors slide open.

"Avery, this is Jared. Jared, Avery."

I should've known this wasn't going to go well.

Avery's eyes look like they're going to bug out of his head.

"Charlotte," Avery says. It sounds pained, like he swallowed glass. I haven't heard his voice that rough in a while. I don't think he's cared about anything I've done in *a while.*

Jared holds out his hand. "Nice to meet you, man."

Avery stands and shakes his hand. "Same. Although, I'll admit, I didn't know you were a *man.*" He glares at me.

I shrug and slide into the booth. Avery sits next to me,

boxing me in, and Jared takes the opposite side. My skin is prickling. It takes Jared a second to get in, and I realize: Avery might not see that Jared is wearing a prosthetic. His jeans cover everything, and he has shoes on both feet. I gulp.

"So, Jared," Avery says. "How long have you known Charlotte?"

Jared glances at me with a question in his eyes. Ever since I was little, I hated being called Charlotte. I associated it with my parents' disappointment. Now, my boyfriend calls me Charlotte and I accept it?

I don't bother to tell him it's my fault—that, in the beginning, I introduced myself to Avery as Charlotte, instead of Charlie, and I never managed to change his habit.

"We were neighbors forever," Jared answers.

My first words to Jared weren't until I was at least seven. He wasn't remotely interested in hanging out with a girl, and by eight, it was my personal mission to yell hello to him whenever I saw him outside and giggle when his ears turned red. And then, at nine, his family moved in with mine and we became friends. Then best friends. Then... nothing.

Avery forces a smile. "Oh?"

I roll my eyes. "He moved away when I was fifteen. We didn't talk for a while."

"I regret that," Jared says. "I wish I hadn't left you with—"

I jerk my head to the side, the motion instantly silencing Jared. Avery glances at me, quick, and purses his lips. I've only vaguely told Avery about my past. I didn't want the judgement, or his anger. I'd imagine he would say something like, *How on earth did you fall for that, Charlotte?*

"Okay," Avery says. He looks a little hurt, but I imagine he feels like I did when I learned about Elaina's arrival.

"I still have my same old job that everyone wants me to

move on from," I say. They both turn to look at me. "What? It's true. I was just…" *changing the subject.*

Avery looks back to Jared once the waiter takes our orders. "I am trying to convince her that she is much more capable than she thinks she is."

I snort. It isn't true—he's been trying to convince me that I am stuck in the mud.

"No," I disagree. "I like my job. He just doesn't like that. Avery, that's something you and Jared have in common."

Avery looks at me like I'm insane.

Jared laughs. "Don't rope me into this, Charlie, we haven't talked about it in months."

"You two talk a lot," Avery says. To Jared, he adds, "We got into a fight about it after Thanksgiving. She overreacted."

I hear, *Her fault.*

Jared grunts. "It's good that Charlie stands up for herself."

My boyfriend shrugs and puts his arm around my shoulders. I wasn't expecting Avery to be territorial, but his arm feels like he's staking his claim over me. "Even so."

We sit in silence for a moment. There's an elephant sitting on my chest. The tension is growing, but I don't know how to fix it.

"What do you do for work?" Jared asks.

I allow myself to breathe. Before Avery can answer, the waiter comes by with our food. Once he leaves, Avery says, "I'm an accountant. I'm hoping to jump up the ladder and then move onto a bigger company. This one is fine, per say, it's just too familial."

"What's wrong with a familial work environment?"

He's told me before that firefighters are like family.

I take a large bite of my Caesar salad.

Avery shrugs. "Nothing is *wrong* with it. I just prefer not to gossip about my weekend while I'm trying to make money. I don't need that distraction."

"Except Steve," I cut in. He always mentions Steve outside of work, and we went with him to that club on Halloween.

Avery's lips press together. "Yes, well. His last day was last week."

"It's tough to lose a friend," Jared murmurs.

I clear my throat, and we all look down at our food.

Once we're almost done eating, Avery nods to Jared. He coughs, then asks, "What do you do for work?"

Jared grimaces. "Unfortunately, nothing right now. I got into an accident on the job, and since then I've had to collect disability." He raises an eyebrow at me, and I slowly shake my head. No, I didn't tell Avery.

Jared sighs, but he doesn't look at me like he's disappointed. "Firefighting is my profession," he says.

"Ah," Avery answers. "I noticed a little limp. A bum leg keeping you out of the game until it heals?"

Jared smiles. "No. The amputated leg sidelined me permanently."

Avery's face turns red, which is a telltale sign of danger. "Excuse us, Jared." He practically drags me out of the booth and only stops when we're outside the restaurant. "Is it your goal to make me look like an idiot?"

I rear back. "What?"

"Come on, Charlotte. First you didn't tell me that your friend is a *man*."

I think, *He definitely isn't a boy anymore.*

Avery continues, "Which I might not have had a problem with if you had been honest with me. And then, you forget to tell me that he's missing a leg?"

I snort. "I'm sorry, Avery, but you haven't really paid

attention to anything I've been saying the past few weeks. We just end up fighting. When was I supposed to tell you?"

He hisses, "That is ridiculous. I've been right here. Living beside you. Sleeping next to you every night. I give you attention."

"Right. You give me your attitude. You give me *annoyance*, like you forgot we are supposed to be in love. You have not been living *with* me. Not sleeping *with* me." I rub at my face, trying to get a handle on my emotions. "Everything is my fault? All the time?"

He laughs, but it's emotionless. I flinch. "Yes, Charlotte, you have to accept it when you mess up."

"It's not *just me!*" I yell. Passers-by look at us, but we ignore them. "We are supposed to be partners!"

My eyes widen when he sneers are me. "As my *partner*, I expected more." I don't recognize him. In his place stands Colby, sneering at me like he did when we were in high school. Colby says, *Don't be such an idiot, Charlotte. It doesn't suit you.*

Except Colby never called me Charlotte—I was always Charlie to him.

I wonder, as I blink at Avery, if he actually said that to me. I might've hallucinated it.

"I think you should take a walk," Jared says.

Avery and I both turn to look at him. Neither of us had heard him approach, and he stands close to us. We continue to watch, in silence, as Jared walks toward us and slides into the spot between Avery and me.

My nose almost brushes his back.

"Seriously, man. Take a walk."

I hear Avery sigh, say, "Fuck," and then... nothing.

In slow motion, I lean forward and press my forehead against Jared's shoulder blade. "Thank you," I whisper. That took a lot of energy.

I straighten when he moves, but he just turns toward me and gives me a hug. He's solidly there, so much more-so than Avery was. I didn't realize it until now, but when I hug Avery, I feel a spark of fear that he will leave me. My mother always said that actions speak louder than words. And, as much as I hate to admit it, Avery's past actions say, *I'm out*. He left me in New York City. He actually ended any expectation of romance in Chicago—technically our first date. He's pulled disappearing acts throughout the beginning of our relationship, even last year.

Hot and cold.

Jared has left me, too, but his hug doesn't elicit the same fear.

"Does he always treat you like that?" Jared's voice is hoarse, like he can barely force out the words. His arms tighten around me when I don't answer.

"Did you give Colby the same hell you just gave your boyfriend?"

I shake my head. "No," I whisper. "I grew a backbone in college."

His chest moves as he inhales and then slowly exhales.

"I'm so sorry, Charlie, I shouldn't have—"

I shake my head again. "Stop it."

We pull away from each other, and he glances back toward the doors of the restaurant. "Uh, we should probably pay." When I follow his gaze, I see the waiter standing there, holding our bill.

"I left my purse," I murmur.

Jared lifts his hand, producing my forgotten bag. "I'll give this back if you don't give another thought to paying."

It makes me want to cry even more.

Chapter 53

PAST

"IT'S YOUR LAST SESSION BEFORE COLLEGE, Charlie. How do you feel?"

I shrugged. "Kind of sad."

Dr. Sayer looked at me over the rim of her reading glasses. She didn't usually wear them, but when I walked in, they were perched on the tip of her nose, and she had yet to remove them. I wished I had thought to count how many appointments we'd had together—it would've been more impactful to think, *This is my two hundredth appointment in over two and a half years, and I am done.* Instead, all I had to go on was: I was in therapy for two and a half years, and I didn't really feel that much better.

Funny how that worked.

"Let me tell you my thoughts, yes?"

I nodded at her.

Dr. Sayer leaned forward in her chair. "When we first met, you were a child who had been traumatized. You were angry about it and unable to express yourself. Over the years that we have known each other, I have seen you accept what happened to you. You've matured in how you carry yourself, your writing, and your thinking. You are now a fine young woman who can hold her own. You're leaving for college tomorrow, and I have complete faith that you have an arsenal of tools at your disposal to help you cope and flourish."

I swiped at tears.

"I still feel it," I told her. "The anger, the... disappointment in myself." The latter was harder to admit.

Dr. Sayer smiled. "It's alright, Charlie. You're allowed to feel it. You can't dictate the healing process."

I put my hands on top of the notebook on my lap. "Do you think I should ever show Jared? If I have the chance, I mean." I rolled my eyes. "I'm not saying he's ever going to talk to me again. I know that it could be well outside the realm of possibility."

I appreciated that she took a minute to consider my question.

"I suppose it would depend," she said.

"On?"

"If he would be receptive to it, then I would say yes. I don't know him, though, Charlie. I can't give you his answer."

Chapter 54

JARED AND I ENDED UP WALKING HOME TO BURN
off our energy. I'm shocked that Avery isn't home and
worried about to where—or whom—he would run.

"Did you expect him to run home?"

I squint at Jared. "Where else would he go?"

He shakes his head at me.

"I'm going to call him."

Avery doesn't answer his phone. He texts me, though, and
says, *I'm cooling off like your 'friend' told me to do. I'll see you
tomorrow after he's gone.*

I drop my phone onto my coffee table and try to breathe.

"He's not coming back tonight."

Jared shrugs. It probably doesn't bother him at all.
Somehow, he's managed to retain his ability to not care what
people of unimportance think. "Guy's kind of a tool. No
offense."

"I'm going to insult your boyfriend and then tack on *no offense* so you don't get mad," I mock.

He chuckles. "Sorry."

It's easy to sink on the couch and ignore the issues in my life right now. Sometimes they seem overwhelming. When Jared is here, they aren't as drastic.

"It's okay. Here." I pat the seat next to me until he falls into me with a groan. I laugh at him.

"Can I take off my leg? Is that weird?"

"No, it's not weird. It's weird that you have to ask."

He hoists himself up. "In that case, I'm putting on shorts and exposing you to the greatness of my scars."

"You've come a long way," I tell him once he's changed and seated next to me again. I tap on the leg he still wears. "How do you take it off?"

He points to a button toward the top of the prosthetic. "When you hold that down, it releases air into the socket. It is basically held on by suction, so that makes it so I can pull it off." He does it as he's talking, and there is a faint hissing sound for a few seconds. When he takes it off, I'm somewhat surprised that there isn't just skin underneath. "This is the rubber flap that seals in the air. It's attached to the liner. And my leg has started shrinking, so I wear this band to help fill the socket."

My eyes are wide.

"Your leg is shrinking?"

Jared bursts out laughing. "It's because of the swelling, and blood flow. I wear a shrinker sock at night to help. Eventually, I think it'll be okay to stop."

It's hard not to stare at his leg until I realize that it's Jared: he never cared when I couldn't stop staring at him as a kid, either. "I don't know much about amputation," I mutter. His leg is scarred, angry red and silver raised marks disappearing up toward his hip that are likely burn scars.

"I should've been able to get started with a prosthetic closer to the amputation, but they had to wait for the burns to heal more. That was the true torture. And even then, they didn't want me to wear it so much that it damaged my 'newly healed' skin. I had to work up to wearing it every day."

"Wow." It's all I can think to say.

There is a scar where his leg ends that looks more like a tucked seam.

"You never asked why I wanted to come visit," Jared says suddenly.

My skin prickles. "What do you mean?"

"I mean—"

"You had to have a reason to visit?"

He grimaces. "Stop putting words in my mouth."

I tip my head back and stare at the ceiling. "If you have something to tell me, Jared, just spit it out." I add, "I'm sick of surprises."

"I'm leaving Massachusetts," is what comes out of his mouth.

I jerk forward, turning to stare at him. "Are you serious?"

He smiles. "Remember that I told you I had worked out west for the Hotshots?" I blink at him, and he elaborates, "Interagency Hotshot Crews. The hand crews that fight the wildfires on the front lines?"

"Oh, right. What does that have to do with..."

"I applied for a position that just opened up last month. I was surprised as hell that they considered me, but I guess I had made a good impression on the Superintendent."

He grins at me so hard, I can't help but smile back.

"Are you going to tell me what they hired you for, or am I going to have to pretend I'm pulling teeth?"

"Assistant Superintendent. Can you believe that?"

I hug him. It's impulsive, but he is ecstatic about this. I feel a trickle of sadness seep into me, but I push it back. I only just got my best friend back—and now he's leaving.

"Where?"

"They're called the Baker River Hotshots. It's in Everett, Washington."

My hands are shaking, balled in my lap.

Jared grabs my hands, steadies me. "What do you think?"

I can't help but love that he asks me.

I put my hand on his cheek. There's just a little bit of stubble, adding a shadow to his jawline. My thumb skates along his cheekbone. His skin is hot, and I let it drop. "I am so happy for you, Jared. Honestly."

"I was afraid to tell you."

I raise my eyebrows at him. "You were?"

He nods and looks at our intertwined fingers. "I was afraid that you would tell me it was stupid. That I couldn't do it because of my leg."

There's a lot to be said about insecurities. Jared is one of the most confident people I've ever known. He holds himself so steady in the face of *everything*. Even losing his leg and suffering from burns didn't mess with his self-assured demeanor. I would strive to be more like him.

But his words reveal that, just maybe, he isn't quite as sure of himself as he appears. That's just wrong—that was me in high school, listening to Colby and then explicitly not listening to anyone else once he was gone. Jared shouldn't be anything like the old me.

"Jared," I whisper. "You can do anything you want to do. Okay?"

He just stares at me.

"Don't listen to the few people who will tell you that you can't do it. You can."

And then he says, "You should take your own advice."

I wish I could work up the courage to throw my book of letters—to Jared, to my therapist—in his face. I wish I could say, *I did do that. I stopped taking pills. I started healing myself. I developed my courage.* Something stops me, though. Some insane fear presses down on my chest and hugs my lungs.

"When did you apply?" I ask him.

"I didn't officially apply until just before your birthday. But I had been emailing my old captain, who is now the Superintendent, for a few weeks before that. I wasn't sure what I could do, but I knew that was the happiest I had been." He shakes his head. "If only I hadn't torn my ACL..."

"Everything would be different," I answer.

It's true. His life unfolded in a strange, tragic way.

Would we even be talking?

Probably not.

I wish something magical had happened while Jared was here. He chose to go home on Saturday afternoon, because he didn't want to put out Avery any more than he already had. The rest of Friday, though, was peaceful. It felt like, for the first time in a long time, I had a missing piece of myself back.

I am not sure how I feel about that. I have always believed that a partner would simply complement me, not complete me. And yet, I see so much of my childhood in Jared; I'm having trouble pulling apart the threads that keep me just Charlie.

Saturday afternoon, we take the T to South Station, where Jared's train will be departing, and ride in unusual silence. South Station has always been one of my favorite places. It's crowded, but it's organized in a way that makes you feel like you cannot get lost. Plus, I'm not sure how old the building is, but it feels as old as Boston itself. We get coffees and sit at one of the small tables by the board that announces the arrivals and departures, and my eyes fill with tears. One of the things we talked about last night was when he was leaving for Washington. His answer: in a week. He was doing the groundwork here, and there seemed to be a lot of it. Find an apartment. Hire a company to get his D.C. apartment furniture moved to Washington. Book a plane ticket. Transfer his medical files. Schedule an appointment with a new doctor. One last appointment with the PT to get a new prosthetic socket, which will hopefully be the last one for a while.

"Don't cry, Charlie."

I hadn't realized he was paying attention.

He looks at me. "Do you remember what Colby said to you in the woods that day?"

I tilt my head. "The day you beat him up?"

He doesn't laugh like I expect. Instead, he says, "Yes, do you remember?"

I shake my head.

"What do you remember?"

"Just—feeling trapped. I've tried to block out everything else."

I look down at my coffee. It's hard not to shudder, but I push away the memories.

"Well, he said something and you didn't deny it. And I just wanted to say, I felt the same. Never stopped."

Jared is staring at me so intensely, it's hard to look away

once he's caught my gaze. I've always loved his eyes and the way he looks at me. We both flinch when his train is called, and he stands.

I try to recall the day he's talking about, and those specific words, but... "I don't remember," I say as I stand, too.

"It's okay, Charlie." We hug, and then he shoulders his bag. He touches my chin. "We'll see each other again."

I nod.

"Stop crying," he says again.

I nod again.

Once we've started repeating conversation, it's time to leave.

"Bye, Jared," I whisper.

"Goodbye, Charlie."

Chapter 55

A VERY COMES BACK.

He doesn't say anything about Jared, and neither do I.

Things stay the same.

Chapter 56

I HOLD THE NOTE IN MY HAND, BARELY ABLE TO read it because I'm trembling. *I love you*, it says in an unfamiliar writing.

She couldn't fucking say it—so I left. Avery's words that I haven't thought about in months ring in my ears. It's a soundtrack I can't break. They hold the entirety of his misery that's endured since we met in Chicago.

I pace around the apartment, wondering if I should start moving my stuff out.

I already know that he smiles at me like he would smile at someone he almost loved wholeheartedly, except fell short; his smile becomes sunshine when he looks at her. She has ruined him for any other girl. Maybe he just used me to help him put the pieces back together, until Elaina was ready.

Her name hurts to think about. With her name comes her face, and the way she looked at me, the way she looked at Avery.

With her name comes her voice, and her handwriting floats in front of my face. She had been *gone* for two months! I had asked Avery—with less and less frequency, I'll admit—if he had seen or heard from her since the night she came over for dinner. Every time, he said no.

I wonder when he started seeing her again, and when she slipped him that note. I wonder how long he's been lying to me.

I call Avery.

"Hey," he answers.

"Where are you?" My fingers fold around the note. *I love you*, it mocks.

He pauses. "I'm at a friend's place. I thought you had plans?"

Did I have plans? Yes, I was supposed to meet Rose at eight thirty. *Fuck.* I had completely forgotten the minute that I found the note. I switch my phone to speaker and text Rose, *I'm so sorry—something came up.*

"Charlotte?"

I ask, "Are you with her?"

"Am I with who? Charlotte? Are you alright?"

Before I know it, I'm choking on a sob. My legs give out, and I fall to my knees in my kitchen, shuddering and trying not to let him hear me cry. "Sorry," I sniffle.

"I'm coming home, okay? I'll be there soon."

I nod. I am about to say something else—*I love you*, or *Thank you*—but Avery hangs up without another word.

I tuck the paper into my front pocket, and I keep sliding my index finger in to make sure it's still there. That little paper is grounding me, while obliterating my world at the same time. By the time he gets home, I have moved past tears—temporarily, I think—and into a blank state of shock. Am I fighting for him? Am I letting him go? My mind moves to the ring in his underwear drawer. Was that even meant for me?

I can see our life laid like brickwork ahead of us. But I didn't see this coming: the orange *detour* sign screaming at us to get off of the path. I'm going left, while he's going right.

He zeros in on me as soon as he is through the door. He comes over to me and cups my face, and it's the first time he's touched me in four days. "Talk to me," he whispers. A tear falls from my eye, making a mad dash for the floor. He swipes it with his thumb, and lowers himself until he is kneeling before me. "Tell me what's wrong."

Slowly, I pull the paper from my pocket. I let my fingers uncurl, palm up, and watch him lift the note from my hand. He reads it once, twice, mouths it. I don't think he can look at me, and I wonder if he's reading it for the first time. My head cocks to the side, and I take in the man that is breaking in front of me.

"She loves you now."

He squeezes his eyes shut.

"That's why she's been here. She's fighting for you." That isn't the reason she gave, but it's the real reason.

I'm not angry. My heart is breaking along with his. Because I know, the minute a tear slips from his closed eyes, that I've lost him.

"Avery..."

I wait until he looks at me. There is a thunderstorm of emotion dancing across his face, and I know that I am part of the cause. I can hardly swallow, can hardly breathe, and the tears have started anew.

"You still love her, don't you?"

He only hesitates for a split second, and then he nods. "I've loved her since I met her," he says. He says it like a prayer. He says it like it gives him relief.

I say, "I found the ring."

"You..."

I shake my head, holding up my hand. "Why did you bring it into our home if you weren't planning on proposing to me?"

"I was," he whispers. I tilt my head back and stare at the ceiling. The road that we had planned to walk together still stretched in front of me. I could see it: moving to the suburbs, buying a house, being adequately happy. I had got myself on board for that future, I had talked myself into it over the last few months. He clears his throat. His voice sounds stronger as he says, "I was going to propose, Charlotte. I brought the ring back after I was home for the holidays. It was my grandmother's, and she gave it to me when she passed. After I saw Elaina, and nothing had changed, I knew I had to move on. So, I brought the ring back with the intention of proposing to you in the next few months."

And then, Elaina came for him.

The decision that I have to make is clear to me, but still I ask, "Why did you hide the note from me?"

For a moment, he says nothing. "I hadn't read it. She left it for me when she was here for dinner, and I was putting it off." He attempts a sardonic laugh, but it falls flat. "I thought it was a goodbye letter, honestly." He sobers quickly, the small smile slipping off his face.

And then, he says what I've been waiting for: "I'm sorry." He leans forward and kisses my temple. "I am *so* sorry, Charlotte."

I stand, and he rocks back on his heels to give me room. I step around him. My eyes have dried again, and I am back to the state of numbness. I like this feeling of not feeling anything at all. I float in it. Mechanically, I grab the suitcase I had packed after I called him and hidden in the closet. "I'll come back for the rest," I tell him. "I am going to crash at Rose's... figure out what to do in the morning."

His mouth drops open. "You packed? You're leaving?"

I shake my head, as if to say, *I'm not a moron.* "Yes, of course I did. You told me you only left because she didn't tell you she loved you, and here she is. *She fucking said it.*" I pause. "I don't know if a note counts, though. You may want to get the actual words out of her mouth." I shake my head again. "Either way, you made a decision, and so have I."

"Oh, god," he mutters. He looks like he's about to throw up. "I'm so sorry, Charlotte—"

"Please, stop." I tilt my head back and exhale. I may throw up, too, but I sure as hell won't do it while I'm standing in front of him. "I love you, Avery. But I think I know you. You're going to go back to her. You'll be happy." I am speaking in a damn monotone, and I can't stop. "Please be happy."

He finally nods, and my heart shatters. I practically run out the door with my suitcase and purse, just as the numbness breaks like a dam and rushes away.

Part IV

THREE MONTHS LATER
SEPTEMBER

For the first time,
My future is wide open.

Chapter 57

S EATTLE.
  The city reflects my mood, which is something akin to desolation.

On the bright side: Georgia's condo is spotless.

Henry comes into the kitchen when I am halfway under the sink. Their cleaning products surround me, and I have been wearing bright yellow rubber gloves so long that the skin on my hands may never *not* be tinted yellow.

"Charlie?"

I blush because I'm sure he has an unflattering view of my backside. I keep scrubbing the metal P trap, determined to get rid of the grime build up.

"Charlie..."

"Okay," I mumble. "Okay." Withdrawing, I rock back onto my heels. Henry is bundled in his cap and rain trench coat, his special, waterproofed leather briefcase already in his hand.

What kind of dork owns a *trench coat*?

And then, *Avery would never wear a trench coat.*

Traitorous brain. I try to keep breathing.

"Georgia wanted me to make sure you're leaving the house today."

I take a second to look at him. I can't concentrate on his eyes—golden brown, a bit like Avery's—without imagining Avery looking at me, and that's just too damn depressing. Instead, I focus on the space between his nose and lips. He's been trying to grow out his facial hair, but it just hasn't been working. His hair is too patchy, and he's already starting to get some grey on top of his head. Still, he hasn't given up yet. A sad-looking mustache is all he can do well. I want to tell him, *I sympathize with the sad-looking part.*

When he raises his eyebrows, I realize that I didn't answer him. There was a period of time where I had lost my voice—with Colby—and part of me is terrified that I'm losing it again. It's just so easy to not talk, to let people fill in the silence for me. Dr. Sayer would tell me that I'm self-destructing. So, I answer, "Yeah." *Yes,* my mother whispers in the recesses of my mind. "Yes, yes, I'm leaving the house today." I glance out the window and then wave my gloved hand around. "Although, it's raining."

"Welcome to Seattle," he says sarcastically. He has said that every single time I use the rain as an excuse to stay inside, which only works half of the time. "Georgia has a raincoat you can borrow." He glances at his watch. "Look, I need to get going." He stops and stares at me for a minute. "You're going to be okay."

I offer him a small smile, but I can't hold it with any amount of power. I waver, and he nods. Maybe he's been through this sort of thing; maybe Georgia told him to take pity on me. One day, I'll want to find out. One day, I'll want to know how he has such power to read me and sympathize. But today, I don't want to talk.

"You're going to be okay," he says again. "Leave the house. Go apply for some jobs."

"Find my own place?" I joke.

He grunts, and it actually looks like my words bother him. "Charlie, you're family, even if you don't share the same blood as Georgia. That means you're welcome here as long as it takes you to get back on your feet."

I frown, because I'm sure that while Georgia loves me, it can't be easy having a soggy friend—soggy from the tears, which have mostly dried up—moping around. Henry isn't even my friend yet, so he doesn't really have to afford the same leniency. Uncomfortable with the way this conversation is going, I look down at the cleaning products around me and say, "You just like that your apartment is spotless."

He laughs. It's a rich, warm laugh that makes me fall in love with him for Georgia. She got a good one, if how he's treating her stray friend is any indication. "That, too."

After he leaves, I finish cleaning under the sink, run a vacuum across the area rug in the living room, and decide, finally, that I should shower and try not to beat my head against the tiles. My movements feel sluggish. By the time I am ready, it's late in the afternoon.

I walk down the stairs. I put my hands on the door, ready to push myself out onto the street, and then I stop. I'm not sure what's recently come over me. Some sort of agoraphobia? Maybe, like the wicked witch, I will melt away. I take three quick steps backwards, until my back meets the rows of mailboxes. They dig into my skin, but I can't move.

When I fled the apartment after Avery and I ended our

relationship, trying to hold myself together, I didn't stop. I pulled my suitcase behind me and took a cab to Rose's apartment. She knew I might be coming, but I think she was holding out hope that Avery and I would fix ourselves.

She hugged me. She tucked a blanket around me on her couch and put a steaming mug of tea on the table beside me. At that point, the tears were slow. I was in denial. When the lights turned off, it was like the curtains were swept open. I buried my face in her pillow and sobbed so hard, I got dizzy. I think, too, that she knew I wanted to be alone. My attempts to mask my crying were failing, but she didn't come out of her room.

I stayed in her apartment for two days. Georgia threatened to fly across the country for me to kick his scrawny butt. On Monday, Rose dragged me off the couch and into the shower. "Clean. Dress. Come to work." I nodded. It felt like my mother was leaning over me, whispering, *This is not how you are supposed to behave, Charlotte Harper Galston. Do not disappoint us.* I couldn't even fathom, at that point, what her response would be. She *loved* Avery. He was so much more perfect than I was.

I had pulled myself together. I didn't put on makeup, because I was sure that I would burst into tears and ruin it, anyway. Rose and I walked together. We went into the office, where I swore people were staring at me. Pointing. Whispering, *Has she been crying?* I sat at my desk and counted the seconds. When Tom's final meeting of the day ended, I slipped into his office.

"Charlie," he greeted. "What's up?"

I thought I'd ask for a few days off. To recollect. Instead, what came out was, "I'm giving my notice. I can give you a month."

Everything at work promptly exploded.

Come here, Georgia texted me when I had one week of work left.

I went.

I have been here almost two months.

Go, I tell myself now. *Avery didn't follow you because he doesn't care.*

The rain is cold and refreshing. I tip my head back, letting the drops run down my face. I just need to do more simple things. It isn't like I haven't left their apartment since I've been here. I've managed a walk around the block, trips to the grocery store and coffee shop, but no further. There are still moments when I get stuck. On autopilot, I make the trek to get coffee.

My phone vibrates with a call as I am leaving the coffee shop, from a Boston number I don't recognize.

"Hello?"

"Hey, it's Rose!"

I breathe a sigh of relief, because I was afraid it might be Tom. "Rose, hi. I didn't recognize your number."

"Oh, yeah. I left my cell at home, so I'm calling from a work extension."

"How's Tom?"

Tom and I had been developing a great working relationship, but that went out the window when I gave my notice. He turned back to the snapping, piranha boss that I knew from when I first started. It was almost unbearable; I was tempted to tell him to fuck off and to leave sooner. In the end, I couldn't do that to him.

"He's gone through four temps already. I thought one had potential when she lasted more than a week, but then he threw something 'in her general vicinity' and she quit on the spot."

I rub at my face. "Oh, man." And, quieter, "I miss you guys."

Rose was my life support. I lived with her, cried on her, and let her guide me around the streets of Boston as if I couldn't walk alone. To be fair, I couldn't. She and Eve banded together and tried to distract me from everything.

"Maybe give him a call?"

I let out a harsh laugh. "He wouldn't want to hear from me."

I can hear her rolling her eyes. "There was a reason I called," she says. "Has Avery called you?"

My heart stops. Avery may as well have taken a knife and shoved it in my gut. All sorts of emotions won't stop sliding around inside of me, and I hate that he had the power to do that. He and Elaina, who actually seemed nice until she played dirty to get her boyfriend back.

"I haven't heard from him," I say.

"Well..." Rose sighs. "He stopped by the office. He looked appropriately screwed up. I guess he said he was trying to call you about the apartment..."

"I blocked his number." I shake my head at my own foolishness, because I had completely forgotten about the stupid apartment in my name. "I kind of assumed he and Elaina would just stay there forever. Maybe the building will burn down around them."

There is a silence, in which Rose is probably trying to decipher my sarcasm.

"I told him you weren't going back to it." Her voice drops lower as she says, "You're not, right?"

I snort at her stupid question. God, I feel like crying. "No."

"That's what I thought. He said he would take care of the rent for the rest of the lease. His name was on it, too?"

"Yeah," I whisper.

I hear someone shouting in the background. I've been yelled at enough to know that it's my former boss making the racket, and my stomach flips at the memory.

"I have to go. He's..." She sighs. "Yeah."

"Okay. Bye. Miss you."

"Miss you, too. Stay safe."

My phone starts vibrating again, this time from my mother. I immediately decline the call. She has no idea that I quit my job and got on a plane to Seattle, and I'm afraid to tell her. I've been avoiding her calls for two months, now.

Face your fears, I tell myself.

I hold my breath and dial her back.

"Charlie?"

I exhale. It's been *way* too long since she's called me that. "Hey, Mom, I'm sorry."

"I would hope! My god, girl, how long were you going to make me wait before you answered my calls? Your father and I have been worried."

"I texted you," I murmur. I had, sometime around the second week: *I'm fine, super busy, can't talk.*

She huffs. "Well, that's not quite adequate."

"I said I was sorry," I reply.

"Honey, your father and I were thinking of coming up to the city for a performance at the Boston Symphony Orchestra. We can get you and Avery tickets, as well."

Here we go. "Actually, Mom... Avery and I broke up."

She gasps. "What?"

"He was still in love with his ex-girlfriend, and she moved to town to win him back."

She makes a strangled noise in the back of her throat. "Oh, honey, when did this happen?"

I swallow. "Three months ago."

"*What?* Why didn't you *tell* us?"

"I just—"

"Why didn't you come home? Are you still living with him?"

Here was the hard part. "Actually, I let him keep the apartment. Georgia invited me to stay with her for a little while..."

My mother pauses. Then she says, calmly, "I thought she moved to Washington."

"Yes," I say. "I, uh, I'm in Seattle."

She's quiet for a minute. "You've been in Seattle for three months?"

"Two," I say. "I gave my boss a month to find a replacement..."

I imagine she has sunk into the chair in her office, rolling her eyes at me. Instead, I hear her sniffle.

"Mom?"

"Did you think you couldn't have come home?"

I shake my head. I'm finally back at Georgia's apartment, and I lock the door behind me. "No, I just..." Breathe. "I've been so stuck, Mom, I feel like everyone could see it. I needed to go somewhere new so I could try..." I stop talking. I don't know what I wanted to try.

"You're on an adventure," she supplies.

I blink.

Her voice is soft, like it used to be when she would read stories to me before bed. "You and Jared used to be obsessed with adventure. And then," she pauses to clear her throat, "when Colby... happened... it was like that spirit was gone. In her place was my careful, cautious daughter that hated any sort of fuss or intimacy."

I wince. "No—"

"You wouldn't let us hug you," she says. "It took you months to put on the weight you lost, because you refused to eat. You refused to speak. You just sat in your room and wrote in those journals."

"My therapist told me to do that," I say.

"You were affected by Colby, and he is *still* affecting you. You still run from true intimacy. You don't like the idea of romance. It clearly had an impact on your relationship with Avery, even if you don't see it."

"Are you blaming me?"

All I can hear is her breathing. It's so calm and steady, unlike me. I feel like I'm coming undone. "Honey, no," she answers. "I'm saying that I'm proud that you're taking steps toward helping yourself. You used to *love* adventures, even when you were too young to go out on your own. Your father and I would follow you at a distance, letting you have your freedom while making sure you were safe." She sniffs. "We can't do that now. We can't make sure you're safe."

"I don't know what to say."

"You're finally making real progress. Keep going. Keep pushing yourself."

"I love you, Mom."

"I love you, too, Charlie."

Chapter 58

I NEED A JOB.

As much as that realization pains me, I miss the work. I miss doing something productive. There is also the factor of money, and my sad checking account. I twirl around the ideas in my head, looking around Georgia's apartment. With a jolt, I realize that I had barely recognized a painting I had done in college. It was when I was experimenting with black and white oil paints, with a pop of a single bright color. This one was a black and white child, facing sideways and leaning forward to blow on a dandelion. The color, orange, was the feather-light wisps that the child's breath caught in the air. She had it encased in a wide, black frame. It looks like a professional painting—so much so, that I hadn't noticed it in the months that I've been here.

It feels like I painted it a lifetime ago.

When Georgia gets home, I am sitting at her table with a

cup of coffee from down the street. Proof, I want it to tell her, that I am stable. She's been watching me like a hawk.

I turn the cup slowly in my hands. "I need to get a job."

"Yes," she says simply. "Do you know what you want to do?"

"I think I could sell my paintings."

She freezes, and then she grins wide enough to split her face. "Charlie!" she yells. "That's fantastic!"

It was on a whim, but then—yes, maybe. "Yeah?" I run through it in my mind, and I'm surprised at the excitement that awakens inside of me.

"Absolutely! Yes! We can work on a website and have Henry's friend take photos of them, and you can learn how to put a watermark on everything, and then we just need a gallery to be interested—"

"Okay," I laugh, "The first thing I need to do is paint more. My collection has shrunk quite a bit."

Georgia glares at me. "Oh, my god. You left half of your paintings in your Boston apartment, didn't you?"

"No—no, they're in storage."

She nods and plops down on the seat across from me. She picks up my hand and threads our fingers together. "You've got this. I know the perfect place to get supplies for you, but it's a drive."

"Thank god tomorrow is Saturday," I say. "What if no one wants them? What if I can't make any money?"

Georgia frowns. "Stop that. Listen, what we need is supply and demand. You just need to create the demand, and then give it to people."

I roll my eyes. "We both read the book where the guy painted confessions and only sold them once a month, Georgia. I can't copy that."

"Hey, that guy was a business genius."

"It was a sad book," I say. "And it's famous. Everyone would know. Plus, isn't the idea copyrighted?"

She shrugs. "I don't know. I guess we can figure something else out."

I smile, but then it drops. "You just want me gone, huh?"

She stands up and comes closer, putting her hands on my shoulders. "Chuck, you listen to me. You're welcome here forever, for all I care. I doubt Henry would object, either, since he loves you." I start to respond, but she gives me a look that she must've perfected from her mother—that woman is scary—and says, "We will figure your life out together. It doesn't mean I want you gone. I just want you happy."

I hug her. "Thanks, Georgie."

Later, we sit close together on the couch, sharing a blanket, when I say, "I told you about Jared, right?"

She glances at me. "Um?"

My face turns red, and I pick at my fingers. "Well, just, you know, that he left Massachusetts?"

She knows that he came to visit, but I never went into detail about what we talked about. She pauses our movie. The firefighter—my reminder of Jared—freezes on the screen mid-action. "Seriously? Where'd he go?"

"Uh..."

"Charlie."

"Everett, Washington?"

Her jaw drops. "That's less than an hour from here! Have you told him you're in Seattle?"

I squeeze my eyes shut. "Nope."

She smacks my arm. "Why not!"

"I don't know, Georgia. He left and we've only been friends for like..."

"Forever," she finishes. "You've been friends forever."

I can't stop staring at the actor on screen. "He said something weird right before he left."

She mutters, "I can't believe you haven't talked to him." And then, "Wait, what did he say?"

"He brought up the time that he beat up Colby in the woods. He asked if I remembered what he said."

"And do you?"

I groan. "I've been blocking out that day for so long, I can't remember what Colby was even wearing."

"I'm glad he's in jail," she mutters. "Or else I'd go put him there."

"I think I'm getting over it," I tell her. When she raises her eyebrows, I add, "I had a nice chat with my mother today about it."

She starts laughing. "A nice chat about your abusive ex-boyfriend?"

"Exactly."

She squeezes my hand. "It's about time."

Chapter 59

THE NEXT MONTH IS A FLURRY OF ACTIVITY, and life is getting brighter.

Georgia and I take her car to the art supply shop, where I spend too much money on nice paints, different brushes, and a roll of canvas. I order wooden frames online, to stretch the canvas onto by hand and staple into the wood.

"What are you thinking about painting?" she keeps asking me as I touch tubes of paints.

I don't answer her. Everything goes into bags except for one paint that I can't seem to let go of: a deep, sapphire blue.

"Portraits?" she guesses on the way home.

I shrug. "I'm not sure yet."

From that moment on, painting becomes my full-time job. Henry helps me build a website, and his friend comes over one day to photograph the paintings I have already completed and framed. Robert is tall, dark, and handsome: a complete package with a beautiful smile. Once he is done, he asks me, "How much are you charging for these?"

"How much would you pay?"

He points at one painting: a spider hanging by the barest of threads in a window looking out onto an ocean. "Two hundred?"

"Really?" I can't believe that he sees that much potential in my work, that it would be worth that much.

He blinks. "Okay, I'd do three."

Before I can answer, Georgia walks in the room and tells him, "Deal."

And thus, I make my first sale.

By November, I have sold six more paintings. My website gets regular traffic—all thanks to Georgia's marketing strategies, if we're being completely honest—and I've been churning out different pieces to experiment with which style I like the best. To say the least: I've been busy.

It hasn't been enough to pay the bills, though, so I have been doing an online customer service job. I chat with people and help them with basic inquiries over the phone or through an online chat program. Part-time work, usually in the mornings, is enough for me to contribute a bit to the rent, groceries, and bills.

Robert calls me out of the blue—he comes by once every other week to photograph my new paintings so I can add them to my website—and says, "Charlie. I found the perfect spot."

"The perfect spot for what?"

"Our *gallery*."

My jaw hits the floor. "What?"

He laughs. "Any friend of Henry's is a friend of mine. I started my photography business from nothing, and I've been looking for someone to sign a lease with—and not many people have the raw talent that you have. I don't think you realize how much you can profit from that talent."

I swallow. "I'm not sure if I'm ready for that."

"Neither of us can do it alone in this city. Rent is insane. I've been wanting to showcase my photos somewhere for quite a while, and I think you're the perfect person to partner with—at least, in terms of a lease. Obviously, we only make money on our own work. Now, can I show it to you tomorrow?"

"Wait—"

"Yes?"

I sigh. "I feel like... I don't want to date you or have sex with you or anything like that."

His laughter fills my ear. "Thank god, Charlie! My boyfriend would be quite upset with me."

I realize how much of a terrible friend I've been—to him and everyone around me. We don't know anything about each other, and I consider him a friend. I'm lucky if I manage a ten-minute chat with Henry without Georgia there. Why didn't I know he had a boyfriend? Why didn't I ask?

"I'm sorry, Robert, I think I've been narcissistic lately—"

"Oh, god, Charlie. No. I assumed you were trying to keep things professional. Small talk, nothing too personal... I understood."

"But—"

"We're good."

I breathe a sigh of relief. "What's your boyfriend's name?"

He chuckles. "Paul."

"Well, I look forward to maybe meeting him someday. I'd

love to see the place tomorrow."

Robert and Paul are waiting for me at the address that Robert texted me. It's downtown, and the Uber driver grumbles under his breath at the traffic. They stand in front of a tinted glass storefront, and they both wave as I climb out of the car.

"Paul, Charlie."

"Nice to meet you," I say as we shake hands.

"Likewise."

Robert waves his hand at the storefront and awning. "So, we can put a sign up here with our logos and 'Art Gallery' so people know what the hell is going here."

People pass us on the street; it's surprising how busy it is. We're surrounded by other stores, a few restaurants, and a cute looking coffee shop across the street. *Sold*, I think.

Robert produces a key and swings the door open. It's open and airy, and the tinted windows let in a surprising amount of light. "This actually used to be an art gallery before, so in the back there are still the temporary walls that we can put up. They also have some lights for displays."

The walls are black, and the whole place has an edgy feel to it. I instantly love it.

"This is amazing," I whisper.

Robert grins, and Paul nods. "Have you seen Robert's photos?"

I shake my head. "I'm sorry to say, I've only seen what I was able to find on his website." I shoot them a look. "It seems to be a little outdated."

"Yeah," he answers. "I stopped updating it because it wasn't a good source of income. It just became a hassle."

I nod. It makes sense.

"There's a room in the back, and there's also an apartment upstairs that is included in the lease. We were thinking you might like to take the apartment and I'll convert the back room into a darkroom."

"As in, I can live there?" I think my jaw is on the ground again.

Paul smiles. "I told you she would like that idea."

"Robert." He turns to me. "I want to go over the finances and make sure it's something that I can afford. Otherwise? It looks perfect."

Robert sticks out his hand. "Deal."

We shake. And it's done: we have a gallery.

Chapter 60

OPENING NIGHT.

It took longer than I would've expected to open this place: nearly three months of hard work. In that time, I couldn't keep up with the offers on my paintings. I ended up selling some, and other offers received an email stating that there would be a gallery opening soon where the paintings would be available for purchase. *Supply and demand*, Georgia had said. It seemed like people really appreciated that I didn't turn my paintings into prints—except for the one that I made for myself as a way to catalog and remember. They were original and one of a kind. It terrified me, though, because I knew that my art was finite. It wouldn't last forever, especially once it left my hands.

And then, two days before we were set to open—February 1st—I started running out of ideas. I panicked and called Georgia, and she immediately came over to my apartment above the gallery.

I'd been avoiding going outside, and when she came in with enough layers to be an Eskimo, I knew I had made the right decision.

"Help," I said.

I was sitting on the floor, surrounded by canvases and metal. I had recently begun doing some painting on thin sheets of metal, which created an interesting ability to layer and texture. I'm not in love with it, yet, but it's been giving me some new inspiration.

It took Georgia a century to pull off her hat, gloves, coat, sweatshirt, and boots. "Okay," she said. "Where are your paintings that you're putting in the gallery?"

I pointed toward my bedroom and let her browse. They're a mix of style, but all of them have a dark-versus-light theme.

"Charlie, these are amazing! You've been hiding your skill from the world for far too long."

I shook my head. "Don't say things just to flatter me, Georgie."

She reappeared holding one that I did of her profile: in it, she looked to the left, and the light source appeared like it was coming from the viewer. The background was black, with flecked white, like stars. "Wow, Charlie."

I shook my head again.

"No, this is..." I almost missed her swipe at a tear. "You made me beautiful."

"Georgia, you *are* beautiful."

She choked on a laugh and glanced at me. "I can't believe we just went there."

I stuck out my tongue at her. "We were bound to get dramatic and disgustingly cute eventually."

She came over and sat down next to me. "So, let's talk about inspiration. What've you been working off of lately?"

I told her that I had been inspired by the feeling of being a good person, while also having the ability to hurt people. "There's good and bad in everyone. That's kind of played out in light and dark schemes, so I just expanded on that."

Georgia smiled. "Yes, I can see that. What about your past?"

"My past?"

"Colby? Avery? Jared? Hell, take your pick."

I thought about it, and came up with a lackluster answer. "I don't know. I feel like it would come out as anger for Colby, sadness for Avery, and... disappointment. At Jared."

She leaned forward. "There has to be more to Colby than just anger."

"You're right." I scrunched up my face. "I've tried to block it out, but maybe I shouldn't. I just don't know where to start."

"Do you still have those journals? You should start there."

I froze. "Georgia."

"What?"

"That may be genius."

She cracked a grin as I scrambled upright. It only took me a few minutes to find the journal that I've carried with me since Thanksgiving of last year. "Okay, I need you to leave."

"Really? I don't get to watch the master artist at work?"

I scowled. "Absolutely not."

She started to pull on her outerwear. "Hey, I forgot to ask—how was your Christmas?"

I had gone home for a few days, which was nice because I hadn't been able to fly back for Thanksgiving. The Browns' house was dark—I couldn't stop checking until my mother informed me that they were meeting Jared in Alaska for a family Christmas vacation. I had brought a painting for my parents, albeit a small one that fit in my luggage, and my mother couldn't hold back her tears. "Excellent," she kept whispering.

I took it as a sign that she approved.

My father gave me tips for improving my business strategy, which I diligently wrote down and then shared with Robert.

I gave my parents a handwritten invitation to the gallery's opening. I wrote it on the back of our new promotional fliers. *C & R Art Gallery* had printed fliers designed by Georgia, and then we—Robert, Paul, Georgia, Henry, and I—smothered Seattle in them.

I hoped they came. I hoped *everyone* came.

"It was good," I told Georgia. "How was Henry's family?"

They had went down to Alabama, where his grandparents lived.

She gave me a shy smile. "It was really nice."

"I'm glad. Okay, out."

I had a lot of work to do.

Now, I stand in a gold and black dress, wondering who is going to show up. We hired a catering service from a local restaurant to serve hors d'oeuvres and champagne, and they're setting up in the living room of my apartment.

"Charlie!" I jerk and turn to see Paul rush toward me. He looks nice in a light grey suit and crisp white button down. "Are you freaking out?" he asks. "Robert is in meltdown mode in his black room."

"You mean the darkroom," I say with a smile.

"That's the one."

I glance around at all the work we've pulled off. We have sectioned off the gallery with the removable walls based on themes, and a combination of photographs and paintings that seem to go well together. The atmosphere is of a dark warehouse, with the only lighting focused on the art.

"Well, we open the doors in a few minutes. Is he going to be okay?"

Paul nods and moves to one of the paintings. It was one that I just barely finished in time—it's a girl standing on the threshold of a house that is completely engulfed in flames. The force of the fire blows her clothes back, and her hair whips out. When I first had the idea, I wanted her to be fluid. I wanted the girl to be unwavering in front of such danger.

I think I managed to accomplish at least a little of that.

"Charlie," Paul whispers. "This is terrifying. And beautiful."

Avery's voice comes back to me: *You're wholly terrifying*, he had once said.

I swallow. "Thanks."

Someone bangs on the front door, which makes both of us jump. I hurry to the door, waving in Henry and Georgia. "Welcome!"

Henry helped us hang the last of our art yesterday, but he left before we set up the lighting. There are big fluorescent lights in the ceiling that have been on every time they've been in here that are off now. "Wow, guys. I can't believe how amazing it all looks."

Georgia elbows him. "He means, we never had a doubt." She comes over and hugs me. "You look beautiful, Charlie, and this is so cool. Did you decide on...?"

I nod as Robert comes out of the darkroom. "Oh, hey guys. Sorry, I was—"

"Puking," Paul finishes.

Robert scowls at him.

I tell them, "For anyone who asks, all the artwork is for sale except this one." I point to my most recent, the girl and the fire. "They take the number on the card next to each painting or photograph, and bring it to the desk. Once it's paid for, it'll be marked with a 'sold' sticker on the card."

Georgia snorts. "Yeah, you definitely didn't steal that from that book."

"I'm pretty sure *most* galleries do it that way," I tell her.

"Sure."

We both crack smiles, and I feel myself relax a bit.

My phone starts going off, and I realize it's time. "Okay. Okay. Places, everyone. Paul, can you tell the wait staff—"

"On it."

"Henry, open the door—"

"Yes, ma'am," he replies.

Georgia squeezes my hand. "You've got this."

I inhale and exhale.

The first people through the door are my parents. They're grinning from ear to ear, and I wonder if they're going to be the only people we see tonight. That fear is squashed, however, when my father holds the door for more people. Rose and Eve. Tom and his wife. Strangers follow them. And then more.

Inhale.

Exhale.

Yes, I've got this.

Chapter 61

"THANK YOU ALL FOR COMING," I SAY. I'VE
been through this speech twice before: once, when
we opened, and again on our second showing.
Robert and I decided that we needed to limit the supply of the
paintings, and give ourselves time to create. So, we have a small
showing every other Friday night. It's now the first week of
March, and I have a small crowd in front of me. I have a glass of
champagne in one hand, and a card of brief notes in the other.
"We appreciate you all for coming out with us tonight. Robert
and I have been blown away by all of your words of
encouragement and support." There are some familiar faces
who receive my grateful smile.

I take a deep breath.

"Tonight, we are doing something a little different. We only
have three paintings, and four prints." They are currently
spread around the open room. Next to each piece is a standing

table wrapped in string lights. The art is covered in black cloths, so our guests have not seen anything. "Instead of setting a price, we've set up a silent auction. It will only go on for an hour." I gesture toward Robert, who holds a stack of cards with numbers on them. "Register for a number with Robert, and bid with that number."

I give everyone a large smile.

"Have a fun evening, everyone."

People form a line, and between Robert, Paul, and Georgia, we get everyone registered quickly. While we do that, Henry pulls down the black curtains. As with the last two showings, I meander amongst the people, answering polite questions about brushes and how long it took me to perfect one thing or another.

And then, I see Julianne, Jared's mother.

"Charlie," she says. She pulls me into a tight hug. "Congratulations! Your mother told me what a big star you were turning into, and I had to see it for myself. You didn't do the photographs, too, did you?"

I shake my head, a bit bewildered that she's standing in front of me. She's only ever reached out to me about her son, so it's easy to I assume she is here about Jared this time, too.

I pray she doesn't recognize his eyes in one of the pieces on the wall.

"Are you in Seattle for vacation?" I manage to say.

She laughs and pats my shoulder. "I flew in to see Jared, and today's the last day I'm here. My flight leaves tomorrow morning."

"Does he know—"

"No," she says. "Although, I may have accidentally left a flyer there that your mother had given me. I just can't seem to remember." She laughs as I turn red. "Now, Charlie, can I get a number? I would love to put a bid on one—oh, goodness, is that you?"

She points to a photograph on the far wall. Robert had caught the rare photo of my uncontrolled laughter. One hand rests on my stomach—because, at that point, it was starting to hurt to keep laughing—and the other is in the action of brushing a tear from my eyes. My mouth is open, my eyes are squinted shut. I had been painting all day, and I had dark smudges on my hands from the charcoal that I used to sketch it out beforehand. There was a streak of grey in progress under my eye.

We meet eyes, and it isn't the first time that I'm reminded of Jared: they have the same eyes. Most everything else of his comes from his dad, except the hair color, but the eyes are purely his mother's.

"You managed to capture his spirit," she says. She points to the one behind me.

One of my paintings tonight is inspired by Colby: one of toxic anger, in abstract—kind of like how a black hole swallows stars—and the other is his face, as crisp and accurate as I could get it, crying and looking repentant. At the last second, I splashed it with red paint, which dripped and spotted the canvas.

The last is Jared: his back, with a backpack, as we follow him through a blur of forest. It was a recreation of the day we went to the lake, before it spiraled. His head is partially turned in my painting, so we can see the strong outline of his nose, chin, throat. One blue eye. Pink lips, parted, and white teeth.

I don't have anything to say, because she's right: I know Jared's spirit. It's easy to put it on my canvas.

"He cares about you a lot, Charlie," she says as she fills out the information for her number. "He would want you to call him."

I sigh. "I know."

She fixes me with a stare. "Then, why haven't you?"

I purse my lips until I say, "I haven't been ready. I wasn't really... healed."

She knows exactly who I'm talking about.

"He got out of jail a few months ago," I tell her. "I didn't tell anyone, but I think it messed with my head a bit. I kept thinking he would show up. It wasn't this... conscious fear, but it was making me anxious to go outside. I didn't realize it until I found my old journal."

Julianne touches my arm. "Oh, honey."

I shake my head, shifting until her arm drops. "It's okay. I just wanted you to know that I wasn't ready before. And I wasn't over Avery."

She grimaces.

"Georgia makes that same face when Avery's name is mentioned."

We smile at each other.

"Charlie, it's almost time," Henry says at my elbow.

Julianne looks him over. "A new boyfriend?"

Henry snorts.

"No—" I elbow him, "he's my best friend's boyfriend."

They shake hands, and I move to slide past Julianne. "One last thing, Charlie," she says. She holds out an envelope. "In case you change your mind."

She moves away from us, and Henry mutters, "Change your mind about what?"

I roll my eyes. "Who knows. That was Jared's mom, by the way."

"Oh my god!"

I glance at Henry, who gives me a large smile.

"Nope. Don't start, Henry," I warn.

Robert is at the podium when I arrive, making small talk

and generally getting the people's attention. He hands me a glass of champagne, and we clink glasses. "Alright," he says to the crowd. "Let's see who's going home with a one-of-a-kind piece of art, yes?"

Henry fiddles the lights, and the whole room goes dark except for a light on Robert and me. "The first is a painting titled, *Swallow Me Whole*, by Charlie Galston." Robert leans forward. "That's the lovely lady standing beside me, if you were confused by the name." Henry lights up the painting, and the crowd turns to look at it.

The crowd chuckles.

Robert moves through the line, naming the winning bids and the amounts. The people then shuffle over to Georgia and Henry, who help with the paperwork and money collecting. The last photograph is the one of me, and my mouth drops open when Julianne wins. She winks at me as she heads toward my friends. And then it's just the painting of Jared left, and I feel a sharp stab of regret over letting it go. Robert reads off Julianne's name again, and I can't help the tears that fill my eyes. There is a sob in my chest, ready to break free.

"I'm so sorry," I whisper to Robert, my hands over my mouth, as I rush to the door that leads up to my apartment.

I'm an idiot. I painted a boy with two legs, I painted a boy who hadn't had the trauma of life affect him yet. I should've done something else. I shouldn't have made it so clearly *him*. And now? Julianne is going to go home with that painting and hang it somewhere, and it'll remind everyone of who Jared isn't.

"Can I come in?"

I spin around, shocked to see Julianne standing in my doorway.

"Your friend said it was okay to come up. Georgia, I think it was."

I wipe the tears away and clear my throat. "Yeah, sorry."

"That was quite the dramatic exit. Are you okay?"

I pull myself up onto the kitchen counter. "No."

She comes over and leans on the island across from me. "Charlie, it's okay to remember him as who he used to be. It's okay to paint the young him, the new him, the man you never met... It's okay."

I shrug.

"I bought it for you."

"What?"

"I think you're stuck on that year, in the back of your mind. Even now. It's all you can paint."

"It's inspiration," I tell her.

"You're using paint to work out your feelings, which is great. You've flushed out Colby, I think. You're only now beginning to reconcile your thoughts and feelings about Jared."

I shake my head and laugh. "My feelings about Jared? What does that even mean?"

Julianne gives me a tiny smile. "I'm headed back to Massachusetts tomorrow. Don't let any sort of fear keep you from living your dream. Right?"

"Right."

She steps forward and hugs me, kissing my cheek. She's always been like a second mom.

"When you sent Jared away... I kind of hated you."

She pats the cheek she just kissed. "I know. We had to do it, though. He is the sort of boy that, without direction, would self-destruct. He needed a more strict lifestyle than we were able to give him." She frowns. "Plus, your mom and I figured you guys would be married by twenty if we kept you together."

I gasp.

"*Married?*"

She laughs. "I need to get going."

I nod and slide to my feet. "It was nice to see you again."

"Likewise." She looks around my place. "And I love your apartment."

There are half-started paintings everywhere. Things happen in layers, and so each individual painting moves more slowly than I would like. It's organized chaos and it's small. But, yes, I love my apartment, too.

I finally like my life, even if it feels a little too empty sometimes.

Chapter 62

I HANG THE PAINTING OF JARED IN MY LIVING room, so I can stare at it while I eat my breakfast. Every day, a little bit more of that day comes back to me. It plays in my dreams like a movie reel. And, one day, everything clicks.

In the water, Jared was making out with Leah.

My heart seized, and I turned and fled.

I ran like my hair was on fire, following the barely-there path. Eventually, I collapsed to my knees. Ugly sobs burst out of my mouth, spit flew everywhere, I choked and tipped my head back and howled my agony.

That was how he found me.

"Charlie," Colby said. I looked over my shoulder, and he stood on the path with his arms crossed. "Jesus, you're making a fucking racket."

I swallowed my groan.

He stepped toward me and smiled. It looked so wrong on

his face.

"You saw Jared and Leah, yeah? I thought you might be in love with him." He shrugged. "Oh, well."

I stood up when he walked closer. My fingers tightened on the strap of my backpack, every muscle tensing. He was close enough to breathe in; I didn't want to do that. I wanted to step back and back. In fact, that's what I did—right until I bumped into a tree.

He touched my face. I knew this moment would haunt me, but fear kept me paralyzed.

"Colby!"

I jerked, and tears started streaming down my face. I met Jared's eyes over Colby's shoulder. He looked angrier than I had ever seen. A whole tropical storm brewed on his face.

Colby swiped at a tear with his thumb, and then dropped his hand from where he had traced my jaw. He turned to face Jared, and my legs gave out. I slid down the tree.

The rest was a blur: Jared yelled about leaving me alone; Colby said something about Jared not owning me. Jared shoved Colby away from me and crouched down. He brushed away more tears. There was an endless supply of tears. But then he was pushed sideways, and Colby was on top of him with a manic look in his eye. He was possessed; I had never heard the sound of flesh hitting flesh before.

Colby and Jared rolled on the ground, each trying to get on the upper hand. Finally, Jared landed on top. He straddled Colby and hit him once, twice, three times.

"Jared," I whispered. I said it again, louder, on repeat until I was screaming. I didn't realize I was standing over him until I was close enough to grab onto his arm. "Stop," I sobbed.

"He can't fucking touch you, Charlie," he said.

I thought you might be in love with him, Colby had said.

And Jared, months ago, had told me, *He said something and you didn't deny it. And I just wanted to say, I felt the same. Never stopped.*

When Jared had said that, I had Avery.

I had been in no position to accept love from someone else.

When we were fourteen, *Jared loved me?* Does he still?

I look at the boy in my painting. I don't have to ask if I feel the same way. It's been there all along.

My next phone call is to Georgia.

"Hey," I say. "I need to borrow your car."

Chapter 63

IN THE ENVELOPE JULIANNE GAVE ME WAS THE address of Jared's apartment. It was like she had superpowers, because she knew that I would need it. I could blame her and my mother for repeatedly meddling later. Now? I have a man to confront.

When I pull into Everett—which is a lot closer to Seattle than I thought—I'm shocked at how big the city is. I think I was expecting something tiny. And yet, with the help of my GPS, I don't have an issue finding Jared's apartment.

I hope he's here, because it will be awkward if he isn't.

When I knock on his door, I don't have a clue what I'm going to say to him. It depends on his reaction. It could go badly, I suppose. In the time that it took me to figure out what I wanted—*Jared*—he could have moved on. Some other girl could answer the door and shatter my dreams.

See, this is why I should've called first. Gave him time to tell his girlfriend about the crazy old neighbor.

That, and it didn't appear that he was home.

I sat in my car and waited for another ten minutes before I gave up. I could try again another day.

Traffic crawls into Seattle, making the drive feel eons longer than it did when I was heading toward Jared's home. The door to the gallery is unlocked, which is unusual. Robert should've been the only one here today, and he religiously locks it behind him. His darkroom blocks out sound, so there would be no way to tell if someone walked into the gallery.

But then, I hear Paul say, "I'm not sure where she is. She doesn't have much of a social life, so I'm sure she'll be back soon." He laughs. I roll my eyes, because I know he means well. It's true, though, my social life has been nearly nonexistent since I moved to Seattle.

I round the corner and freeze.

I would recognize the back of Jared's head anywhere.

"Ah," Paul says. "Charlie, this man was asking for you."

I nod, struck mute, as Jared turns around. His look holds all the warmth in the world. It melts my heart into a puddle.

He holds up one of our fliers, and then shows me the back. His mother, I presume, had written, *C is for Charlie!*

I, in turn, hold up the note she had written with his address on it.

"You went to Everett?"

A smile breaks across our faces when I nod again. I'm not the only one who can't stop staring this time.

Paul looks awkward standing there. "I'll just, uh..." He turns, opens the first door to the darkroom, and closes himself inside without hesitation.

"We might've passed each other on the highway," I whisper.

He takes a few steps forward.

"Why didn't you tell me that you were so close to me?" he whispers back. I realize, immediately, how much that information must hurt.

"Because I needed to sort through my shit," I reply.

Inhale, exhale.

"And," I say, "I drove to Everett to tell you—"

He shakes his head.

"Charlie, I don't—"

"I love you," I blurt out.

It's awkward, and the words trip over my tongue and past my teeth. My cheeks turn bright red. Three words have undone me. It's the first time I've said them first; it's the first time I've meant it with my whole being.

We stare at each other for a minute before he crosses the distance between us and crushes me to him. He says, "Oh, Charlie."

I close my eyes when he runs his finger down my jaw, and his other hand cups the side of my neck. His fingers brush into my hair at the nape of my neck, and it's like I have a lightning storm under my skin, crackling wherever he touches me. When he leans down and presses his lips to mine, I know that his kiss is better than any I've experienced. I feel it everywhere, all at once, like I've been frozen and now I'm alive.

When he pulls away, I whimper. It elicits another smile from him, and he touches my lips with his finger. "I've been waiting way too long for that," he says. "I'm going to kiss you again, and then we're going to look at your artwork. I'm going to admire all of it and tell you how proud I am of you at least a hundred times." He chuckles at whatever dazed expression is on my face. "And then I'm going to take you on a proper dinner date, and maybe you'll invite me up to your apartment after."

Everything happens exactly as he says.

I am perfectly okay with that.

"I did tell you our mothers like to meddle." He kisses my collarbone. I've never fit so perfectly together with a person before; I didn't know this kind of peace existed.

"You did. She came to one of our showings and bought a photograph and a painting."

He smiles. He has so many smiles to give out, and I feel compelled to match his expression with a smile of my own. "She is clever, we can give her that."

"She gave me the painting," I tell him. "She said it was..." I let my eyes trail down to his left leg. "She said it's okay to remember you as you were."

He kisses my temple. "Which one?"

I pull him standing, and he follows me into the living room.

"You painted one of our adventures. You always did fall behind so easily," he laughs.

"You were too fast! I could probably keep up with you now."

"I wanted you to follow me. I thought that if you did, it meant you liked me more than just as a friend."

I step into to his side, loving the way he pulls me close. "I did, Jared. I knew it then, and you made me fall in love with the adult version of you, too."

"I love you, too, Charlie. Every piece of you."

The way he kisses me after that, I know we're headed to the bedroom.

After, we lay in silence. I study his breathing, trace the taut muscles in his stomach, taste his skin; he breathes and sighs and rubs circles into my back. I've been debating telling him about the journal. The guilt of it is tearing me apart, and I don't know how to shut it off.

"There's one more thing," I eventually say. "And I would understand if it changes everything."

Jared pulls his head back so he can look me in the eyes. "What is it?"

I roll away from him, digging through the drawer in my nightstand until I find the notebook. "When you went away, I wrote to you. It... it isn't pretty. I've recently reread them, and it shows..."

He gently takes it from me.

"Why are you giving this to me?"

Tears fill my eyes. "Because, Jared, you missed such a big part of my life. I missed a big part of yours that I'll never get back. But I think you need to see this, to understand—"

He silences me with a kiss. Once on my lips, once on each eye, and once on my forehead, where he lingers for a moment. Then, he says, "I know who you were when you were a child. I know who you are now. Reading you in pain... I do want to know. And I will read it. But you need to know that this will not change my opinion of you. This will not change my feelings. I love you, and that doesn't just disappear."

"I don't know," I say. A thought crosses my mind: if he were like Avery, this already would've turned into an argument. I shake my head to clear that mental image away. "It's a vulnerable part of my life."

He hugs me. "I know. It'll be okay."

I get up and slip on a shirt. "We need food," I say. My cooking skills, since living alone, have improved. I hear the notebook rustle open as I walk out of the bedroom, and even after I've finished cutting the cheese and putting crackers on a plate—okay, my cooking skills aren't *that* improved—I stay away from the bedroom.

Eventually, Jared comes looking for me.

We meet eyes, and the same amount of love is in his expression now. His eyes are bloodshot, though, and I raise my eyebrows. "You made me cry," he accuses with a small chuckle. "Charlie, I'm so sorry for what you went through. I felt like I just went through the journey with you."

I shake my head. "I don't want you to feel guilty, okay?"

"I might, a little. You are *not* to blame for Colby's manipulation."

He looks at the crackers and cheese. "How about I make us some omelets?"

"Please."

Our transition from single to taken and in love is seamless. He has a few months before the fire season starts, which means most of his job is at the office in Everett, organizing preparation, construction, and support for the structural fire crew. I busy myself painting. Because I can do it anywhere, I stay with Jared in Everett most nights.

Our parents come and visit, and I've never seen them so thrilled for Jared and me. They already love Jared, and my dad revealed, unsurprisingly, that our moms had been rooting for this match up for a *long* time.

The best part about my new life, however, is that all the people I love are with me.

One day, I turn to Jared in the middle of working on a latest creation. I say, "You were right."

"About what?" he asks.

"I had settled in my life. I was content to just... let everything be, because it wasn't messy or bad."

He comes up behind me and kisses my neck. "And now?"

"Now, I am extremely happy."

"I can work with that," he answers.

Epilogue

HAPPY ENDINGS ARE HARD TO COME BY, BUT they are not impossible. I learned, as I grew up, that my parents had a good marriage but not a great one. I learned that happiness is fought for and hard-earned and shouldn't be taken for granted.

I learned that family isn't just blood. It's who you let into your life. It's who fills the missing pieces. It's for whom you want to crack yourself open, who you feel can crawl into your darkest spaces and bring the warmest light.

In Jared, there was a darkness that emerged when the people he loved were in danger. In me, there was a darkness that hid all of my insecurities, deep inside of me. But, somehow, we figured each other out. We overcame our obstacles *for* each other, and *because* of each other.

In October, just eight months after we began our relationship, Jared proposed to me.

Washington was beautiful in the autumn, on the mountain we frequently hiked. Yes, I got into hiking. Jared had a special prosthetic made for more intense exercise, and I told myself, *If he can do it, so can I.* I wasn't afraid to admit that he inspired me to work harder. We were all alone at the top of the world when he gave me his own special words.

You and I have something special, Charlie. I have loved you for an eternity, and I will love you until both of us have returned to ash. You are my light, you are my happiness, and you are my best friend. I never want to lose you. I never want you to want for anything. I love you because you understand me. And I understand you.

Charlie, if you asked me for the moon, I would get it for you.

I answered, *I would never ask the impossible of you, Jared. That is another reason why I love you.*

He got down on one knee. The ring wasn't in a box. It had just been in his pocket, and then it was just pinched between his thumb and index finger. It was a simple band with a row of inset diamonds that shimmered in the morning light. It was perfect. It was not a public display of romantic affection, and I felt myself fall even deeper in love with him in that moment. A moment where my heart skipped and then sighed, and it said, *He understands.*

Yes, I told him. *I'll tell you yes every day, for as long as we live.*

I didn't believe in happily ever afters until that day, but for once, I'm happy to be wrong.

THE END

Acknowledgements

This book was a long time coming. It had been my goal for a very long time to publish a story, and it could not have happened without the fantastic support in my life.

To Rebecca, who has read every word of every draft I've written: thank you for encouraging me to keep writing. Thank you for giving me positive feedback, for loving my words, for helping me develop my characters, and for listening to me talk out everything going through my head. Without you, there would be no story on paper.

To my beta reader, Dave: thank you for your thorough critique, guidance, and support. You gave me a boost of confidence in this story when I needed it the most.

To my parents, who never stop supporting me: thank you for letting me choose this path, and for giving me a life that inspires creativity. Thank you for not asking about my story as I was writing it (or, rather, for not getting upset when I refused to tell you), and for accepting that only one person could read it before it was done. I love you guys.

To Akyanna, who promised an honest review: thank you for giving me your truth, and for reaffirming to me, "You are a writer." I really needed to hear those words.

And last but not least, thank you to my editor, Josiah Davis (JD Book Services), for polishing my manuscript and restraining my (probably toxic) love of commas. Thank you to Murphy Rae and Ashley Quick for *Something Special*'s gorgeous cover, and Alexandria Bishop (AB Formatting) for the amazing interior design.

About the Author

S. Massery grew up in Pittsfield, Massachusetts. She has a Bachelor of Arts degree in English Writing from Emmanuel College in Boston, although she has been writing much longer than that. Her short story, *Lightning Storm*, was previously published in Foliate Oak Literary Magazine. *Something Special* is S. Massery's debut novel.

When she isn't writing, you can find her at www.smassery.com.

Join her on Facebook:
https://www.facebook.com/authorsmassery

Sign up for her monthly newsletter: http://eepurl.com/dFfHQP

Made in the USA
Middletown, DE
29 October 2018